"You can't go back and change the beginning, but you can start where you are and change the ending." —CS Lewis

Also by the Author:
*Funny Bones Make A Very Fine Stew (and Other Stories)*

# Road Trip

By Heidi Lacey

Cover art by Jana Montgomery

**ISBN:** 9781999010607

Dedication:
To *Thomas Robert Lacey*,
1986-2017
My little hell-raiser. Always and forever.

*"Hijole!"*

A demon stood beside my bed, drenched in moonlight, and looking at me with a mixture of longing and pity. I knew right away he was a demon because (a) he was looking at me with longing and (b) his eyes were glowing. I flipped on my bedside lamp and fumbled for my glasses.

On closer inspection, this demon was not what I would have expected, given the jaunty nature of his well-cut three-piece suit, crisp white shirt, and natty blue and green striped tie. A demon in a Brooks Brothers suit casually sipping a Diet Coke is not something you see every day. Or any day. Lucky me.

I remained calm. Glowing eyes aside, he didn't look menacing; in fact, his bland expression made him appear rather cow-like in a disconcerting but not unattractive way.

He continued to stare at me until I found my voice, albeit strained and a little higher pitched than usual. "Well? What is it? What do you want?"

His glowing red eyes opened and closed with reptilian precision, but he still didn't speak.

"Are you going to tempt me with offers of unlimited wealth or fame or sex in exchange for my soul? Because if that's your plan, the joke's on you—I'm not interested."

His mouth began to twitch. Was he about to laugh at me?

"What, then?" I snapped. "Come on, I haven't got all day. Or night." Actually, I did, since I was in between lovers and had drunk a little too much coffee that evening. Not that I would admit it to the strange apparition currently throwing daggers at what little sanity I still possessed.

"Ah, Hector—patience, please. All will be revealed to you in time."

I jumped in surprise when he used my name, especially given the familiar way it rolled off his black tongue. It occurred to me he had to know a lot more about me than my name—like every nasty detail of my pathetic life. Perversely, it gave me a little thrill. With some effort, I turned on the charm. "Since you know my name, perhaps you'll tell me yours. If you have one."

"Certainly, I have a name. It's—well, never mind. You couldn't pronounce it. Call me Art," he said, with a bow. His voice was thick and rich, like cream over honey. "I have been cast out of hell." Then he sighed, a pathetic little sigh, followed by an expression of woefulness more suited to a golden retriever than a demon.

"Seriously?" I fought to restrain the smile tugging at my lips. I had learned all about the volatile nature of demons from my grandmother, although this demon, with his fine attire and soothing voice seemed ridiculous, not at all like the raging demons of my grandmother's lectures.

"I am not wicked enough." This time, he sighed so wholeheartedly my nose prickled in sympathy. On the other hand, it could have been his fruity aftershave.

"How is that possible?" I had never heard of such a thing. Angels cast out of heaven, yes. People cast out of paradise—at least two. Undocumented aliens out of certain western nations—all the time. But a demon cast out of hell? "Does this mean you have to return to heaven?"

He recoiled in shock. "I should hope not!" His eyes pulsed, shooting out red sparks. Steam escaped from the tips of his ears. The poor demon looked seriously offended. "Besides, there's no going back, if you've never been."

"What, then?" I stopped short of apologizing. Saying *sorry* to a demon seemed a little like apologizing to the alligator before it ate you because you might give it gas.

"I have to prove I'm evil enough for hell." A waspish tone crept into his voice.

Given he was a demon, I didn't see the problem. Or what it

had to do with me. "How hard can it be?"

"Harder than you might think, given today's political and moral climate in which even the most atrocious acts go unnoticed." A bit of steam escaped from his nostrils, dropped to the floor, and curled around his feet.

"Oh, people notice. For a day or two, at least." The news media is full of such events, although I avoid the news. It gives me heartburn. "There's just so much of it—" I stopped, realizing I was about to validate his argument.

"I'm an old-fashioned kind of demon," he continued. "I miss the time when there was less moral ambiguity and people weren't so accepting."

I snorted. "You think people are accepting? What planet are you talking about?"

"This one." He raised his hand to tidy a stray lock of hair that had fallen across his forehead. "I miss the old days when adultery was punishable by death, stealing meant you got your hands chopped off, and blasphemy led to a nasty bonfire or a brisk stoning." Another sigh. "Not so much of that these days."

"Thank God."

He recoiled at that, looking horrified. "Please, there's no need to be insulting."

"I meant no offense," I said, clutching the edge of my blanket as if it might offer me some protection. "What do you want from me? I'm sure I can't help you. I may not be a paragon of virtue, but I would hardly consider myself evil. I admit sometimes I straddle the fence when it comes to what's right and what's wrong, but I'm only human."

"I know," he lamented. "I had intended to seek someone far more diabolical, but upon meeting you, I think you'll do just fine. Plus, this is as far as I got."

Great. Lucky me. "What? Did you run out of gas or something?" I imagined him traveling back and forth between earth and hell on a little red scooter, complete with a wicker basket and a shiny brass horn. *Beep, beep.*

"Not gas. Fire. I am out of fire. Hellfire, to be exact." His eyes dimmed to a dull, dried blood red, which enabled me to see him better. He had a thin face and a weak chin, a little recessed; otherwise, he appeared as an average late-twenties, early thirties whitish male with heavy black hair and perfectly aligned teeth that glowed a faint pink.

"Ah." I understood. Out of fire. Out of steam. So, yeah, out of gas. And he managed to land in my bedroom at—I glanced at the clock on my bedside table—three in the morning. "I still don't understand how I can help you. Or why I would want to."

"Because the world is about to end, Hector." His voice turned wispy and wavered as if he might fall to pieces right in front of me. "But it's too soon. It can't end yet. Not before I can prove myself worthy of my rightful place in hell. That's where you come in. I need your help."

"How can I help you? I'm nothing. And why should I?" I was on a roll. End of the world! As if! "You're a demon! Now, if you were an angel—"

He grimaced at the word *angel* and cut me off. "It's because you're nothing. That's your greatest virtue. That's what makes you the perfect accomplice. They won't even notice you until it's too late to stop you. And as for why you should…" His voice trailed off as he contemplated the question. He looked genuinely flummoxed. "Because you're a nice person and you like helping people, and I need help." His voice rose at the end as though it were a question.

"That's the stupidest thing I've ever heard," I said. "I'm not a nice person, and I hate helping people. In fact, I hate people. Most of them, anyway. Try again."

He sighed. Little puff balls of white steam shot out of his ears, rose above his head and then dispersed into the semi-darkness. "Okay, how about this—we'll save the world and have a little fun at the same time."

"Fun? You say the world is ending and you want to have fun?" I shot him the strongest look of incredulity I could muster, fluffed up with a heavy dose of sarcasm.

"Well, sure. Haven't you ever wanted to cause a little mayhem and mischief? Blow up things? Start a war? Slay a few people?"

"That's your idea of fun?" Actually, I was beginning to grasp the appeal. I do have my perverse side. And a little list ….

He shrugged. "It's all relative."

"You're rather sad."

"True," he agreed, with a little snivel. "But I'm trying to change."

I swore under my breath and flung back the covers, realizing he was trying to provoke me—and he was succeeding. Well, damn him. "Go away. I don't believe you. The world is not going to end. You're trying to trick me. I'm not going to help you, so go away. There's already enough evil in the world, thank you very much. I'm certainly not going to contribute to it."

"Well, aren't we a self-righteous paragon of misplaced virtue. You do evil every day and you don't even realize it." He paced between my nightstand and dresser, picking up steam (literally) with each step. "Meaningless evil, at that. Random evil without a greater purpose. I'm offering you an opportunity to do a little evil for a worthwhile cause."

My jaw tightened. A coldness snaked up my spine. "What do you mean I do evil every day?"

"For a start, you work for your cousin Iggy."

That made me laugh. Iggy! "I fix cars. How is that evil?"

"Iggy makes you fix cars that don't need fixing, and charges people a lot of money. He makes you talk people into paying for services they don't need, and you go along with it."

"He doesn't—"

"Yes, he does."

Well, okay, sometimes. "He's my cousin—"

"He's a crook."

"Yeah, but he's family." And the only member of my family who still spoke to me.

"Hector—" The way he said my name, loaded with reproach, made me shiver with shame. He was right. Iggy was a crook, and I willingly enabled him. I told myself I had no choice—I needed the job. So what if I looked the other way when he padded the bill, scammed a customer, or told a little lie? No skin off my teeth.

Let me tell you, there is nothing worse than being called out by the devil on the duplicity of your morality.

"Demon," Art corrected. "I'm not *the* devil. I'm not even *a* devil. Not yet, anyway. I'm simply a lowly demon."

A demon who could read minds. The realization shook me more than anything he had said to me.

"You've spent your entire life sitting in the backseat, letting other people drive you around, haven't you, Hector? And what has it gotten you? Diddly squat. *Nada.*" He leaned in, his Diet Coke breath hot on my face. "Wouldn't you like to stick it to Iggy? He may be your cousin but he's a first-class lug nut, isn't he?"

He almost had me. I would, I had to admit, do just about anything to get out from under Iggy's festering thumb. Still, there had to be a catch. Wasn't there always a catch when you're dealing with a devil—demon? "This isn't about Iggy, is it?"

"Nope. But I'm willing to help you settle the score if you'll help me on this other project, and then I'll leave you alone."

I could feel myself crumbling. Iggy had been a pain in my butt since I was a kid. He made me work long hours and paid me peanuts. He is one nasty SOB, but he'd loaned me money a few years ago when I had been desperate; money I couldn't pay back when things went bust. And now, he owned me. Lock, stock, and *cajones.*

"Come on, Hector—you know you want to." He grinned. His perfect teeth glowed hypnotically. I couldn't take my eyes off them. So perfect. So pink. So sharp ....

"I'll be free of him?"

"Free as a bird." His hands fluttered in such a way that I imagined the flapping of honest-to-god wings, sailing upward, disappearing into the ceiling.

I blinked. What? Was I hallucinating? Perhaps I dozed off. But I considered it, bending down to pick up a single black feather the size of my thumb. Now, where had that come from? "Nothing violent," I declared. I had standards. A few, anyway.

"Whatever you say, Hector."

Silly me. I believed him.

~2~

Five minutes later, I found him in the kitchen, surveying the contents of my fridge. "See anything you like?"

"Alas, yes." The light from the fridge cast him in eerie shadows and I shivered. I could see the evil clinging to him the way iron filings cling to a magnet, forming a dark halo.

My fridge was well-stocked; I could open a small deli with the contents of my fridge. Food, in all its various incarnations, has always been my weakness. While other kids played video games, I read cookbooks. I love to eat. Fortunately, I don't gain weight easily. It is my one and only superpower. But more than anything, I love to cook. I specialize in the Cuban dishes my grandmother taught me to make while I was growing up, but I don't limit myself. French, Italian, Chinese—I love them all. I must admit I took some satisfaction at the look of longing on the demon's face.

"You should open a restaurant," he said.

I laughed. Not because it was funny. No, I laughed at the irony. He had unwittingly discovered the one enduring fantasy of my paltry existence, but I had already failed once; hence, my debt to Iggy. I wasn't cut out for success and I couldn't afford to take another risk.

"I could help you," Art said, with a gleam of lavender swirling in his red eyes.

"No—"

"Think about it."

Ah, temptation. Thou dost pop up in unexpected places. I did think about it. I couldn't help myself, but it was pointless. I knew all too well how it would end.

"I would fail. Again. Oh, I can cook well enough, but there is more to running a restaurant. I have zero people skills. Large crowds make me anxious. Too much pressure brings on anxiety attacks. Even if I was successful, I wouldn't enjoy it."

The demon grinned—ah, those perfect teeth. They now glowed faintly green in the semi-darkness of my kitchen. "With my support, you would not fail, and your success would be every bit as sweet as you imagine."

I turned away abruptly and busied myself making coffee. I didn't want him to see even the tiniest glimmer of interest lurking behind my glasses. I could not let him tempt me.

"Coffee?" I avoided looking at him. "Or perhaps a sandwich? I have some nice ham—"

"No, thanks." He produced a lengthy sigh. "Another Diet Coke would be welcomed."

When the coffee was ready, I took my cup and his Coke to the kitchen table. "Are you sure I can't make you a sandwich? You look … hungry."

"Ah, indeed. However, I dare not indulge." Another deep, theatrical sigh. "I am, sadly, an addict. Food is my weakness. My Achilles' heel, if you will. My heroin. My crack—" I coughed, which broke his revelry. "But it doesn't stop me from enjoying the scent of food. Smelling is almost as good as tasting." He plucked a plump red apple from my fruit bowl and held it against his nose. "I can smell where this apple was grown." He closed his eyes and took in a deep breath. His face softened. His jaw went slack. Then his whole body relaxed and swayed precariously. I thought he might slide off the chair, but he rallied. "British Columbia. A Canadian apple—well, isn't that interesting? Just north of Oliver, in the Okanagan. Beautiful country, by the way. Ever been?"

I shook my head. I'd never been out of Florida; I'd rarely been out of Miami.

"It grew on a twenty-year-old tree on the west side of a gently sloping hill," he continued, eyes still closed. "It contains sixteen percent sugar—a little higher than usual for the variety. It will be sweet, crisp, and satisfactorily juicy. It has a tiny bruise on the top, which occurred in transport. You should eat it soon." He returned the apple to the bowl and sighed, a long, deeply painful sigh as if he had discovered the one, true shortcoming of his eternal existence.

I choked back a sudden urge to stuff an apple into my mouth. "So, you don't eat, but you drink Diet Coke?"

"An exception. It helps curb the craving. I'm not perfect, you know. None of us is."

Well, he had that right. "So, how are you going to get me out from under Iggy's thumb?"

"Don't know yet." He ran his finger around the rim of his Diet Coke can, producing a faint hum. "I have to think about it. But don't worry. It will be spectacular."

"Spectacular?" I didn't like the sound of that. "What am I going to have to do in exchange?"

"I told you. Save the world."

That again. "Is that all? You're kidding, right?" Save the world, my ass! He had something else up his sleeve. Either that or I was deep into a psychotic break.

He gaped at me, confusion written plainly on his thin face. "I never jest about such things."

"How can you possibly expect me to save the world? I can't even save myself." I sputtered, drooling coffee down my chin.

"Patience, my friend. You underestimate yourself. And me. I don't want to tip my hand, but don't worry. You cannot fail."

It was on the tip of my tongue to remind him I had, in fact, failed at everything I had ever attempted but, instead, I shrugged. "Either you don't have a clue what you're doing, or you don't want me to turn tail and run."

"Yes!" His exuberance nearly knocked me off my chair. "Do you have any more Diet Coke?"

I obliged him.

By his fourth Diet Coke, the poor demon was a mess, weeping and wailing with great vigor. Who knew you could get drunk on caffeine and fake sugar? There was nothing I could do except watch him weep. I mean, how do you comfort a demon? It was as if the poor devil had lost his soul.

His soul?

A devil with a soul?

"A demon," Art corrected. "I have many, and I have ceased to torment them. They no longer take me seriously."

I was beginning to understand his dilemma.

"They laugh at me. They make fun of me. I, like you, am a complete failure." He shook and swayed, precariously close to breaking down. If he'd been a tree, he would have dropped all his leaves.

I ignored his last comment, one I assumed he constructed as a ploy for my sympathy, to make me think we had something in common—the two screw ups: of course, we should join forces. *We'll show them, by Jupiter.* "Let me guess—the other demons won't play with you anymore?" I didn't even try to hide the sarcasm. I wanted to go back to bed. And I wanted to laugh, but I didn't. I'm not a complete fool.

"You have no idea what it's like," he sobbed.

How much longer was this going to go on? "Oh, for heaven's sake—"

He paused long enough to glare at me, his eyes now a fathomless black, big and droopy and oh-so-pathetic. Think demented basset hound. A deeply offended, demented basset hound from hell who would no doubt turn me into a glowing ember without so much as a second thought if I didn't watch myself.

I tried again. "Come on, man. Get a grip. You're going through a slump. Stop acting like the world is ending."

He snapped to attention. "The world *is* ending, you moron. Haven't you been listening?" He commenced wailing again.

"I'm just a simple mechanic," I countered, "and not a very good one, either. What do I know? I'm really very stupid. It's amazing I can even change a tire. If you say the world is ending, who am I to say differently?" I said this to placate him, of course. I didn't know what else to do.

He sagged and dropped into a chair. "I'm sorry. I'm a little on edge."

No wonder the poor bugger had been thrown out of hell if he went around apologizing for his actions. I took the high road and changed the subject. "Would you like another Diet Coke?"

He immediately perked up.

I handed him another can, and then took a detour to the bathroom to pee. I ran a comb through my hair, checked my reflection to make sure nothing was caught in the gap between my front teeth. I stopped short of brushing them, even though they needed it because I had a hankering for a stiff jolt of whiskey. Have you ever drunk whiskey with the minty taste of toothpaste still in your mouth? Ick.

I toddled back to the kitchen, but Art was gone. I thought briefly about making a run for it. It would have been easy. The front door was only a few steps away, but all I was wearing was a pair of boxers. My keys, wallet, and clothes were in the bedroom. I calmed myself by opening the bottle of whiskey Iggy had given me at Christmas and pouring a healthy dose into a glass.

I found Art stretched out on my bed as if he owned it, his head propped up on a mass of unfamiliar pillows. I wondered where they had all come from. He held the Diet Coke can against his chest. His eyes were closed, and he was very, very still. Then he let out one hell of a burp, causing the window to rattle. I wrinkled my nose in disgust at the sulfury fumes.

Cradling my whiskey, I climbed on the bed as far from him as I could and settled against the headboard. I took a sip and savored the burn. "What did you do to put your damnation in jeopardy, anyway?"

The bed creaked as he stiffened. "I don't want to talk about it."

"You must have done something really, really good to be in this much trouble." I stressed *good* and was rewarded by a grimace of epic proportions.

"You don't know the half of it." He folded his arms across his chest and puffed out his cheeks like a petulant three-year-old.

"So tell me. You might feel better." Which might get him out of my apartment sooner.

"I doubt it," he said, answering both the spoken and unspoken comments.

"Then what do you want from me?" I whined. My turn to be a three-year-old.

"I told you—I need your help to save the world."

"But why me?" I stopped short of stamping my feet, only because I was in a semi-prone position.

"I can't do it alone. Believe it or not, I have limits. All demons have limits. I know what needs to be done—more or less, but I need a living human to do the legwork. As for why *you*—why not you? I suppose I could do better—you can always do better, but time is running out, and you have certain qualities I find most attractive and advantageous." He leveled an intense, glowing stare at me. "You underestimate yourself, Hector. That's your biggest problem."

I met his stare and gave him one of my own. "So, let me see if I've got this right. You want this puny, mortal, nearsighted gay guy with a gap between his teeth, and a somewhat ambivalent moral code as your sidekick?"

"Yes."

I was, in a word, dumbfounded. "No wonder they kicked you out."

"They didn't exactly kick me out," he said indignantly. "I'm just not sure they'll let me back in."

"Well, I suppose you could learn to do good deeds. You know, embrace the light." You might think I was goading him, but it was an honest suggestion.

"I'd sooner stuff slugs up my butt."

In other words: *no, thanks.*

"I like being a demon. It's very freeing. Being 'good' is nothing more than an anxiety-ridden trip on an out of control, downward-spiraling roller coaster. All that people-pleasing, which is mostly impossible, by the way, and all those moral-slash-ethical dilemmas lurking around every corner, just waiting to trip you up. The constant striving for perfection. Do more. Sin less—talk about crazy-making!"

As his agitation increased, the bedroom lights flickered precariously. I tried to placate him, lest he blew a fuse and plunged all of Miami into a blackout.

"Maybe you need a vacation. You know, recharge your batteries. A few days of doing nothing and you'll be back to your old, evil self." He looked at me as though I had suggested he kiss a puppy. Then it finally hit me. "Holy *hijole*—you're serious, aren't you? The world really is about to end."

He turned on his side, away from me.

The freaking bastard. I wanted to punch him; instead, I downed the rest of the whiskey in one quick gulp, ignoring the fiery pain that enveloped my throat.

"When?"

He didn't answer.

"When? Damn it, Art, tell me!" I started to pull pillows out from under him and toss them across the room. "When! Tell me, or I'll sprinkle holy water on you." This was no idle threat. I had some in the drawer in my bedside table, a gift from my grandmother shortly after I told her why I wasn't likely to give her any great-grandchildren.

That got his attention. "Two weeks," he said flatly. "Give or take a day or two."

"Two weeks?" I fought back the panic. Breathe, I told myself. *While you can.* Two weeks. Today was Tuesday—no, Wednesday. So, two Wednesdays from today. I paused long enough to consider the irony of the world ending on a Wednesday—my bowling night.

"What's going to happen?" My tone, I confess, was slightly mocking, or maybe it was panic. "Is Jesus coming in a flaming chariot, driven by winged unicorns, with a chorus of angels singing hymns?"

"You're confusing Jesus with Ben Hur." He was calm now; his eyes were bright—in a nearly normal way. All traces of melancholy had vanished.

"What, then?"

"Some guy named Stanley Waterman is going to start a war with Canada."

"Stanley Waterman?" I couldn't hold back the laughter. "You mean the president of the United States? *That* Stanley Waterman? With *Canada?* Get serious. Why?"

"Haven't you been paying attention? Since Waterman pissed off the Arabs, he's going after Canada—they have the third largest oil reserves in the world, and Waterman thinks the Canadians should hand it all over to the Americans. Manifest Destiny, and all that."

"That's ridiculous."

"You think so? Maybe you should read a newspaper now and then, Hector. Or, gee, I don't know—watch the news."

"What's Waterman going to do? Invade Canada? Bomb them?"

The demon looked at me, waiting for me to catch up.

"He wouldn't! Why would he do something so stupid?"

"Well, for starters, he's not that bright. Of course, if the bombs actually landed in Canada, it would simply destroy half the northern hemisphere, including the oil fields he wants so badly but, as I said, Waterman's not that bright. The rest of the world would barely notice. They might even applaud. But the bombs will overshoot Canada and land in Russia, which will get the Russians, the Chinese, and the North Koreans a little hot under the collar and they'll retaliate with gusto. And glee. Lots and lots of glee. Those guys are nutso, you know. Especially the North Koreans. And then, one thing leads to another, as is prone to happen in these situations, and the next thing you know—*kaboom!* Bye-bye, civilization. Bye-bye, Starbucks. Bye-bye, cable TV. Bye-bye—"

I got it. "But what am I supposed to do?"

"Stop it," he said. "Then I'll have more time to unredeem myself."

"How am I supposed to do that?"

"Assassinate Waterman." His voice brimmed with triumph.

I opened and closed my mouth three times before I could get the words out. "Are you kidding me? The man is the President. He's surrounded by a zillion Secret Service agents. Those guys don't mess around. You'll never get near him. Besides, you'd have to get in line."

"Not me. I can't assassinate anyone. I can only suggest it," he hummed, seductively.

The magnitude of what he was suggesting made my head spin. "Are you crazy?"

"No," he said grinning, "but you are. Or will be."

My biggest mistake was in not taking any of this seriously right off the bat. But do you blame me?

Think about it. You wake up in the middle of the night and there's this weird guy with glowing red eyes and shiny pink teeth standing next to your bed, claiming to be a demon and drinking your Diet Coke. Not the devil, mind you. Just a demon. One of the troops. A foot soldier in the War for Universal Damnation. I mean, what would you conclude?

You're having a bad dream?

You should lay off the booze?

Reduce the stress in your life?

Up your meds?

Or do you wonder what in the name of heaven and/or hell did you do that was so bad that an honest-to-God demon thinks you would conspire to assassinate the leader of the free world, even if that leader is an asshole?

I mean, I'm not a bad guy. Okay, so I could shower more often, drink less beer, leave a bigger tip, and call the girl the next day instead of forgetting her name. But, hey, life's short. I got things to do. Places to go.

And I'm gay. I never call the girl.

~4~

Iggy was in a fine mood that morning. He's a wiry little bastard—barely five-three. Big hands. Tiny heart. Smokes cheap cigars like the proverbial chimney. (Given our heritage, you'd think he'd have better taste in cigars.) He has the voice of a Sumo wrestler and the brains of a codfish. He's married to a flat-bottomed woman named Bella Florio. Bella's okay, but why she sticks with Iggy is a mystery. Maybe there's more in the trunk than there is under the hood. They have three flat-bottomed kids who call me Uncle Hector, even though I'm not their uncle. Truthfully, I kind of like it.

"I'm gonna fire your ass," he yelled as I walked into the shop. I was only 15 minutes late. Hardly a capital offense. "I don't care if you are my cousin."

I ignored him. "Is there coffee?" I had a slight hangover, and I really needed the caffeine.

He waved me off with a vulgar phalangeal gesture. I blew him a kiss. Tit for tat.

There was no coffee, but that suited me fine. Iggy couldn't make coffee worth a damn. I made a pot, reaching behind the can of Folgers for my stash of the good stuff, then flipped through the newspaper while it brewed.

The paper was filled with the usual bullshit: death, destruction, mayhem, corruption, wars and rumors of wars. The usual political shenanigans. The latest on Waterman's rhetoric with the Canadians. I had skipped over such reports before. Nothing to do with me. Besides, who takes Canada—or Waterman—seriously? But now I read carefully, scanning for signs of an impending war. The Associated Press quoted him as saying, *"Our northern neighbor is no friend of the US. You can't trust them. First, they burn down the White House, now they won't share their oil. What next?"*

Burn down the White House? Perhaps I really should pay more attention to the news.

On the editorial page, there were several opinion pieces on the state of Canadian-US relations—some for, some against. (Can't trust a country that has English and French as their official languages. Two official languages? How un-American can you get?)

On the back page: CANADA PLEDGES TO RETALIATE AGAINST NEW ROUND OF TARIFFS. What were they going to do? Stop sending maple syrup? Recall Justin Bieber and William Shatner? *"All they have to do is give us their oil," Waterman told the Associated Press.*

It occurred to me Art was on the wrong track. Shouldn't he be encouraging Stanley Waterman, not trying to stop him? I mean, if your business is EVIL, wouldn't causing a nuclear holocaust be the ultimate triumph? I would never encourage such a thing, of course. I was just playing devil's advocate.

I lapsed into a fit of coughing.

Damn it. He was doing a great job of manipulating me, but I still didn't believe him. I didn't believe *in* him. And I certainly wouldn't do his bidding. I was a Christian, damn it. Sort of. This was God's problem, not mine. Well, let God handle it. Leave me out of it. I was perfectly happy being a mindless member of the flock, thank you very much.

I flipped on the radio, hoping for a brain-numbing blast of salsa music. Instead, I got the news:

*"Canadian-American tensions are at an all-time high, according to reports coming out of Washington and Ottawa. Ottawa has recalled its ambassador. American citizens living in Canada, some of whom have lived there for decades, could face deportation. This has led to riots along the border and civic leaders fear it could get worse. As a result, the Canadian military has moved troops into Northern Alberta to protect the oil sands."*

I changed the station. *"The world is ending, Brother Cooper. God has told me it's time to prepare."*

*"Amen, Brother Knutson."*

*"The signs are all around us. It won't be long now. Repent, brothers and sisters. The time for His return is soon."*

Brother Cooper and Brother Knutson sounded far too cheerful. This disturbed me more than riots along the border.

I turned off the radio.

The coffee was ready, so I poured some into my over-sized insulated travel mug, added enough cream and sugar to turn it into pudding with a few good shakes, and took my first glorious sip.

Then I got to work.

The day passed well enough. Engines to tune. Carburetors to clean. Oil to change. Tires to balance. Nothing requiring much concentration, which was a good thing. I was distracted by thoughts of my late-night visitor. I mean, really, who wakes up with a demon standing over them? And a rather wimpy demon, at that. A demon who isn't "bad" enough for hell? A demon who needs help from a living human? With pink teeth and a Diet Coke habit?

Ridiculous. I needed to get a grip and lay off the late-night fried bologna sandwiches.

I tried to get Art out of my thoughts by constructing elaborate meal plans in my head while I worked. Today's menu featured beef tenderloin in a red wine sauce, eggplant casserole, and a multi-layered pastry with strawberries and creme-fraîche. Every so often I sensed something like a sigh—wistful, vague, hungry. Very, very hungry.

"Drink another Diet Coke. You'll feel better," I finally mumbled.

"You talking to me, butt-face?" Iggy came up behind me, scaring the crap out of me. "Where's my friggin' wrench? Did you take it again?"

"I haven't seen your stupid wrench." I wiped my hands on my overalls and glanced at the clock. The day had passed much faster than I had expected. "I gotta go."

"You just got here."

"Eight hours ago," I said. "I'm done working overtime for you, Iggy. You never pay me for it."

"I pay you. What do you mean I don't pay you?"

"Not enough to stick around any longer than necessary. I got a life, you know."

"Since when? You don't go drinking. You don't gamble. You don't got a girlfriend." He made a face. "Or a boyfriend. Hell, you don't even got a dog. You got a life! Right!"

"I have a house guest." One who would happily munch on your face for a snack, Iggy, *mi primo.*

"A houseguest? Is that what you call it?" He snorted most unattractively. "Your mother must be real proud of you."

My mother forgot all about me the day after I was born. This is no exaggeration. Dissociative Identity Disorder mega-sized. The day before I was born she was Consuela Sanchez, a waitress/dancer of Cuban descent with a fondness for dill pickles and Bourbon; the day after, she was Suzy Maguire, an Irish florist with a foul mouth, a preference for gin, and an amazing ability to color-coordinate plant matter. She's been Suzy ever since. Forgot all about being Cuban. Forgot every single word of her native tongue, except the swear words, which is why, except for a few choice phrases, I don't speak a word of Spanish. It's put me to a real disadvantage, let me tell you, among my Spanish-speaking peers and relatives. It's also why I have a slight Irish lilt when I get drunk. The doctors tried to treat her, but nothing worked. She was Suzy, from 'Derry, damn it. Get over it.

It made for an interesting childhood. She regarded me as a changeling child, left by the faeries—so to speak—for her to raise, or not, as she saw fit.

If it weren't for my grandmother, I'd probably have ended up in jail.

Granny Inez was an amazing woman—strong, beautiful, highly organized, a fine cook, and unforgiving of even the smallest defect. She fled Cuba in the 1950s, and ended up in Florida, like so many other Cubans. She ran a little corner store, married a cigar maker named Jorge who left her with three kids, my two uncles and my mother, while he went to New York to become a "star". (It didn't happen.)

She never talked much about her life in Cuba. She quickly became Americanized and did her best to stay clear of the Cuban community. After she died, we discovered letters that suggested she had once had a love affair with a high-ranking aide to Fidel that turned messy. Apparently, her opposition to all things Cuban was not just political.

Which also meant she was perfectly happy when Consuela became Suzy.

By the time I was born, there was plenty of family in the area, all somehow spirited out of Cuba by means of which to this day I have no clue. I'm not close to any of them—kind of hard when we don't even speak the same language. Iggy's the exception, but his mother is Anglo. Besides, most of them had me pegged as queer before I was out of diapers. At least one church nearly burned to the ground from the number of candles my relatives lit to pray me "normal."

I had a long, lonely childhood.

Iggy tried again. "Come on, man. We got all these cars—"

"Perhaps you should hire another mechanic." I studied my overalls. Should I wash them, or could they wait another day? I opted on waiting. "I've been telling you that for months."

He scowled. "Maybe I will. Maybe I'll hire one and give you the boot."

"Then you'll need to hire three." I packed away my tools.

"Is that my wrench?" He snatched the thing out of my toolbox before I could answer. "You little thief. You keep your hands off my tools."

"Screw you, Iggy. I'm out of here." I slammed the lid down on my toolbox and snapped shut the padlock.

"Fine. Whatever. Just don't expect no bonus."

"Ha! Right. Like that would ever happen." I checked my pocket to make sure I had my keys. "*Adios, amigo.*"

I almost made it to the door when he called after me, "Hey, Hector, you gonna go bowling tonight?"

"Nope. I have company. I told you."

Iggy harrumphed. "Yeah, well, Mike said to tell you if you missed another practice, you could kiss the team goodbye."

"Tell Mike to eat shit." I didn't care. I was tired of bowling. Being around all those back-slapping, ass-snorting, ball-busting "friends" with their blowhard, antiquated delusions of mid-century grandeur had become a migraine-inducing ordeal of late. Pity. I was a pretty good bowler. Not a single one of them could call me "limp-wristed."

Iggy yelled something I couldn't make out as I slid out the door. I wasn't interested enough to get him to repeat it, but I gave him a cheery back-handed wave.

I unlocked my Subaru and stood by the open door for a moment to let the worst of the day's stored heat escape before I got in. I pushed my glasses back up my sweaty nose. It was hotter than—

A figure stood at the head of the alley, watching me. I couldn't make out any features, but I'm pretty sure it was male; tall, broad shoulders, black hair that gleamed even in the shade, little flashes of red coming from his eyes. I could make out the silhouette of a trench coat.

A trench coat? When it was 96 degrees in the shade?

I pushed my glasses right up against my eyes and squinted—I hate being nearsighted—but whoever or whatever I saw was gone. I had a sudden need to get out of there.

The feeling intensified, hitting me square in the chest, building into an instinctive, primal urge to sprout wings and fly.

But being the naturally talented and well-coordinated creature that I am, I fumbled for my keys and dropped them between the seats. When I finally fished them out and got the key into the ignition, I flooded the engine.

Buckets of sweat poured down my face, and I whimpered like my true girly-boy self. I couldn't breathe. My primitive brain screamed *run, RUN, you stupid moron*.

I stumbled as I got out of the car and fell face-first into a puddle of dog piss and motor oil, which turned out to be a good thing because a second later, the alley exploded, and a freaking blast furnace catapulted over me.

That damned demon had killed me after all! I was dead now—I had to be—and it was completely and entirely his frickin fault. We were going to have words, Art and I. Evil, nasty, ugly words. *Híjole*.

Then it got very, very quiet. Middle of the night quiet.

End of the world quiet.

Slowly, I turned my head and flexed my fingers, my toes. And the pain hit—a dull, pulsing pain like a two-ton pachyderm had stomped on my chest. But I could still breathe.

So, I wasn't dead.

Well, halleluiah and call me blessed.

I turned my head but all I could see were undefined clouds of smoke and pulsing orange light. I must have been in a protective bubble because flames passed over me without so much as singeing a hair on my head. I got a faint whiff of burning oil and gas, mildly pleasant and far away as if someone had juiced up the barbecue.

My ears were ringing so loudly I couldn't hear clearly, but I had a sense of sirens and people yelling, along with the crackling and popping of flames and things exploding, including my car. A war zone, I thought. The back alley had become a war zone. Had the Canadians finally had enough of Waterman and launched a pre-emptive strike?

If they had, they'd missed him by several hundred miles.

Wait—did the Canadians even have bombs? Or airplanes?

You think of strange things when you're semi-conscious and in shock.

I tried to stand, but I was too dizzy, so I stayed down and doubled up, resting my head on my knees. At some point, I started rocking myself and possibly muttering incoherently while flaming bits of debris rained down around me. Oddly, none of it touched me.

After a while, I dozed a little. I know, I know. Hard to believe. I jerked awake mid-snort and discovered I was still in my bubble, but I wasn't alone. I'd lost my glasses, so I had to squint. Art stood in front of me, grinning like a banshee.

"You did this." I meant it as an accusation, but Art's grin widened.

"Guess you won't have to worry about going to work for a while," he said.

"You frickin asshat." The urge to strangle him intensified. "Where's Iggy? Did you kill him? Is he dead?"

"Hector, buddy—would I do that to you? Kill the only member of your family who talks to you?"

"Yes."

He looked ponderous for a fraction of a second. "You're right. But I didn't. He's fine. Although the police may arrest him at some point. Like when they discover the insurance on his business is ten times the actual value."

I glared at him. Pointlessly, I might add. Because I realized it was exactly the kind of stupid thing Iggy would do.

"He wanted me to work late." My anger faded into flaccid helplessness.

"Good thing you didn't." He let that sink in and then added: "He has insurance on you, too."

~5~

Shortly after midnight, I crawled out of the alley and headed home. I had to take the bus since my car didn't survive the explosion. No great loss. The transmission was about to fall out.

Without my glasses, I couldn't see clearly, which made getting on the right bus an ordeal. It didn't help that I looked like I'd been dragged through the streets by a league of marauding elephants. More than one bus sped away when the driver got a good look at me.

I found Art lounging in my living room, downing the last of my Diet Coke. "You need to buy more," he said, apparently forgetting I'd nearly been blown to pieces. Then he got a good, long look at me and waved me off. "Tomorrow will be fine."

I didn't argue, protest or swear at him. I simply stripped off what was left of my clothes, right in the middle of my living room, and headed for the shower.

I stayed under the pulsing spray until I ran out of hot water. Screw my water bill.

As I drip-dried, I dug around in the drawer next to the bathroom sink until I found an old pair of glasses. They made me look like a wiggle-headed moon monster and they weren't up to my current prescription, but at least I could see well enough to find the toilet and some clothes.

I looked longingly at my bed, but hunger pains struck so hard I nearly keeled over. I can't sleep if I'm hungry. I hadn't eaten a thing since I'd had a meatball sub at lunch. That meant I'd gone more than twelve hours without food, which had to be a record.

It also meant I had to go back to the kitchen and face Art.

To my surprise, he had set the table with my good dishes and had already poured the wine. The air was ripe with the smell of butter and cheese. I wiped a bit of drool from my mouth as I pulled my chair up to the table. With a flourish and a grin, he produced a towering souffle from the oven. I gasped in appreciation. It was a thing of beauty, puffed sky-high, golden brown, flecked with bits of cheese on top, just the way I like it.

He spooned the steaming souffle onto my warm plate and I whimpered in anticipation, my fork already in my hand. "I hate you, you know."

"I know. I wouldn't have it any other way."

Yes, yes, I'm weak. Spineless. Possibly without morals or scruples. But it was cheese souffle. Cheese souffle! Light and tender and deliciously tart. I couldn't make a souffle to save my soul. Lord knows, I've tried. After the first mouth-melting bite, I forgot my anger and threw myself into savoring every single forkful. I couldn't even be jealous at Art's culinary skill. I morphed into the miser in his counting house. *Mine, mine, all mine.*

"There's dessert," Art announced as I polished off the last crumb.

I looked at him in child-like wonder. "You made dessert?"

"Chocolate cake," and then, with a giggle, he added, "devil's food."

I moaned. Yeah, it was corny, but it was also my favorite dessert.

He served it with homemade vanilla ice cream. Where did he get an ice cream maker? I didn't own one, although it was on my wish list. The cake was splendid. Dark, moist, and sweet, covered in a layer of chocolate buttercream icing that made my heart flutter and my arteries gasp.

"My god, that's good." I licked the last bit of chocolate off my fork. "You are a genius."

He bowed. "I'm glad you enjoyed it." His lower lip quivered. "Was it really good?"

I nodded. "Beyond good—the best food I've ever eaten."

"I should have made a salad, but I ran out of time. And frankly, your lettuce is a little wilted."

I brushed that thought aside. "This was perfect. Really. No

salad was needed. Thank you." He frowned a little. "But I'm sure if you had made a salad, it would have been excellent, too."

He brightened. "Yes, it would have been, although I don't understand the current craze for eating leaves."

"How did you learn to cook?"

He poured more wine into my glass, which I sipped with great contentment. "Food channel. I have a lot of time on my hands."

The wine must have gone to my head because I said, "If I ever opened a restaurant, I would hire you in a heartbeat."

He glowed at that. Literally, come to think of it. Not just his eyes. I swear I saw a green cast emanating off his head and hands. Kind of like his own personal Aurora Borealis.

The wine and food had done a good job of dulling the trauma of the day. I still wanted to kill him, but the urgency had faded, and I had trouble remembering why.

"You should get some sleep," he told me. "You have a busy day ahead of you."

As soon as the words were out of his mouth, the exhaustion took over. I staggered into the bedroom and collapsed onto the bed.

"Mind if I hang out?" I heard him say from a million miles away.

"Uhhhh ... busy day. Busy, busy ..." and then I was asleep.

6

I woke up the next morning with a powerful ringing in my ears, compounded by pounding. It took a moment to realize the pounding wasn't in my head. Someone was at the door. A very impatient someone.

I am not at my best in the morning, even when I haven't recently survived being nearly blown to pieces and/or roasted to a crisp. I staggered to the door wearing nothing but a pair of boxers and flung it open with a snarl. "What?"

Iggy filled the doorframe, leering at me. He shoved the door open so hard it banged against the wall, knocking the door stopper right through the wall. "You asshole! You could have killed me." He leaped at me and knocked me to the floor.

For a little guy, he's wiry, and he had the element of surprise, but I outweighed him by 50 pounds. I pinned him down by sitting on his chest. It's not often I can out-wrestle someone. (Never.) I was pleased with myself. Then I remembered he attacked me.

"What's the matter with you?" His chest rose and fell with such force, I thought he might injure himself in his attempts to buck me off. "Relax, man. You're gonna have a coronary. And you're turning me on." Not really, but I was desperate for him to stop moving.

"I'm gonna kill you," he snarled, bucking with renewed vigor.

It was an idle threat since I had the upper hand but still, I proceeded with caution. You can never tell with guys like Iggy. They can be full of surprises.

"Is this about the garage?"

He spit at me. "Yeah, it's about the garage, you moron."

"Let me guess—you think I'm responsible for the explosion."

"Damn right."

"Now, why would I do such a thing? Really, Iggy, you're not thinking straight." He bared his teeth and growled. "I swear it wasn't me. You realize that I'm out of a job now, don't you? And a car."

He swore a streak in Spanish, adding a few new words to my vocabulary, and then gave a rousing effort to free himself, complete with a bellow that would have intimidated a bull moose.

I held my position. "Iggy, Iggy. This is getting us nowhere. I swear I did not blow up your garage. For one thing, I don't know anything about explosives, and for another, I really don't give a crap about you or your garage. Obviously, somebody was extremely pissed off at you. Unless it was an accident. Or you did it for the insurance money."

That earned me another bellow and an energetic squirm. This was more action than I'd had in months. Too bad Iggy was family. (I do have a few standards.) I let out a big, overly dramatic sigh to make a point and tightened my grip on his arms.

Iggy roared in a most unbecoming way. "Let me up, you moron."

"Not a chance. Not until you cool off."

"I ain't never going to cool off."

"Then we're going to be here a while, aren't we?" I hoped it wouldn't be too long. I had to pee. "Come on, Iggy, I know it's hard, but think. Who would do this? Do you owe anybody money? You piss someone off? Well, I suppose that's a given. You always piss people off. You charge too much. You make people buy things they don't need. You really are a cheating moon fart, Iggy. I'm surprised someone hasn't blown you up long before this."

He let out another string of curses and tried to claw my glasses off my face. He could be one little hell-fighter. I wondered if Art should have chosen my cousin for his sidekick instead of me.

Where was Art, anyway? Maybe he could talk some sense into Iggy.

I heard someone cough. I glanced up to see two cops standing in the doorway: one white, one black. A variety of looks passed over their faces—amusement, disgust, confusion, disbelief:

interpretation, misinterpretation. The usual.

I offered them my best shit-eating grin. "Morning, officers. Me and my cousin are having a tickle fight. Nothing to concern yourself." Iggy snorted.

I climbed off Iggy and stood up. I even offered my hand to help him, but he rolled away and got up on his own. "Were we making too much noise? The guy below me is always complaining. I can't even make toast without him jabbing the ceiling with a broom. I bet there are lots of holes in his ceiling. You should check."

The black cop stared at my crotch. I think he liked what he saw, but I wasn't in the mood anymore.

"Mind if I go to the bathroom?" I did the pee-pee dance, like when I was a kid.

He looked away and then pulled out a notebook. "Make it snappy."

A few minutes later, bladder successfully emptied and fully, if not immaculately, dressed I rejoined them in the living room.

Iggy must have been regaling the cops with one hell of a story, judging by the epic glares they shot my way. "Coffee, anyone?"

They waved me off, although the black cop perked up a bit. Screw them. I went into the kitchen and put on the coffee pot. I made a full pot. Experience has taught me that once the smell of coffee is in the air, people change their mind.

Sure enough, they took the mugs I handed to them a few minutes later. Even Iggy, who didn't look quite as angry anymore. Maybe the cops had validated his feelings and commiserated with him about his crazy cousin, and that had temporarily placated him. Most people lose a lot of steam if you just empathize with them. *There, there.*

We sat at the kitchen table and I served them slices of leftover chocolate cake. I swear the cops swooned and forgot why they were there. Iggy ruined the moment by reminding the cops about the explosion. Then we proceeded to have a nice little chat.

Why, no, officers, I have no idea who would want to blow up Iggy's garage.

No, I didn't see anything or anyone suspicious.

No, I don't hold any grudges against Iggy. We're family, man. All families have problems, but we stick together, man. Gotta. You know. It's a Cuban thing. Us against them. Cultural, and all that.

No, I didn't think it was racially motivated. Everybody in the neighborhood loves Iggy. Most of his customers are Latino. We stick together, you know. He always treats people fairly, Iggy does. He's got that kind of reputation. The black cop, apparently more attuned to sarcasm than his partner, snorted into his coffee.

The white cop glared at his partner and then turned back to me. "Your cousin says you left early last night."

"I didn't leave early. I left at six o'clock. I'd put in a full day. I was supposed to go bowling. I'd missed a couple of nights and the boys threatened to kick me off the team if I missed another practice, isn't that right, Iggy? What could I do? I had to leave. Couldn't disappoint the boys."

Iggy glared mightily, but he didn't contradict me.

The cop tapped his notebook with the end of his pen. "But you never made it?"

I shook my head. "I got caught in the explosion in the parking lot."

Iggy's head jerked up sharply. "You were in the parking lot?"

"Yeah—" Too late, I realized I'd made a mistake.

"How the hell did you survive that?" the black cop asked. "It was an inferno back there. It looks like frickin Ground Zero."

I shrugged. "I don't know. Guess I fell into a pocket in the space-time continuum." No one laughed. I continued. "I really don't know. I must have been knocked out because when I woke up, it was dark, and the fire was under control, so I went home."

"How did you get home?" the white cop asked. "Your car was destroyed. Did someone pick you up?" Like, maybe, an accomplice?

"I took the bus. Four buses, actually. There's no direct route. Took forever. And I still had to walk a couple of blocks."

They looked at me like my nose was on the back of my head. I picked up my charred pants, still laying on the living room floor, and pulled my bus transfers out of my pocket. I handed them to the black cop. He glanced at them and then handed them to the other cop.

The white cop finished his cake and coffee and then closed his notebook and stuffed it and the bus transfers—without looking at them—into his pocket. "That's enough for now, but don't think we're done with you. Either of you."

Iggy feigned indignity.

"Thanks for the coffee," the black cop said. "And the cake. Damn good cake, by the way." I could tell he meant it. I'm sure if the circumstances had been a little different, he would have asked for the recipe. And possibly my phone number.

"Sure thing. Any time." I even kind of meant it.

I locked the door behind them, deadbolt and all. I could see Iggy nattering to the cops all the way to the parking lot. He watched them drive away, arms on his hips as if he couldn't believe that they would just drive away like that. He glanced in my direction, flipped me the bird, and then marched away.

I thought about turning off my cell phone before Iggy had a chance to plead his case to the rest of the family. Most of them would take Iggy's side. I didn't need that kind of pressure.

Instead, I made steel cut oatmeal with fresh blueberries. I was feeling the need for something healthy after last night's dinner.

Last night's dinner—had I imagined it?

Apparently not. There was a sink full of dirty dishes to bear witness.

I groaned. Couldn't the little shit at least do the dishes?

Speaking of which—where was Art this morning? Did he decide I was not the sidekick he envisioned and bugger off? I could only hope—but it was, of course, premature.

7

I finished the last of the dishes and was about to start rearranging the cutlery drawer when Art appeared, standing in front of the stove, grinning like he'd ended world hunger.

"How did you get in here?" I was sure I had bolted the front door. Had he flown through a window?

"There is no lock that can keep me out," Art said, answering my unspoken question with eerie precision. He dropped the large bag he was holding on the table.

"What's that?"

He brightened considerably. "Oh, just something you're going to need."

"What?" I was curious but wary. I didn't want to look.

He shrugged coyly. "Any Diet Coke?"

"I haven't been to the store yet. Sorry." Wait—why was I apologizing? "You went shopping." I pointed to his bag. "You could have picked some up."

"It doesn't work that way. You have to supply it. I'm not allowed to buy my own."

"That's stupid."

"Tell me about it." He gave me an engaging smile. "Think you could get some soon? I'm starting to go into caffeine withdrawal."

"Yeah, sure. As soon as I'm done in the kitchen, I'll go to the store." I was willing to do anything to get away from him.

He rubbed his hands in gleeful anticipation and then stopped suddenly and sniffed the air. "You've had people." Was that reproach in his voice, with a hint of jealousy?

"It's not like I invited them." I hated sounding defensive. "Iggy showed up, pissed as hell." Art flinched. Was it something I said? "He thinks I blew up his garage."

Art busied himself rearranging the salt and pepper shakers on the table. "Well, that's just stupid, isn't it?"

"Then the police showed up. Iggy made all kinds of accusations. I think I got them straightened out, though."

"Oh, I wouldn't count on that." Art frowned and continued sniffing the air as if trying to determine the source of a gas leak.

"What does that mean?"

He stopped mid-sniff and flashed me a smile full of charm and orange teeth. "They'll be back."

"That wouldn't surprise me." How could anything surprise me at this point?

"It might surprise you when they show up with a search warrant and find traces of explosives in your closet." He had that look on his pasty face—you know the one—as if he'd swallowed a plate of shit and found it tasty. "I'd clear the cache on your computer if I were you. Better yet—get rid of it."

My head spun. Like I'd eaten one too many hot dogs, topped by a candied apple and a fried Mars bar, and then hopped on the roller-coaster. "What the ...? Why are you doing this?"

"I'm not doing anything, Hector, except trying to save you unnecessary grief. Things have been set in motion, over which I no longer have control."

"Bullshit, Art, *buddy*, this is all you. I demand you put an end to it."

"I can't do that, Hector. It's too late. And I need you. I really, really need you."

"I won't be of much use to you if I'm in jail."

"Oh, you won't go to jail."

"And how do you know that?"

"Because we're leaving."

"*We're* leaving? Where are *we* going?"

He shrugged. "We're taking a road trip. It'll be fun. You'll see."

"Are we going to Canada, by any chance?"

He stared into space as if considering it and then shook his head. "Nope."

"So, the president isn't going to launch a nuclear attack?"

"Oh, that. Well, yes, if we don't get busy and stop him. If *you* don't get off your high horse. How's your aim, by the way? Ever fire a gun? Convincing you to help me has proved harder than I expected. Your resistance has put us behind schedule, so now we have to hustle."

I crossed my arms over my chest. Hustle? "My answer is still no. I'm not going to help you. And you can't make me." I almost stuck out my tongue. So there.

"Don't be stupid, Hector. Of course, you're going to help me."

A sharp pain bit into my head. The pain increased until I crumpled to my knees. "Okay, okay." The pain faded. Did I mention I don't like pain? "Why are you doing this to me?"

"I'm not doing it *to* you, Hector. I'm doing it *with* you. And I told you, I need you, bud. I need your expertise. Your cunning. Your brains. Your feisty spirit. Your impeccable aim. Your trigger finger. Your Diet Coke. You and me, we're a team. I have evil to do. Lots and lots of it and you're going to help me because I'm running out of time and there are things you can do that I can't."

"But I don't want to!" I stopped short of stamping my foot.

Like that mattered. "So you've said, but listen, buddy, it'll be fun—I told you. You'll enjoy it, trust me. I mean, aren't you glad Iggy's shitty little garage blew up? Don't you, deep in your heart of hearts, think he's a pig-bastard who deserves to have a little comeuppance?"

I twitched all over and I wanted to cry. "Why me?" I wailed, my voice rising an octave or two. "Just tell me that, Art. Of all the schmucks in the world, why me?"

"Oh, don't be such a whiner, Hector. We already went over this. Why not you? Answer me that. Why the hell not you?"

"Because ..."

"You have a right to wreak a little havoc in this wretched world. It's time you exercised that right. Show a little initiative, Hector, my buddy. Live a little. Sin a little."

"I've sinned plenty." Ask my grandmother.

But Art was on a roll. There was no stopping him. "You

might actually enjoy your life for a change instead of trying to slide through it without making waves. This safe, secure, predictable life you've been living is a killer, Hector. Keep it up and you'll kill, all right. You'll kill yourself, and half the world or more. Do you want that on your conscience?"

I gestured helplessly. "I don't see—"

"Oh, you see, Hector, my boy. You see just fine. With or without those glasses of yours. You should be thanking me. And sure, it's kind of random, but like I said, why the hell not you?"

"But I like being safe, secure, and predictable." It sounded weak and silly, even to me.

"Too bad. We have about fifteen minutes before the police return, Hector. Get packing and be quick about it. You won't need much. We'll pick stuff up on the way."

"Where are we going?"

"On a road trip, Hector. We're taking the road to glory. Yes, sir. Halleluiah and amen. Now get moving. The police may or may not get here before Iggy. Did you know Iggy keeps a gun under his mattress? He's gone home to get it. He's a man on a mission, Hector, which is what you should be. I suggest you stop wasting time."

"But I'm his cousin."

"You think a man like Iggy cares about family when his world is in chaos?"

He had a point, but I couldn't move. I stood in the middle of my kitchen staring at him, my mouth opening and closing like a fish drowning in air. He gave a little "get moving" swish of his hands.

In the distance, I could hear the faint whine of approaching sirens. Art cocked his head. "Make that five minutes."

I jumped, overcome with an irresistible urge to run, hide, pee myself, dive into a deep hole....

Art pulled a black backpack out of the bag he'd put on the table and tossed it to me. "Here. Get moving."

The backpack smacked me in my face. That snapped me out of the last of my stupor and launched me into a panic. I stuffed a change of clothes, several pairs of underwear, socks, a jacket, my toothbrush, my stash of mad money, my passport, my laptop, a roll of duct tape—don't ask—and a picture of my grandmother into the backpack.

On the way out the door, Art grabbed a coupon for Diet

Coke off the fridge. I crammed a bottle of aspirin into my pocket.

By now, the sirens were close, so close I could taste them. I was on the verge of full-blown panic by now. What was I doing? Where was I going? I had to escape. Run. Hide. I could see the flashing lights, coming right for me—

And then they sailed right on by, right on down the street, with no sign of slowing down. I plopped down on the sidewalk, in a hyperventilated stupor, tears welling up in my eyes.

"What the fuck, Art?" I sobbed.

"Got you moving, didn't it? Come on. We don't have all day. They are coming for you, Hector. Now we can have a decent head start."

I didn't have the strength to protest. Besides, what was I going to do? Sit around and wait for the police to show up and drag me off to jail? Or wait for Iggy to return with a gun and blow my brains out? He would do it, too. He was that crazy.

For the first time in my life, I understood fear. It coursed through my veins, perverting my judgment. Yes, I would run because I wanted to live more than I wanted to be right. And that led to a bitter truth: expediency wins every time. "To hell with it." Yes, indeed.

~8~

Art had arranged an orderly escape, complete with a nondescript SUV with tinted windows and Internet access. It was waiting for us at the curb, all bright and shiny and ready to roll.

Before we left town, we stopped at my bank and I drew out my life savings, which had mysteriously doubled—no, tripled. Then we went to Walmart where we stocked up on Diet Coke, cheese strings, and pepperoni sticks.

I also bought a ball cap to shade my eyes since my prescription sunglasses had been destroyed when my car exploded. I suppose I didn't need them. The tinted windows in the SUV were more than adequate, but the cap made me feel like I was wearing a disguise. The whole thing was ridiculous, but we were on the run, so of course, I needed a disguise.

Didn't I?

I was torn between wanting to retch in fear and wanting to giggle.

I had no idea where we were running to—Art's directions were vague. "Just drive."

So, I drove. And drove. And drove. North, since there's not really any other way out of Florida.

We stopped once so I could pee and once again because I was hungry. Art regarded all these stops as petty indulgences, complete with heavy eye-rolling and deep sighs. In the meantime, he polished off two six-packs of Diet Coke and we had to stop a third time to replenish his stock.

"That stuff's going to stunt your growth," I told him. By now I was sick of Coke and had switched to Dr. Pepper.

"Whatever. Just keep driving."

"We're going to need gas soon." We'd been driving for a while and the gas gauge was dangerously low. Finding a station without a lineup was going to be difficult, given the current gas crisis. Damn Saudis. No, wait. This wasn't their fault. Not entirely. No, this was the president's fault. He had to insult the entire royal family and then make things worse by further alienating the entire Arab world. Way to go, genius. Now they'd taken their oil and gone home. *Nanny, nanny, poo-poo.*

Art pointed me down a side street and then directed me to take several more turns. We ended up on a quiet street that ran along some railroad tracks. There, in the center of the block, was a gas station without another car in sight. I quickly filled up the SUV.

"How did you do that?"

"I know the city."

Of course, he did.

"Where are we going?" I asked once we got back on the highway. "We can't drive forever."

"Actually, we can."

"Maybe you can, but I'm getting tired. I'm going to have to stop soon and get some sleep unless you want me to fall asleep at the wheel, which means we will probably crash, and I might die. In which case, you could have saved yourself a lot of trouble and let Iggy finish me off."

He considered this. "Have another Dr. Pepper."

"No, thanks. I want real food. And if I have any more caffeine, I'm going to start flying."

He considered that. "If only you could—"

I stopped at the next decent motel with a restaurant attached. It was close to ten o'clock. Enough, already. "I'm done. I'm not driving another mile. I want food and a real bed to sleep in."

I geared up for his objection, but he said, "Fine. Whatever. Don't use your credit card. Pay cash."

The clerk behind the desk was a middle-aged woman with flat eyes. She looked us over thoroughly. "Just you?"

"Me and my friend."

"Your friend?" She took a long look at Art. I wondered what

she saw that was so interesting. Did she see his glowing eyes? Or did they seem normal to her? I made a mental note to ask him about that later.

"Yeah," I repeated. "Me and my friend. We need a room."

"One room?"

"Yeah. One room."

"One bed or two?"

"Doesn't matter." It's not like Art needed a bed. "Whatever you got."

Her eyes narrowed and her upper lip curled into a little sneer. "Well, I don't think we have any rooms for you. Or your friend."

"You didn't even look."

She smiled oh-so sweetly. "Sorry, hon. We're real busy."

Like hell. There were only two cars in the parking lot.

Art sauntered up to the counter. "Is there a problem?"

The woman's sneer deepened. "I was telling your *friend* that we don't have any vacancies. Maybe you should try the Motel 6 down the road."

"My *friend* likes this motel. I'm sure if you look again, you'll find something."

"Oh, I don't think so." Then she made a mistake. She tried to stare him down.

Art leaned across the counter and hissed in her ear, "I'm preparing a special place for you, Edith. Wanna see?"

Her eyes grew wide and her puffy face turned bright pink. She clutched her hands to her chest as if her heart was about to fall out.

"And that's just for starters. *He* loves you, you know. People like you. Really, really loves you. He depends on you to do his work, and you are succeeding beyond his expectations."

She stood rooted to the spot, unable to move, unable to turn away from the images he streamed into her head—unable to protest, or speak, or cry out.

She was so still, I thought he had turned her to stone, but finally, she blinked and snapped out of the trance. "We have a very nice room on the second floor, next to the vending machines. It's recently been renovated, and we put in a new air conditioner. There are two king-sized beds and a Jacuzzi tub. Will that be all right?"

"That will be fine." I signed the register and offered her cash, which she refused.

"It's on the house. For your inconvenience." She handed me the key and a voucher for two free dinners at the adjoining restaurant. "It's the least I can do."

"Well, that turned out well," I said, as we parked the SUV. "But I think you let her off a little easy."

"Don't be so sure. I poked a hole in her belief system. She has no anchor now. When she's done work tonight, she'll step into the bar, take her first drink of alcohol ever, get drunk, and run off with the trucker in room 104. When she sobers up, she'll be in Memphis, alone, completely broke and so desperate she'll rob a convenience store, hijack a Chevy pickup, and end up in a Mexican jail where she'll eventually die of food poisoning, but not until she's infected half the police force with syphilis. A gift from the trucker."

I stared at him, awestruck. "You're making this up."

He shrugged. "Maybe. Maybe not. But you'll never know, will you?"

Point taken.

We went to the restaurant as soon as we dumped our stuff in the room. Art ordered a Diet Coke with extra ice. I had spaghetti and meatballs, a mixed salad, and a piece of surprisingly good pecan pie.

Art watched me eat with a mix of envy and lust, while he nursed his Diet Coke. He let out a series of sighs. "I suppose you're going to want to sleep now." It sounded like an accusation.

"I'm too wired. Too much caffeine. I think I'll watch television for a while."

"The food channel?"

I didn't really care one way or the other. "Sure. Why not?"

So that's how I ended up in a lumpy motel bed with a demon, watching a bunch of disparate people attempt to construct a meal out of strawberry jam and pigs feet for cash, prizes, and international acclaim.

The show ended, and I yawned. "I'm going to check the news and then brush my teeth. Then I'm going to sleep."

"Mind if I keep watching the television? Chef Walter is going to demonstrate fifteen ways to cook zucchini in an outdoor pit."

"Whatever."

"Great. Oh—I'd skip the news if I were you."

Too late, I had already switched the channel.

There was lots of coverage about the gas crisis. A bunch of senators went on ... and on ... about taking a stand against the Arabs. *("It's about time.")* Someone pointed out this all could have been avoided if Waterman hadn't shot off his mouth but that was glossed over pretty quickly since his approval rating was at an all-time high. This was followed by the usual rhetoric from Waterman who was all fired up at the Canadians. *"The Canadians are the kind of false friends who will stab you in the back. After all we've done for them, and they won't give us their oil. What kind of neighbors won't help in a crisis? Damn selfish of them, if you ask me. Well, America won't let them get away with it. I won't let them get away with it."*

I went to the bathroom, brushed my teeth, and returned in time to catch the tail end of the story about Iggy's garage explosion, complete with video of the damage, Iggy's oh-so-sad, pity-me face, followed by information of where to send donations to help him and his family weather "this unfortunate storm."

Then they flashed a picture of me. The announcer looked grim-faced. *"The police are looking for this man in connection with the bombing and possible links to other area bombings. He is believed to be armed and dangerous. Approach with caution."*

Other bombings? What other bombings? Approach with caution? Armed and dangerous? Holy hockey Hannah, that was like giving permission to shoot at will in this stand-your-ground gun-obsessed part of the world. I was as good as dead.

I looked at Art in horror. "Told you not to watch the news." He took the remote out of my hand and flipped back to the food channel. "Good night. Sleep tight. Don't let the bedbugs bite."

I crawled under the covers and turned my back to him. I tried to say a prayer. You know, something like, "Dear God, get me out of this."

*Too late for that*, a voice whispered in my head. *Nothing but fun times ahead.*

~9~

We were back on the road by eight the next morning. I grabbed coffee and a box of granola bars at a convenience store. The coffee made me gag. This traveling business wasn't turning out to be all that much fun and I still had no idea where we were going. I was pretty sure Art didn't know either. He pointed west once we cleared Florida and that's the way I drove. *Like a lemming to the sea* ....

He didn't say much for once, which was fine with me for the first hour. Truthfully, he was more than quiet. He was downright morose.

"What's bugging you?" I finally asked when the silence turned from pleasant to freaky.

He gave a pathetic little sigh and stared out the window.

After another hour of his Gloomy-Gus routine, I reached my breaking point. "Look, buddy, what's up your ass? I'm doing you a favor and you're treating me like shit."

He gave me a long, cool look. "Well, if you must know, I have to kill you and I'm trying to figure out the best way to do it."

I slammed on the brakes, swerving from one side of the highway to the other, narrowly missing a milk truck, until I came to a precarious stop. "What the hell are you talking about?"

"The word has come down from the Prince himself. He thinks you're a liability. A bad influence, if you must know. You have to go."

"So, I'll get out on the next corner and go on my way," I said. How hard was that?

"You can't do that. You have the police and Iggy after you. You won't get far. I can't let anything happen to you. Not like that, anyway."

"You make my head hurt."

He continued as if he hadn't heard me. "The problem is not everyone thinks Waterman's plan to blow up half the planet is such a bad one. Turns out, he has a few friends. These 'friends' think I should mind my own business and let nature take its course, so now the Boss is all, 'whoa, Art. Back off and ditch the breather.' I have to obey. My eternal damnation depends upon it."

"Seriously? You're pulling my leg, aren't you? You just want to mess with me."

The cars were lining up behind us now—the butt end of the SUV jetted into traffic. I ignored the blaring horns. Then a guy the size of Texas popped up beside me. "Move your ass," he yelled.

I smiled and waved. I stopped short of blowing him a kiss. He started banging on the window with those over-sized bearpaws of his, which made the glass vibrate precariously, so I gassed the SUV and rolled over his foot. Then I left him in the dust, hopping on one foot while holding the other. It was oddly satisfying. I suppressed a giggle. This is what hanging out with a demon was doing to me, I realized. I used to be a pretty nice guy. Miserable as crap, mind you, but nice.

I drove until we came to a rest stop and then I pulled in, parked, and turned on Art. "Well? Surely you can come up with a loophole or something. Aren't you supposed to be good at that kind of thing?"

There was no emotion in his red eyes; they mellowed to a dull shade of mauve. "If only I could ... I don't want to kill you, Hector. I like you. You have potential. I mean, you'll never be a serial killer, but my guess is you could do some serious damage to the moral fiber of the universe, given half a chance."

"Thanks," I mumbled. "That doesn't explain why you need to kill me. You could just give me a head start and let me take my chances."

He sighed. "It's complicated."

"Bullshit. Music theory is complicated. String theory is complicated. Making fondant is complicated. This is not complicated."

"Actually, string theory is pretty simple, once you understand some basic concepts, but I agree with you about fondant. So many variables—"

I punched him. "Ouch," he said, rubbing the spot. "You don't have to get physical."

"You felt that?"

"Yeah? So?"

I punched him again. "Did you feel that, too?"

"Hell, yes. Knock it off."

"Why is that, Art? Why can you feel me hitting you? If I slashed you with a knife, would you bleed?"

He opened his mouth, sputtered, and closed it. "I'd rather not find out."

"Well, maybe I would." I wiggled my butt until I reached the Boy Scout pocketknife I'd kept in my back pocket since I was 12. It was a little rusty, having gone through the wash a few times. Was it still sharp? I flipped it open and studied the blade, running it across my finger. A bead of blood seeped out of the shallow cut I'd made. Sharp enough.

"Put that thing away. You're going to hurt someone."

"There's only you and me, Art."

"You'll hurt yourself."

"Why do you care? You want me dead."

"*I* don't want you dead. That's what I'm trying to tell you. I like you. But I can't disobey the Prince."

"Why the hell not? Isn't disobedience his stock and trade? Don't you think that maybe he's testing you? Only not by getting you to obey him, but by seeing if you have the balls to defy him, plus stand up for what you believe?"

He considered this, although the logic clearly confused him, which wasn't surprising. It confused me, too. But, hey, I was desperate. Perhaps if I flung enough shit, some of it would stick.

"You could be right," he said finally, to my amazement.

I relaxed some but I kept the knife in clear view. "You need to think about this, man. Not act rashly. Think loophole—"

He nodded absently. Then he reached over and grabbed the knife out of my hand.

"Hey—"

Before I could grab it back—yeah, I know, that would have

been stupid—he drew the blade across his finger. Blood oozed out of the cut.

Well, I think it was blood. It wasn't deep red, exactly. It was thick like blood, but it was pink. Mauve, really. Like his eyes.

He gasped and his composure completely left him. He turned into a quivering mass of pseudo-flesh. I thought for a moment he might even faint.

"Hey, man, get a grip."

"Quick—you got any of those granola bars left? The ones with chocolate chips?"

"I think so."

"Give me one."

"Are you kidding?"

"Now! Give me one now." He was shaking, quivering, and clearly in distress. He still had the knife in his hand, which he pointed at me. I fumbled behind me and dug into the backpack, found one of the granola bars and tossed it to him.

He caught it, ripped off the wrapping and held it to his mouth. He hesitated, calmed himself, and took a tiny bite.

He chewed and then swallowed. Waited a moment and took a big bite. He repeated this process, taking bigger and bigger bites until the bar was gone.

He leaned back in the seat, sighing deeply. His body went slack, including the hand holding the knife. I took the opportunity to remove it from his grasp. He didn't so much as twitch. He sat there, smiling contentedly, in some sort of post-orgasmic-like stupor. "Chocolate ... oh ... chocolate ...."

It was a thing to behold: a dopey demon with a little smudge of chocolate on the corner of his mouth.

It was also creepy. Very, very creepy.

But more importantly, I was still alive.

Art sighed deeply. "I needed that." He patted my knee. "Don't worry, Hector. I'll figure something out. You got any more of those granola bars? Keep driving."

I didn't want to go anywhere but sitting still made me nervous. I resumed driving. The nervousness didn't go away. "Sorry, buddy. There aren't any more granola bars."

"You ate them all?"

"You had the last one." And then it dawned on me. "You *ate* one. I thought you couldn't eat."

Now I was scared. Maybe it was the crazed look on his face or the way his eyes flashed and narrowed as he looked at the empty granola bar wrapper. He buried his nose in it, took a deep breath, and held it for so long I thought he was going to burst. He let out a long, pitiful sigh.

"Were you listening to me at all? I can eat—it's just better if I don't. It's a real slippery slope, eating. But I need to figure out a way to keep you alive, and all that thinking takes calories. So, yeah, I put food into my mouth. Relax. It might save your sorry ass."

"How?"

He waved me off. "I need to think. Are you sure they're all gone? The granola bars, I mean."

"Yes."

"Mind if I check?"

Before I could answer, he was reaching into the backseat, groping for my backpack. He pulled it into the front seat, knocking me in the head and nearly shearing away the rear-view mirror.

"Hey, watch it!" But he wasn't paying any attention to me. He was too busy digging through the backpack. He tossed aside my clothing and other stuff until he got to the bottom.

"How could you eat an entire box?"

"I didn't get breakfast and you wouldn't let me stop for lunch, so yeah, I ate the entire box, except for the one you ate. You're such a piss ant."

"*I'm* a piss ant?" His face blossomed into a bright red balloon. "You're the one who ate all the granola bars."

I was fantasizing about pushing him out the door when he spotted a gas station.

"Stop!" He leaped out of the SUV before I came to a complete stop and dashed into the little store. I took my time. Filled the gas tank. The line was reasonable, fortunately. Checked the oil and the tire pressure. Went to the bathroom. Washed my hands. My face. My glasses. Popped a zit.

He wasn't in the SUV when I got back, so I went looking for him.

And there he was, in the middle of the store, arms laden with a mound of STUFF: chips, candy bars, cookies, pop, popcorn, topped off by three loaded hot dogs and two deep fried drumsticks.

The clerk, a scrawny blond kid with a buzz cut, eyed him suspiciously.

I approached him the way one might approach a potentially rabid dog. "Aren't you overdoing it a little?"

He jumped and I automatically reached out to catch the avalanche of STUFF, which sent me into a frenzied cha-cha-cha as I grabbed at bags and boxes, catching most of them.

When I stopped dancing, he was grinning at me like the proverbial kid in the candy shop, pink teeth shining brightly. "Gotta taste this stuff. You have no idea how long I've wanted to taste—" he giggled—"a *hot dog*. And potato chips."

I didn't have the heart to tell him he was going to be disappointed. He looked so damn cute, with his silly grin and bright eyes without a hint of red.

"Come on." He motioned in the direction of the cashier. "You have to pay for this stuff."

"I do?"

"Well, I don't have any money, now do I?" His eyes flashed red for a split second. Not so cute, after all.

"Come on." I motioned him toward the counter. I added a bag of pretzels and a Dr. Pepper. He eyed them with lust. "Mine," I said sharply.

He huffed and we dropped his stuff on the counter in front of the kid, who approached us in a peculiarly halting manner. "All of this?" He couldn't believe it any more than I could.

"Yeah," I said. "And gas."

He nodded. "Somebody has the munchies." He grinned stupidly. Like he knew exactly what caused the "munchies." Like maybe we'd hit the motherload and he was wishing we would share.

"Is there a decent motel around here?" It would be dark soon and suddenly I was very, very tired.

"There's a couple down the highway a few miles. The Bottom Crusher Inn is probably the best of the lot. They got a Beef Steak Restaurant attached."

Art looked up at that. "Steak ..." He grinned stupidly, like on the verge of drooling kind of stupidly.

I couldn't look at him, so I glanced downward and stared into my very own face on the front page of USA *Today* under a headline that read WANTED FOR DOMESTIC TERRORISM. I nudged Art and pointed surreptitiously.

He glanced down, following the direction of my wiggling finger, and grinned. "Butterfingers! I'm sure I'll love Butterfingers!" and he scooped up six of them and added them to his pile.

Once we got in the car, I slammed the door with particular force. The SUV shook. "You're a twit, you know that."

He was unwrapping a Butterfinger with the eagerness of a five-year-old on Christmas morning. "Relax, Hector. I got this covered."

"Did you see the newspaper?"

"Of course, I saw it. Like I said: relax." He bit into the candy bar, closed his eyes, and moaned with such ecstasy, I blushed. "Oh, yeah. It's a fresh one."

~10~

We pulled into the Bottom Crusher Inn ten minutes later. I left Art in the car while I registered. The guy at the desk barely glanced at me, didn't ask for ID when I handed him cash. "You don't got no dogs, do you?" was all he said to me. I assured him I did not.

I managed to secure adjoining rooms. There was no way I was going to share a room with Art, not the way he was acting.

We settled in and I left Art wallowing in junk food heaven while I took a shower. I should have brought more clothes. One additional set of clothing wasn't going to cut it if we were going to be on the road much longer. I really needed to get Art to tell me where we were going. And what we were doing. Especially, what we were doing.

I came out of the shower and found Art lounging on my bed, staring at the television, a trail of wrappers, bones, ketchup smears, and empty pop cans leading from the door between our rooms.

"What are you doing?" I glared at the mess.

He looked up and waved. "You're on the news again."

Sure enough—there I was. *"We repeat. A nationwide manhunt is now underway for suspected terrorist, Hector Gonzales. Caution is advised. Do not approach. Consider him armed and extremely dangerous."*

My mouth dropped to my knees. "Can't you do something about that?"

"Like what?" Art asked, licking chocolate and mustard off his fingers.

"Well, how about stopping the cops from looking for me? If

48

they find me, I'm a dead man. Those guys aren't going to waste a single second wondering if I'm innocent or not."

Art shrugged. "You worry too much. Pass me the potato chips."

I passed him the potato chips. I didn't want to, but I did it anyway.

He stuffed a hot dog, loaded with chips, into his mouth, followed by up ending a bottle of Pepsi and then a bottle of Coke. "Hmmm—Pepsi or Coke? The eternal debate." He stood up and brushed the crumbs off his shirt and pants. "You ready for dinner? I could sure use a big juicy steak, couldn't you?"

I would like to say I found him amusing or perhaps even charming, in a demented sort of way but, alas, my usual congeniality, such as it was, eluded me. "Do you want me dead? Because if you do, say so, and I'll go outside, stand in the middle of the highway and wait for a semi to run over me."

Art shrugged. "I'm working on that loophole you wanted—"

There was a knock at the door, but when I got up to answer it, no one was there. Art glanced at me over his second hotdog. "I wouldn't answer that, if I were you."

"It's a little late—" I started to say, but there was another knock, and I opened the door again. For a moment, I thought I had crossed into the Twilight Zone; the lights flickered, and I was falling. Then the moment passed, and I was fine.

I stared into an empty parking lot, wondering—not for the first time—if I was losing my mind. "Well, that was weird."

"What?"

"Someone knocked on the door. Twice. Didn't you hear it? But no one was there." A wave of dizziness passed over me. I grabbed the doorframe and then it was gone.

Art just shrugged. "You got any more pretzels?"

I tossed him the bag. "Be my guest. I'm not feeling all that great."

"Well, maybe you should lie down for a while, Hector."

"I think I will."

"Good plan. We'll eat later. Toss me the remote."

$\sim$11$\sim$

I woke up feeling very strange, to say the least, but uncharacteristically calm.

Art took his attention off the food channel long enough to glance in my direction. "About time. Come on, I'm starving. I thought you were going to sleep all night. If we hurry, we can still get dinner."

"Is it safe?" My voice sounded weird. Deeper, as if it were coming from my chest, and with an odd twang.

"As safe as safe can be."

I wasn't so sure. "You're not pulling my leg, are you?"

"Hector! Relax. I've got you covered. As far as anyone is concerned, you're some white dude by the name of Charles Hunter. Oh, and you're straight. I mean, you look straight. No point in complicating things."

"There is no way I can pass as some straight white guy named Charles Hunter." I let my disdain for the name show.

"Look in the mirror, my friend."

Reluctantly, I dragged myself out of bed and went into the bathroom.

Sure enough, there was a big ol' white dude looking back at me. He was really, really white, too. Pasty white. Vampire white, if you know what I mean. And old. At least fifty. Blond, buzz cut hair. Deep creases around watery blue eyes. Bullish neck. He reminded me of someone.

Not me, though. Definitely, not me. "How did you do that?"

Art shrugged. "One of my less appreciated talents. Consider it your loophole." He handed me my wallet. "Now check out your ID."

There was $600 in cash, the usual credit cards and a bunch of bank cards, all embossed with the name "Charles Hunter." I pulled out the driver's license, and there I—*he*—was. Charles Hunter. Apparently, I was 47. Only 47? I swore I looked a lot older. I lived in Dallas. I was 5'11" and didn't need glasses to drive.

I touched my face. No glasses.

"How did you do that? I can see!"

"Consider it a bonus."

I was momentarily gleeful. No glasses for the first time since I was six. I checked my teeth. Straight and pearly white. "Is this permanent?"

He shrugged. "As long as it serves our purpose."

"You mean until the clock strikes twelve?"

"You're a riot, Hector— I mean, Charlie. Is it all right if I call you Charlie?"

"I guess." What did I know? Charles? Charlie? Chuck? Chad? Chaz? Whatever. "Let's eat." I was suddenly very hungry.

Dinner, as it turned out, was spectacular. The steak was perfect. The service was impeccable.

"Is this what being a straight white male gets you?" I asked Art after the waiter had refilled my water glass for the third time without having been asked.

Art was licking the butter off his knife and sighing contentedly. "Are you saying you could get used to this?"

"Definitely." I experienced a flutter of guilt. But just a flutter.

Art flashed me a self-satisfied smile.

"What?"

"So, you can be bought."

"What are you talking about?"

"Nothing. Nothing at all. Are you going to finish your cheesecake?"

I pushed my plate toward him after I secured one last bite. "This is nice, but we can't do this every night. I'm going to run out of money." And get fat. Charles was already a bit on the hefty side. My guess was he didn't spend too much time in the gym.

"Don't worry. Charles Hunter is a multimillionaire. Among

other things."

I know, I know. I should have protested. Or asked a few questions. But the idea of being a multimillionaire was far too appealing to ruin it with pesky questions. Especially if I was fairly certain I wouldn't like the answers.

I took a few moments to savor my newfound worldly gain along with my last bite of the cheesecake. To hell with weight management. But something was nagging at me, and I couldn't shake it. Something important. Something—

I dropped my fork: "What's the catch?" There had to be a catch. Wasn't there always a catch?

Art looked at me in surprise. "Catch? There's no catch."

I wasn't so sure. "I haven't sold my soul to you, have I?"

"Don't be silly." But he shifted slightly and dabbed his lips with the white linen napkin oh, so carefully.

"What, then?"

"Relax, Hector. I mean, Charlie. Your soul is still safe and very much intact."

"But there is something, isn't there?"

"No. There's nothing. Really. You are now a very wealthy man of social prominence. Enjoy it. Consider it a gift from me to you, freely given."

Freely given? That should have been a clue right there, but I was too full of steak, baked potato, and cheesecake to ponder anything deeper than a hangnail. "And how did I earn this new-found wealth?"

"Earn?" He looked puzzled. "Oh, you mean *earn*, as from a job or something."

"Or something."

"Ah ... the usual. Theft. Fraud. Tax evasion. Insider trading. Oh, and you married a rich woman."

"Great." Well, what did I expect? Good deeds don't make people rich.

"Isn't it?" He grinned and thumped me on the back. He cleaned up the last bit of cheesecake and licked his fork. "Mind if I have another piece?"

"Yes. I'm tired. You're going to get sick if you keep eating like that."

"Sick?" He pondered the concept as if it didn't quite

compute.

My hand shook as I handed the waiter one of my new credit cards. What if the card was fake? What if Art was setting me up? I was pretty sure that was exactly what he was doing, but I didn't know how.

The waiter took the card without comment, ran it through his handy portable machine, and presented the receipt for me to sign, which I did. *Charles Hunter,* I wrote with a flourish I didn't recognize. Even my handwriting had undergone an overhaul.

"I trust everything was satisfactory," the waiter cooed.

"It was excellent." I barely recognized my own voice. It was deeper, more mellow. Richer. Oh, yeah.

The waiter smiled, with a hint of *something.*

It hit me after he left. "Was he flirting with me?" Usually, I didn't have to ask. Usually, I knew, but something was off.

"No. That's just how rich guys get treated when they have the power to enhance a mere waiter's life with a generous tip."

"Oh." Did I even remember to tip him? I looked at the receipt. Apparently, I had. I gasped. His tip was bigger than my last paycheck.

Art regarded me with a sly grin. "Do you want me to change you back to Hector?"

I thought about that. "I won't be rich anymore?"

He shook his head.

"And I'll have to wear glasses?"

He nodded.

"And I'll get arrested?"

He nodded again.

"And convicted?" Or shot?

"Quite possibly."

I pondered that for a moment. "Do you still have to kill me? You know, the Prince—"

He waved away my words with a grand sweep of his hand. "Don't worry about that."

"You fixed it? How?"

"Not important, Hector, my boy. Let's just say I found a loophole. Nothing for you to worry about."

But I would worry. It's what I did best. Hell, I excel at worry. Once again, I should have asked a few more questions; instead, I said,

"I hate you."

"Who doesn't?" He stood up and stretched. "Come on. I still have a couple of chocolate bars left. I feel the need to indulge."

When we got back to the motel, I left him to his chocolate. I undressed, climbed into bed and surfed the television, flipping from one news channel to the next. There was a lot about increasing tensions at the US-Canadian border, which I barely noticed. A story about some religious group predicting the End of The World. Again. And there, finally, it was—*Hector Gonzales, suspected Cuban sleeper agent-slash-terrorist ... biggest manhunt in FBI history ... armed and extremely dangerous.*

I checked the mirror one last time before I went to bed. I was still pasty, puffy, and creased. I slept better than I had in several days.

~12~

You may wonder why I didn't freak out more about my sudden transformation into a straight, middle-aged very white dude. The thing is—I don't know. It never occurred to me at the time. I was Charles Hunter on the outside, but I was still Hector Gonzales on the inside. I figured it was one of Art's tricks. You know, making me look different so I wouldn't get caught. A neat trick, I figured. One of his better ones.

I got up the next morning eager to get on with … whatever. I was hungry. I wanted breakfast. I craved scrambled eggs, waffles, bacon, and espresso. "Come on." I rubbed my hands together in anticipation of gastronomic glee. "Let's get breakfast."

Art refused to budge. "I feel funny," he moaned. "Like my middle section is going to explode or fall out."

He did look a little green. "Must have been the hot dogs," I said. And the steak and potato with extra sour cream and the two pieces of cherry cheesecake.

"I think I'm going to die."

"Don't be stupid. You did that already."

"No, really. I feel—" He gazed slack-jawed into outer space … *computing, computing* … "Sick. Yeah, that's it, isn't it? I feel sick."

"Maybe you need to go to the bathroom. You know, lose a load."

He gave me a "drop dead, you titmouse" look, which I happily ignored. "Well, stay here if you want. I'm going for breakfast. You want anything?"

"No." He buried his head into his pillow. "Oh, hell no."

I left him making pathetic little moaning noises into his pillow and made my way to the coffeeshop attached to the motel. I ate my breakfast and read the morning paper. This time, I didn't flinch when I saw Hector's picture on the front page. I regarded it with detachment. Not me. Not my problem. I was positively jubilant. Stupid foreigners. This is what happens when you let foreigners into the country.

Something about that struck me as odd, but I dismissed it.

I could see my reflection in the mirrored wall at the back of the room. Charles was good-looking, in a mature, rich kind of way. And he—I—dressed well, albeit a bit on the conservative side. I was wearing a navy pinstripe suit with a pale green silk tie and a light blue shirt. The absurdity of me, Hector Manuel Ortiz Gonzales, in a suit made me want to giggle.

Wait—who?

Then I heard dogs barking to the tune of *Camptown Races*. I jumped, spilling a bit of coffee. Cell phone, I realized. I found it in my breast pocket.

"Hello?"

"Charles?" The voice was feminine.

"Uh, yes—"

"Oh, Charles. Thank god. I've been so worried. Are you all right?" She stretched out her words like they were infused with gold dust and diamonds. And vodka. Lots and lots of vodka.

"I'm fine."

"Why didn't you call me? I tried to call you last night, but I couldn't get through. When are you coming home?" There was a hint of petulance in her golden tones.

Home? "Uh …."

"I was expecting you last night." Still petulant but now with a hint of smoldering anger. She was used to getting her way. She was not used to Charles disappointing her.

"I got delayed," Charles said in his deep-not-mine voice. "I'll be starting for home as soon as I finish breakfast."

"You might have let me know." Now she was flat out cold. Icy. Poor Charles. All that ice. I hoped the money was worth it. "Don't forget we have the party at the Wilson's tonight. Unless you're going to be too tired to go. I suppose I could make our excuses, although it is rather late to back out. You know how much trouble they go to for these parties."

"Uh, no. That's fine. I should be home in plenty of time." Would I? I had no idea.

"Good." She sounded relieved. "I'd hate to miss it. It sends the wrong message, you know. Like people can't depend on you."

"Yes," I/Charles said. "I know." I wondered what the hell I—*he*—was talking about.

"Oh, by the way, the Feds were here yesterday. They wouldn't say why. Are you in trouble again?"

"No," I said quickly, biting back a wave of panic. I glanced at the mirrored wall again. Still Charles. "Don't worry about it."

I paid for my breakfast and got out of there. On the way back to the room, I stopped at every bank machine on the block and emptied Charles Hunter's bank accounts. They all had the same security code, which I knew without having to think about it. When I was done, I had about $100,000. Not bad for petty cash. I stuffed it into a shopping bag.

I showed Art the cash. "Good work," he said. Then he went stiff. He tilted his face as if listening to a faraway voice.

"What's wrong?"

He raised his hand to hush me. And a moment later, his face contorted. "Shit. Shit, shit, double shit. Did you answer his phone?"

"Yeah. It was in my pocket." I held it out to show him.

He jumped out of bed and grabbed it, and then stomped on it, reducing it to electronic shards. "Never answer the phone!" He scrambled to get dressed and we were out of there before I could ask him why I shouldn't answer the phone.

I followed Art through the parking lot, still feeling slightly out of place. Like I was out of sync, slightly off-key, a teeny bit out of focus; traipsing down a one-way street the wrong way. Weird, but not so weird that I didn't keep going.

Then he stopped in front of a late model silver Cadillac and my anxiety disappeared. The car shone like a star plucked from heaven. I itched to pop the hood. I imagined a pristine engine and more power than the starship *Enterprise*. I had to swallow hard to keep from drooling.

"Where's the SUV?"

"Gone." He handed me the keys and I opened the trunk to

toss in my bag. Inside the trunk was a box of fliers. I pulled one out. The paper was heavy and slick and folded in thirds. In big red letters on the front, it read: *"Restored Missionary Evangelical Gospel Church of the Sacred Order of Anarchy: THE TIME IS NIGH."*

On the inside was a picture of a man identified as the Rev. Peter Knutson smiling benevolently to an audience of slack-jawed devotees. *"The world is ending sooner than you think,"* it read. *"Be prepared. Don't let Armageddon take you by surprise."*

On the back: *"Send your donations today. Every dollar you spend will get you closer to Glory. Don't be left out. There's only so much room in the Ark. Secure your place today."*

"What a load of crap." I flashed the flier in front of Art's face, fully expecting him to agree.

He took it out of my hand and studied it thoughtfully. "Damn it. This is worse than I thought. Come on, we have to get moving."

Also in the trunk was a very expensive briefcase, a small suitcase, and a lumpy leather duffel bag. It was the duffel bag that caught my attention. "Wait." I reached in and grabbed it. I balanced it on the edge of the trunk and unzipped it, half expecting to find it full of dirty clothes.

Art watched me, frowning. He rolled his eyes and tapped his foot. Then he gasped as I opened the bag to reveal it was stuffed with cash. "Holy mother of acid rain," he mumbled.

Apparently, Art was not incapable of surprise after all.

I gaped at all that money. Fives, tens, twenties mostly; a few fifties and hundreds. And a thousand-dollar bill. I had never seen a thousand-dollar bill. "Is it real?" I held it up to the light. It looked real.

Art snatched it out of my hand. "You trying to get yourself killed?" The question, I would realize later—much later—was rhetorical.

"How much do you think is in here? And where did it come from?" Drugs was my first thought. Clever. No one ever suspects the middle-aged white dude.

"Hand over the cash you got out of the bank accounts," Art said. I did so and he stuffed my cash into the duffel bag. It was so full, I wasn't sure he'd be able to zip it back up, but he gave the zipper a little tug and it glided closed. Easy peasy. Then Art shoved the bag deep into the trunk and looked around surreptitiously. "Come on. We need to get out of here."

For once, I agreed with him completely.

~13~

The seats of the Caddie were upholstered in a buttery yellow leather so soft and silky I groaned in pleasure. "Where are we going?" I asked, not particularly in a hurry to go anywhere. Leather does that to me.

Art didn't appear to be the least bit impressed by our upgraded ride. He studied the flier from the Church of the Sacred Order of Anarchy for a long moment, and then he said, "Our first stop is home."

"Home?" My heart leaped.

"Yeah. You live in a very nice house, just outside of Dallas."

He meant Charles. Silly me. "He has a wife. Is she going to be a problem?"

Art shrugged. "Nope. Don't worry."

I wasn't convinced. Every woman I knew was a problem. And most men, come to think of it. "So, how do we get there?"

He tapped the dashboard. "You have GPS. Turn it on and follow the directions."

It was easier than I expected. I read the address on Charles' driver's license. Soon we were cruising along, changing lanes and turning when directed. A few hours later, we were in the kind of neighborhood where Hector Gonzales would have been arrested for walking down the street. I kept looking over my shoulder, checking the rearview mirror, scanning the road around us. This neighborhood was so upscale, it didn't even have sidewalks.

"Relax, Charlie-boy. You're going to have a heart attack if

60

you keep this up."

"I can't help it. What if your spell wears off and I'm Hector Gonzales again? You gonna bail me out of jail? Or stop a bullet for me?"

"That's not going to happen. And what 'spell'?"

"Whatever you call it. Spell. Enchantment. Voodoo. Whatever you did to turn me into a rich white dude."

"Voodoo?" He laughed. "I haven't practiced voodoo in centuries. I'm not a witch or a wizard or some kind of crackpot fairy tale magician, Hector. You won't turn into a pumpkin at the stroke of midnight, so don't worry."

In retrospect, turning into a pumpkin might have saved me a lot of grief.

We made another turn onto a tree-lined street with large brick houses, well-kept lawns, and graceful trees, just like you see in the movies. Finally, the GPS announced, "Your destination is on the right." I pulled to a stop in front of the largest house on the block. It also had the nicest lawn. Bonus.

My knees shook as I climbed out of the Caddie. This house was bigger than my entire apartment building back in Florida. I didn't know whether to be awed or angry. So much money in the hands of one man. How was that even remotely fair?

"No time for revolution," Art said, and pointed to a stone walkway that ran to the side of the house. "Come on."

I unlatched the gate and we followed a meandering path until we reached a sliding glass door. It was unlocked. Not a rip or tear in the screen. Definitely high class.

"Go on." Art gave me a little push. "Go inside."

So, I did.

I was nervous, in an excited, newly entitled sort of way. Like yeah, man, I could *own* this. Revolution? What revolution? Revolution was for the peasants. I was no longer a peasant. Not by a longshot.

I slid open the door and stepped into a spacious mud room. It was cool and dark and smelled of lemon scented floor polish. The silence got to me. It was profound. Religious even, the kind of silence you get when you walk into an empty church. Or a tomb.

Art made little shooing motions with his wrists, so I pressed forward, entering the kitchen.

OMG. The kitchen. It was massive. It was modern. The

refrigerator was the size of a small country. The gas stove had eight—*EIGHT*—burners. There were two full sized ovens. I itched to fling open the cupboards, to hunt down the pantry, to pop open the pot drawers, but Art kept motioning me forward.

From the kitchen, we went through a dining room the size of a banquet hall and then crossed under a broad marble arch into a living room, which resembled something that belonged in a magazine. Did people actually live here? Or was this a set for some television show? A throwback to *Dynasty* or *Dallas*?

Art must have known what I was thinking because he wouldn't stop grinning at me. His eyebrows kept flicking up and down and he kept making these weird faces at me as if we were in the middle of some major conspiracy.

"We're not going to rob the place, are we?"

"Don't be stupid. You own the house. Unless you want to rob it for fun. But that would be weird."

A large hairy gray cat ambled by, pausing to give me the once-over. It might have hissed or perhaps I misheard. In any event, it continued its amble, giving its well-feathered tail a dismissive twitch as it passed. I promptly sneezed.

"Is there anyone home?"

"Upstairs." Art gestured in the direction of a wide, impressive staircase. *Gone With the Wind* impressive. Climbing it was exhausting.

"You'd think they'd have an elevator," I mumbled as I huffed up the last few steps.

"They do," Art said. "But only the servants use it."

At the top of the stairs was a wide hallway, covered in cream-colored carpet so deep I half expected it to swallow me whole.

Cream colored. *Cream.* Pristine. As if it had just been installed. It even smelled new. It looked like no one had ever walked on it. Maybe no one did. Maybe people floated above it. Perhaps I should have removed my shoes.

"It's your house." Art stopped me before I could kick them off. "You have staff to clean up after you."

"Staff," I mumbled under my breath. "I have staff." Probably some brown people named Jesus and Maria. I hoped I was a decent employer.

"You're not the best but you're not the worst, either. You give good bonuses."

"Good to know." I meant it in a sarcastic, tongue in cheek kind of way.

Art smiled at me indulgently. "That's your bedroom." He pointed to a massive set of closed double doors. He made the shooing motion again and I pushed the door open, stepping into a room larger than my apartment. A massive bed sat in the center, with a large mirror perched overhead. There were acres of empty (wasted) space around the bed, furniture so massive the old me would have needed a ladder to see the top of some of it. There was a sitting area with a full size sofa, a love seat, and the biggest television I had ever seen. And a bar. A bar? Fully stocked, from the looks of it. Obviously, Charles spent a lot of time here.

"Not Charles," Art said. "Doris."

"Who's Doris?"

"Your wife."

"Wife?" Not my wife. Charles'. The idea of a wife startled me. I was aware of the concept, of course. I had never thought about what it meant, like having to share an intimate space with a woman. Not that there was anything intimate about this cavernous room. Still, I glanced at the bed and shuddered.

I heard a noise and froze mid-shudder.

The noise came again. A kind of low, slightly off-key murmuring.

Singing. Someone was singing. Although drunken walrus song would be more accurate. It was coming from a room off to the left. A bathroom?

"That is your beloved." Art grinned wickedly, something he did very well, I might add. I must have looked blank because he added, "Your wife."

"My wife," I repeated, trying not to choke on the word. "Doris?" Art nodded.

I looked toward the door where the sound emanated. It wasn't too late to run. If I was quick, I could make it down the stairs and out the door without ever being detected. On this carpet, she'd never hear me.

"Charles? Is that you?" A disembodied voice drifted from the bathroom, light and airy, as if all the substance had been bleached from it.

"Too late." Art's grin broadened until I thought it would cut his face in half. I stared at him; you know, a deer in the headlights stare. "Say 'Yes, dear'."

"Yes, dear," I repeated. My voice sounded flat and nasal, without enthusiasm. It sounded straight. So straight ….

"How was your trip?" The voice was still disembodied.

Art mouthed a reply, and I copied him. "Great. How have you been?"

"Oh, you know. As well as can be expected, I suppose." The voice took shape in the form of a figure emerging from the bathroom, wrapped in a satin robe the color of overcooked mashed peas. Doris, I assumed. Tall. Blondish. Sharp chin. Waspish eyes. Her skin was too smooth, too tight. It made her look like a walking, talking, barely breathing mannequin. She gave me a once over. "You look beat. Do you want to rest before we leave for the Wilson's? Or should I just mix you a drink?"

That perked me up. And I wasn't going near that bed. "Aaa-a drink would be nice."

I watched her amble over to the bar and disappear behind it for a moment, emerging with two glasses, a couple of bottles, and a cocktail shaker. I watched her mix and shake and pour. I had no idea what she was doing, but she did it with ease.

I took the drink she offered. She smiled, raised her glass, and clanged her rim against mine. "Cheers, darling. Welcome home. I trust you had a profitable trip." She emphasized the word "profitable" as if it had a special, private meaning.

I replied with a slight noncommittal shrug and I took a sip of the drink. It was sweet and salty and slightly bitter. It was good. Very, very good. The part of me that wasn't screaming *run* was thinking, *I could get used to this.*

She motioned me to sit beside her, which I did. We sat on a low sofa covered in a pale lime silk that clashed horribly with her mashed pea robe. I could smell lavender and something else. Roses, perhaps. Water-warmed flesh. Expensive soap. My nose twitched but I didn't sneeze. Hector was allergic to perfume. Apparently, Charles was not.

She patted my knee and looked at me oddly. Her robe fell open, revealing an expanse of bare flesh. I sipped my drink. Did I mention it was very, very good? She had nice legs. I had to give her that. Long and lean. And evenly tanned.

"Tell me about your trip." That voice. Like silk wrapped in barbed wire.

I knocked back the rest of my drink. Damn, that was good. What the hell was in it? "Not much to tell. Usual stuff. You know. Business and all that." I held out my glass, hoping she'd pour me another drink. She took the glass and sat it on the ornate brass coffee table in front of us, completely ignoring my imploring whimpers.

"You were successful?" Was she batting her eyes? Was this her idea of foreplay? Grilling Charles? Withholding sustenance?

"Yes."

"Good. I'm glad. You deserve a little success. *We* deserve a little success."

I glanced around the room. Where was Art? I didn't see him. Had abandoned me? My heart jumped. I couldn't do this alone.

"Are you all right?" Her tone was cool and unsympathetic. Calculating. It made me shiver but I forced myself to make eye contact.

"Yes. Of course."

"You seem nervous. What aren't you telling me?"

"Nothing." I swallowed hard. "Dear."

She put her hand on my thigh. "I missed you."

"I missed you, too." Flight mode was about to be engaged.

She let out a little laugh and she pulled her hand away. "How much money did you get from them?"

"I-I don't know," I said, remembering the duffel bag full of cash in the trunk. "I haven't counted it all."

That made her laugh and she snorted into her drink. "Oh, Charles, you're so precious. Well, count it up quickly. I want to go shopping."

"Sure," I said. "I'll do it tonight. After the party."

That satisfied her. Where the hell was Art?

We sat for a few more minutes, nibbling on stale crackers. She leaned back, stared vacantly, a cracker resting daintily between her thumb and forefinger, ignoring me. I was fine with that. I didn't know how to talk to a woman, especially a partly naked one. Finally, she finished the cracker, sighed heavily, and got up. She glanced at the clock on the bedside table.

"We need to leave in half an hour. You have time to take a quick shower." She slipped off her robe and headed for the closet.

"Shall I lay out your clothes?" She started tossing clothes onto the bed without waiting for me to answer.

I didn't want to take a shower, but I didn't want to watch her dress either, so I wandered into the bathroom. I stood in the center of the massive stone floor and gasped. The shower was one of those spa showers with a hundred shower heads pointed at various angles. Take a shower? Oh, hell, yeah. Why the hell not?

Perfectly heated water hit me in a thousand places. I gasped from the pleasure of feeling truly cleansed. The steady pelting on my back eased every ache and pain, erasing both dirt and sin. My mind floated in a warm, wet haze. For a short time, I rode the universe, and nothing mattered. I even broke into song. The acoustics were stellar, and Charles had a fine baritone voice.

I finally emerged half expecting Doris to be yelling at me about the time, but I heard nothing. *Nada.* Not even my own breathing. The silence was unnerving, and my recent feelings of pleasure quickly retreated.

I toweled off and reached for the large, white robe hanging beside the shower. Was this going to be a formal affair, or casual? Suit and tie? Or Tux? Men like Charles Hunter wore tuxes all the time, didn't they? I was pretty sure they did. The last time I wore a tux was when I was best man at my cousin's wedding—what was his name? Oh, yeah—Iggy. No, wait, that was Hector's cousin. Charles didn't have a cousin. He had a cat, though. A gray one of uncertain origin. The thought of running drifted onto the back burner—why would I do that? I had a party to attend. Not that I wanted to go. I didn't even like the Wilsons. A little too liberal for my taste but they did have money. And I liked their money.

I tightened the robe and ventured into the bedroom.

I didn't see her at first. It wasn't until I moved to the other side of the bed that I saw her, lying on the floor. At first, I didn't get it. What was she doing on the floor, in a pool of blood that was seeping into the cream-colored carpet? That will never come out, I thought. Poor Jesus and Maria.

"She's dead."

I jumped at Art's sudden appearance. In the few minutes that I'd been Art-free, I'd forgotten all about him. The reprieve ended abruptly. "Dead?"

"Stabbed. Several times. Someone was really pissed off."

"It wasn't me. I was in the shower."

Art glared at me. "We have to get out of here."

I nodded. Of course, we did. "I have to get dressed."

"So, get dressed."

I studied the clothes on the bed—beige slacks, white button-down shirt, navy tie. Kind of boring, but not bad. I got dressed quickly. "Who killed her?"

"Charles."

"But Charles was in the shower."

"Was he?"

"Well, yeah. I mean, wasn't he?"

"You may want to check your fingernails. I don't think you got all the blood."

I stared at my—Charles'—fingernails, noting a few dark dots under his right index finger. "Shit. Why would he kill her?"

"God told him to. Well, to be precise Pastor Peter Knutson told him to, but he was acting on word from God."

"Who's Peter Knutson?"

Art's eyes spun in their socket. "I really wish you'd pay more attention to things. He's the head of the Restored Missionary Evangelical Gospel Church of the Sacred Order of Anarchy."

There was still a loose connection. "But why would he tell Charles to kill his wife?"

"For her money, of course, and because she's an ungodly greedy bitch, who wanted all that money for herself. You heard her, didn't you? She wanted to go shopping. With church money. Ha! As if already having more money than God—or, in this case, Peter Knutson—wasn't enough."

"Oh. But I was in the shower. So was Charles. He couldn't have killed her."

"How can you be sure?"

"But—" And it hit me as I glanced again at my fingernails: I couldn't. Would I ever be sure of anything again? I pulled on the sweater and after consideration, tossed the tie.

"The cops won't believe you, I'm afraid. Especially when they put together Charles' connection to Peter Knutson. Doris isn't the only rich spouse he's arranged to have murdered, I'm afraid. He really is very good at getting people to do things like that. He'd make one hell of a demon. Now, Charles will inherit all her money and put it to good use." He huffed out a snort of suppressed laughter. "Provided he isn't charged with murder, of course. The police have been tapping his phone. They know what he's been up to, and that means, you really need to get out of here."

I still wasn't grasping the circumstances of my peril fully, but the urge to take flight returned with an instinctive vengeance. "So, let's go."

In the distance, I could hear the faint whine of sirens. "They're coming already?"

"She managed to call 911 before you—Charles—attacked her." As we raced through the house toward the kitchen, Art managed to knock a few things over, creating eerie echoes that stung my ears.

"But I told you, *Charles* was in the shower." I know, I know. I was being stubborn. Call it a character flaw. Or God-given stupidity. "He couldn't have done it."

"Come on, buddy. We need to move. You can wrap your head around this later."

I never did, of course. Not even close.

I drove like a bat out of hell, which is probably the truest thing I've said so far. I mean, those sirens were loud and rather cranky. So, yeah, I drove very, very fast, and Caddies can really move, let me tell you! Out of that upper-class neighborhood, and onto the highway heading north lickety-split. *Zoom-zoom.*

At some point, the sun finally set, and night came creeping, all puffed up and pretentious.

"There's a gas station up ahead. Stop there. You need gas," Art said.

I did what he told me without thinking, without even glancing at the gas gauge. I liked not having to think for myself. It was a pleasant sensation. Kind of left me feeling warm and cozy inside like I'd just eaten a turkey dinner with all the trimmings. I swear I could taste sage and onions.

That all changed when I turned off the engine. Instantly, the air turned claustrophobic. I flung open the door. The air outside was so thick and hot, it was like trying to breathe through cotton candy.

"You get the gas," Art said. "I need something with salt and grease." He hopped out, leaving me behind to fight my way through my mind-fog.

I filled up the gas tank. There was plenty of gas here, but the price was outrageous. Nearly $8 a gallon. Damn Canadians. This was all their fault. Then I went to the bathroom. My nerves were doing nasty things to my stomach, so I was there for a while. When I came out, I found Art inside the station with an armful of potato chips and pretzels. I had a hankering for some grease myself, but he didn't look as though he was inclined to share. I settled on corn chips and a large bottle of Seven-Up.

"Use cash," he whispered.

I nodded and pulled out my wallet while Art lined up our purchases. I pointed to a small bag of cat food. "What's that?"

"What does it look like?" He nudged it forward lest I attempt to remove it.

"We don't have a cat."

"Actually, we do." He grinned in that self-satisfied way of his I was beginning to hate.

I paid for the stuff without asking any more questions and took the bags to the car.

We did indeed have a cat. He was sitting on the backseat, lazily grooming his nether regions. Art opened the door and the cat hopped out, sauntered over to a strip of grass, did his thing and, to my surprise, came right back to the car and hopped in. I half expected him to tip me.

Art poured some cat food and water into a couple of plastic bowls he must have snagged from the gas station food bar and put them on the floor of the car. He rattled the food bowl to get the cat's attention. It glanced at the food, let out a "meow" that sounded oddly like "thanks, man," and jumped down to have a few dainty nibbles.

"That cat looks familiar," I said.

"It's Charles Hunter's cat."

I remembered seeing it now. "Why do we have his cat?"

Art gave me a "well, aren't you stupid" look. "Because he doesn't have anyone to take care of him now that Doris is dead, and Charles is on the run. Charles was rather fond of the beast—I believe he liked the cat more than his wife. In fact, I'm pretty sure of it. It's the least you can do since you killed Doris."

"I didn't kill her."

"He's very grateful, you know—the cat, I mean. He didn't like Doris very much, despite her myriad attempts to win his affection. Cats are like that, you know. Picky, I mean, about who they bond to. He doesn't like Charles very much either, so I wouldn't get too close. His name is Putin, by the way. As in Putin-On-The-Ritz. Not to be confused with the famous Russian dictator."

"What are we supposed to do with him?"

Art shrugged. "I don't know. I've never had a pet before. Except for maybe that maggoty thing that attached itself to me a few centuries ago. Now, he was cute. But alas, one day he flew away."

I got back in the Caddie and started the engine. I needed the cool comfort of the air conditioner blowing in my face before I punched the little prick. "Do we need to ditch the car?"

"Eventually. They're not looking for Charles yet. They will think it was some random intruder. They won't look for Charles for a while. He's not supposed to be home."

"But his stuff—"

"Still in the trunk. No one will remember seeing his car or him and any sign that he's been home today has disappeared. The cops will think he's been kidnapped or worse. Don't worry."

"But I cleaned out his bank accounts—"

"*Charles* cleaned out his bank accounts. Not illegal."

"But suspicious."

He shrugged. "The cops won't figure that out for days. By then, we'll be far away, and you won't be Charles anymore."

I was too relieved to ask the obvious questions—like "who would I be?" and "what will happen to Charles?" My relief must have been obvious because Art slapped me on the back and grinned. "Had you worried, did I?"

I am not a violent man, but I would have happily stabbed him right about then. That is, *Hector* wasn't a violent man; I wasn't so sure about Charles.

"Where to?" I asked, once the cold air had saturated my brain and I had cooled down enough to drive safely.

Art paused in the process of ripping open a bag of barbeque chips and consulted the ether—which is to say, he sniffed the air, tilted his head one way and then the other; paused; sniffed some more and then turned to the back seat. "What do you think, Putin? Should we continue north or go west?"

From the backseat came a long, plaintive, slow-motion meow.

"Hmm." Art gave a few more sniffs, his nose twitching in a most precise way. "Yes, I agree." He turned to me. "West, it is."

Who was I to argue? We got back on the highway and headed into the setting sun.

After a few hours, I said, "I'm tired. How much farther?"

"You really are a lazy sod, aren't you?"

"I'm human," I reminded him. "I have needs. Like sleep. And real food."

"Pity," he said. "All those pathetic needs of yours are slowing us down, you know."

"What's the hurry?"

"Seriously, Hector. You're not very bright, are you? Or have you simply not been paying attention? The world ends—" he glanced at his watch— "in eleven days. No time to linger. Drive faster." Then he stuffed his mouth full of chips.

I didn't press him. I was learning.

It was a good thing we'd come into a lot of cash. We stopped at Mom's Steak House. Dinner cost $79. Of course, Art had to have the most expensive items on the menu. Three bags of potato chips and several bottles of pop and he still had an appetite. I was impressed.

The cheapest motel I could find wanted $225 for a tiny room with sagging beds that reeked of mothballs and dollar store cleaning products.

"Why so much?" I demanded.

The clerk, a beefy teenager with a big red zit on the end of his nose, shrugged. "It's the Canadians. They're causing the economy to tank. My dad says we should nuke them."

I mumbled something in return about those damn Canadians, and the kid grinned. At that point, the father showed up and took over, giving us the *eye*.

"You don't got no animals, do you?"

I shook my head. "Why, no, we don't." What did he think we were? Canadians trying to sneak in a beaver or two under our jackets?

I don't think he believed me. "You have cat hair all over your shirt." His squinty little eyes drilled into me like he expected me to break down and confess my deepest darkest sins. But I was stronger than that.

"I hate cats." I lied with amazing ease. "I'm allergic. I break out into hives." This was fun. "I develop polyps on my scrotum. I start seeing things in 3D. I hear the voice of Howard Cosell—"

"Yeah. Yeah. Whatever." He held out the room key and gave us another once over. "As long as you're not gay. I don't cotton to none of that funny boy stuff. I run a good, clean establishment."

I froze. Then I smiled like the proverbial Cheshire cat. "You have nothing to worry about," I cooed.

And I wasn't even lying. Much.

~15~

Before I fell into bed, I counted all the money. Turned out we had acquired quite the windfall. With the money I'd gleaned from Charles' bank accounts and the cash in the duffel bag, we ended up with a grand total of $346,732.93. I thought about checking the briefcase, but it was locked, and I was too tired to hunt for a key or jimmy the lock. There was nothing in the suitcase but clothes. No surprise there.

All that cash went a long way in cheering me up.

And to add to my cheer, we left a present in the hotel room for Mr. I'm-a-Homophobic-Jerk-Who-Also-Hates-Animals. Putin and I had had a little chat before bedtime, and he had come through with flying colors, bless his malicious heart. This cat and I were going to get along just fine.

I turned the air conditioner off as we left and put the "Do Not Disturb" sign on the door to let things mellow a bit.

Oh, I know, I was being incredibly petty. I would have burned the place down, but I didn't have any matches.

Sometimes, you have to make do with what you've got.

~16~

At some point in the middle of the night, I stopped being Charles Hunter. This proved to be a good thing because Art had been wrong about how long it would take the police to zero in on Charles. His picture was all over the news by the next morning. In fact, the police were driving up as we pulled out of the motel that morning. I guess Mr. I'm-a-Homophobe-Animal-Hater must have recognized Charles. Or he figured out we had a cat.

I was now some beefy black dude with a shiny, bald head and an itty-bitty mustache.

Not bad, I concluded. I like bald black men. Truthfully, I was hot. I had muscles and bulges in places I didn't know you could have muscles and bulges.

I did a fair amount of strutting in front of the mirror before Art finally persuaded me it was time to leave. Oh, yeah. I was hot.

"So, who am I?" I asked Art, as we drove away in a very fine Lexus. We left nothing in the motel, not even fingerprints, Art assured me. I grinned, thinking about how confused the cops were going to be when they searched the room.

"Your name is Leroy Jefferson. You're 39. You're an attorney from San Francisco, on your way home after visiting your parents in Houston."

"Am I single?"

"Divorced."

"Straight?"

"Mostly."

75

"Mostly?"

"Yeah, well, you had a few moments of confusion in your teens. But you straightened out."

"*Straight*ened out? You're hilarious, Art."

"I like to think so."

Then something occurred to me. "Are we still in Texas?"

"Relax, buddy. You're safe."

"I bet you say that to all the black men."

"I got your back."

I wasn't comforted.

Putin must have picked up on my unease because he put up a bit of a howl. Art turned around in his seat and gave the cat his version of the evil eye: red shooting flares with little flashy things twirling on the ends. Putin offered one final spity-hiss. Then he shut up and resumed grooming his nether regions like he didn't give a rat's ass about our stupidity.

"Where are we headed?" I thought we were still going west, but I wasn't sure. It was overcast and I've never had a good sense of direction.

"We're headed to Vegas. Then to Frisco."

"San Francisco," I corrected. Or rather, *Leroy* corrected.

"That's where Leroy lives. We gotta stop and pick something up."

"What?"

"Well, aren't you a nosy Parker."

"Just tell me this—is it going to get me killed?"

He hesitated a split second too long. "Of course not."

"Yeah. Right."

He sighed. "It's not my job to convince you of anything, you know. You're free to believe whatever you wish. But I will tell you this—if we don't get the thing that's in Leroy Jefferson's possession, the world will probably end by next Monday—we won't even make it to Wednesday."

On that cheery note, we drove on.

I took particular care to drive the speed limit, maybe even a shade under. We were driving through too many small towns and backwater burgs for me to be heavy-footed on the gas pedal. Being black was apparently making me a better driver.

Which in turn, make me crave caffeine in order to stay alert.

We stopped several times for gas. There was still plenty available despite a bit of a wait, but the price rose to nearly $10 a gallon. Everywhere we went, people were cursing the Canadians.

Eventually, I switched to energy drinks 'cause coffee wasn't cutting it anymore. Consequently, we had to stop every hour so I could pee. Art didn't mind. He was going through chips faster than a teenage girl through lip gloss.

I made an urgent stop at a gas station-convenience store in some little town by the name of Cockle's Bluff, just east of the Texas-New Mexico border. I was desperate or I would have waited until we crossed into New Mexico, but when you gotta go, you gotta go.

Art did his usual gathering of supplies, although not with his usual vigor. This time, he only had two bags of chips, a large bottle of Diet Coke, and only one chocolate bar, albeit a very big one. I had a six pack of ProPower tucked under my arm and more pretzels.

We got to the counter at the same time as a guy with a ski mask perched on top of his head like a wrinkled crown bounced into the store. The clerk, a skinny guy with an enormous Adam's apple and a name tag that read *Bobby*, gulped and dropped the Coke bottle so it fell onto the floor and bounced a couple of times. I could hear the liquid hiss as it strained against the cap.

The little twerp-robber had an itty-bitty knife pointed at Bobby, the clerk. Before Bobby could react, a dozen people stepped out from the aisles all at once. Every single one of them, including an old woman with blue hair and a guy on crutches, had a gun in their hand, trained on the would-be robber.

"Chancy Weatherbottom, what the hell do you think you're doing?" bellowed a man from the center of the store. He waved the biggest, nastiest gun I had ever seen with distrubing familiarity.

The would-be robber froze, a wet spot spreading from his crotch down his leg, followed by a *plop*. He raised his hand to his face as if astonished that he was recognized. Then he sighed noisily as he realized he'd failed to adequately conceal his face. He backed out of the store and ran off. No one bothered to follow him.

"Aren't you going after him?" I croaked.

The guy nearest to me shrugged. "Ain't worth the ammunition, little ass wipe like that. He won't be back. Besides, we know where he lives."

A couple of the other gun-toters laughed. "God damned kid.

Someone should whoop his ass."

"Don't worry about that," the blue-haired woman said. "I'll have a talk with his mama. She'll give him what-for."

A bearded guy in overalls laughed. "Scared the crap out of him, that's for sure."

"You can say that again," said another guy in a cowboy hat as he surveyed the residue.

Bobby leaned over the counter and let out a disgusted groan. "I just mopped that damn floor."

The guy in the cowboy hat shrugged. "You should get hazard pay, Bobby."

"You're telling me." Bobby grabbed a mop and picked up the bottle of Coke that had rolled off the counter. "You might want to replace this," he said, as he passed me, handing me the bottle, which had stopped hissing but was still bubbling ominously. "Wouldn't want it to explode on you after all that bouncing around."

"Stuff like this happen often?" I asked the guy on crutches on my way to the cooler. He was surveying the meager selection of cookies.

"Often enough." He finally settled on a package of oatmeal cookies. He paused and looked me over. "Chancy is what you'd call 'special.' Of course, if he was black, we'd of just shot him."

I froze.

The guy burst out laughing. "Just kidding. You folks sure can't take a joke, can you?"

"Want some Coke to go with those cookies?" I held out the bottle. "I already paid for it. My way of expressing my gratitude for you not shooting me today."

He grinned and took it. "Thanks."

I didn't bother taking another Coke. I grabbed Art by the arm. "Come on." Sometimes you have to trust that karma comes in a potentially explosive Coke bottle and run before the frying pan hits the fire, and so on.

I resumed driving. The miles and road blurred. Everything blurred. The scenery. My thoughts. Time. I only had a vague idea how long it would take us to get to Vegas. Maybe another eight, nine hours, according to the guy at the last gas station. I was very glad when we crossed out of Texas.

And then, suddenly, we were there, right outside of Vegas.

What the hell? Had I fallen asleep?

Couldn't have, not with all the super-powered caffeine I'd been consuming. And we were still on the road and in one piece. But there we were—Vegas. I could have sworn we just left Texas. My can of ProPower was still cold.

*Híjole!*

Putin was curled up in Art's lap, gazing at me with liquid gold eyes. Art was lost in his own trance. His right arm was frozen mid-air, a rippled potato chip clutched between two fingers, a ProPower in his other hand.

"Art—" He didn't move. "Art!" I poked him in the shoulder. "Art! Wake up!"

Not so much as a shimmer or a shudder.

"What the hell is wrong with you?" I was yelling. I couldn't help it. Fortunately, Leroy Jefferson had a superb deep boom to his voice, which made yelling very satisfying but, nonetheless, completely ineffective.

Putin's left ear twitched, but Art continued to sit staring straight ahead. The potato chip remained firmly in his grasp even as we hit a bump in the road.

I looked for a place to pull over and had to settle for a parking lot beside an auto parts store.

Putin let out a sharp *meow* as I pulled to a stop and put his paw on the door. I leaned across Art and opened the door. "I'm not going to go looking for you, so get your butt back here real quick if you want to keep getting free crunchies." He flicked his tail at me in a most disrespectful manner, but I had bigger concerns.

"Art—" I shook him. Nothing. I slapped him across the face, but not with much force. There wasn't enough room for me to get any momentum going.

Nothing.

He might have been a mannequin. Or dead.

"What the hell is wrong with you?" Yes, I know—what a ridiculous thing to say to a demon. But what else was I supposed to say?

I was about to take another stab at punching him, but this woman popped up on the passenger side, bent over to look into the car through the still open door, and then shot me.

No, really.

She shot me. With a gun.

Forget Texas. It was Nevada I should have been worried about.

Suddenly, there was blood everywhere and I heard screaming. Not the deep, sexy baritone of a bald black man. No, this was the high-pitched squeal of a scrawny gay man of Cuban descent who faints at the sight of blood.

At some point, I stopped screaming. The pain was so intense, it usurped the reflex to bellow.

Then this woman pulled open my door and yelled at me to get out of the car. She waved her gun in my face, I'm guessing, to make a point. Like she was serious.

"Get out. Get out." She spoke in the pleasant tone of a speeding freight train.

In the distance, I could hear a sound I was becoming all too familiar with: approaching sirens. A whole lot of them, too, judging by the expanding chorus.

"I swear to God, I will kill you if you don't get out of the car *now*," the woman shrieked. I would have complied, but I was certain if I moved, I'd pee myself.

Then again, it was probably too late.

She grabbed my arm and tugged but my seatbelt was still firmly in place. She swore. Oh, man, did she ever have a fine vocabulary of curse words, all of them ending with "motherfucker."

I fumbled for the seatbelt latch. I wanted to get as far away from this bitch as I could. As the belt snapped open, she gave me one mighty jerk, and I tumbled out of that car like a cork out of a champagne bottle. I yelped as I landed on the hot asphalt. I sat up quickly, but she gave me another shove with her foot, sending me sprawling once again.

She jumped into the car and started to pull away before she'd closed the door, only to come to a screeching halt after traveling mere inches. She let out one mighty fine shriek and then jumped out of the car, grabbing at her face like it was on fire.

Not fire, I realized. It was the damn cat. Putin was spread-eagle across her face, claws fully engaged, and hissing like a hellcat on steroids.

I might have laughed if I hadn't been in so much pain. And if the sirens weren't getting closer.

And if I wasn't still black.

And if I wasn't concerned the cops would misconstrue the present situation and respond in a way that might prove to be to my disadvantage.

And if the car hadn't started to roll away.

I managed to get to my feet and dive into the car, followed by a blur of gray fur.

Next thing I know, the rear door opened, the woman jumped into the backseat, and I took off without regard to life, limb or local traffic regulations.

Throughout this entire engagement, Art remained stone-faced and immobile, that damned potato chip still in his hand as if he were about to take a bite.

So much for having my back, buddy.

I drove for fifteen minutes before I looked in the rear-view mirror. Perhaps I was experiencing an Orpheus moment. I don't know. Or maybe I was thinking that if I pretended that the crazy woman wasn't still in the backseat, she wouldn't be there when I finally turned around.

More likely, in retrospect, I was frozen in full-flight mode.

Putin had settled into the space between my seat and Art's, his attention fully focused on the passenger in the backseat. He hissed from time to time, offering up the occasional growl and showing off a substantial set of teeth, which kept said passenger in line. It helped that he had somehow managed to fluff up his fur, so he looked three times his size, which was rather substantial to begin with. It turned him into kind of a cross between a lion and a Tasmanian devil.

When I finally did glance into the rearview mirror, all I could see was a big dark eye glaring at me.

"Any particular reason for shooting me?" I finally asked.

She snarled, revealing a set of teeth almost on par with Putin's. "I didn't like your looks."

In the mirror, I could see her shifting positions. Then she settled back and did up her seatbelt. I checked for the gun. I couldn't see it. "Was it because I'm black?"

She started laughing. She laughed for a long moment, much to my confusion. "Honey, take a good look at me."

I checked the mirror again. I couldn't see much. Scratched

face. Putin left her with some pretty nasty gashes. Dark brown eyes with a slight almond shape to them. Long lashes. Brown skin.

Brown skin?

I took a closer look, even venturing a quick glance over my shoulder.

"Holy hell—you're black."

"African American, please, because, really, I'm more of a polished oak brown, if you want to be specific."

"But why did you shoot me?"

"I wanted your car."

"Why?"

"I was in a hurry."

"Why?"

"Because some men were after me."

"Why?" Why, why, why, oh why???

"You got some kind of speech problem? That all you can say? Well, fine. I might as well tell you, you being so nosy and all. I held up the auto parts store back there. It didn't go well."

I let a deep sigh. "For fuck's sake—"

"Don't swear," she snapped. "It's crude."

"Did you shoot anyone?"

"Just you." She smiled. I caught that in the mirror. Bright and defiant. Then she sighed and her shoulders drooped a little. "I'm sorry. It was an accident."

"Uh-huh." Like I was going to believe that.

"Really. I wanted to scare you off so you'd give me your car. Why didn't you run? Most people run when you wave a gun at them. Even big dudes like you."

"You know this for a fact, do you?"

"More or less."

"Yeah, well, for your information, I just drove through Texas. Your little gun didn't even raise my heartrate."

That made her laugh. "So that wet stain on your crotch—I suppose you spilled your coffee?"

I looked down. "Yeah. As a matter of fact."

That made her laugh again; a sharp staccato burst that made my ears pop. She pointed at Art. "What's with him? Is he real?"

"In a manner of speaking."

"He don't look real."

"He's real enough when he wants to be."

That must have satisfied her because she moved on. "Did I hurt you?"

"Hell, yes." I whined for emphasis.

She reached out to pat Putin on the head. The beast let her. He was purring loud enough to wake the dead and was more or less back to his usual size and shape. "I couldn't have hurt you that badly. I mean, you're still talking." She patted the cat again. "What's his name?"

"Putin," I replied, willing him to bite her; instead, he lifted his chin so she could give it a good rub. "Is there somewhere I can drop you?" I was getting tired. Blood loss, lack of food and caffeine was starting to catch up with me.

"I can't go home," she said. "Not like this." She pointed to her face. It was streaked with scratches and bits of dried blood. "My brother will think you did it."

"Maybe I could point out the gunshot wound you inflicted on me as a counterpoint."

"What?"

"Never mind. I can drop you off at a motel. I'll even pay for it."

"You don't need to," she said. "Pay for it, I mean. I have money." She grinned at me in the mirror. A sardonic little grin that would have made the hair on the back of my neck stand up, if I had had any.

I thought of something. "Do you still have that gun?"

"No. I must have dropped it."

I was relieved to hear it.

"But I still have a knife." She pulled a hunting knife out from under her jacket.

"You're quite the little psychopath, aren't you?"

"Actually, I'm a Sagitarias."

"Ha, ha."

We passed a billboard advertising the Wayward Inn. "Oh, stop there," she said. "It looks real nice, don't you think? They have a free 24-hour breakfast buffet."

I was too busy driving to pay much attention to billboards, but I pulled off at the next exit and looped my way around the service road until we found the Wayward Inn. It looked like your average highway motel. I was becoming an expert, I realized ruefully, on highway motels.

I pulled up to the entrance and waited for her to get out. She didn't move. Did she expect me to open the door for her? That seemed a little excessive considering she'd shot me.

"Well," she finally said, "aren't you coming?"

"Coming?" She had to be kidding.

"Yeah, man, you look exhausted. I'd hate for you to get into an accident."

And then, quite suddenly, I was exhausted. More than exhausted. Bone-weary and close to absolute meltdown. I didn't think I could move an inch. My brain clouded over and threatened to implode.

"Fine," I managed to say. "Let's go."

I paid (of course) for two rooms. "My sister," I mumbled. Then I remembered this was Vegas. The woman who checked us in didn't even grunt.

She did, however, look me over as if I were a slab of prime beef. "Don't you go getting no blood all over my new bedspreads," she said. She reached under the counter and pulled out a roll of bandages and some tape along with a bottle of antiseptic as casually as if bleeding dudes walking into her motel was an everyday occurrence.

Then she pulled her ample backside out of the chair, went to a sagging metal cabinet and pulled out a couple of dingy towels. She handed them to me with a bored, narrowed-eyed, down-the-nose look, even though I towered over her, that very clearly communicated that I was not, under any circumstances, to use the good towels to clean up my bloody carcass.

Or else.

I nodded curtly, a nod of complete and utter understanding. She grunted and went back to Dr. Phil, dismissing me from her mind and memory.

~18~

As soon as we reached our adjoining rooms, much of my exhaustion vanished. Funny, that. With the woman's help, I managed to get Art inside, and deposit him on one of the beds. Putin sauntered in and took up residence next to Art.

I went back to the car to get the cat's food, the suitcase, the briefcase, and the duffel bag. I put the duffel bag in a corner beside the other bed, hoping I didn't give away its importance to the crazy woman now habituating herself to my motel room.

"Your room is next door." I handed her the key.

She took it and stared at it for a moment without moving. "My name is Felicia, by the way."

She looked about 12 as she stood there in a pair of skimpy shorts and a tee shirt that barely covered her belly button. That brought me up sharp. "How old are you?"

"Old enough," she said, laughing. "You're a strange one, aren't you?" She aimed her hand toward my thigh.

I jumped. "I'm gay." It shot out of me like a chunk of projectile vomit.

That made her laugh. "Sure, you are, honey." Then she noticed her scratched face in the mirror hanging over the dresser. She winced and raised her hand to her face. "Oh, lord, I hope these don't leave scars. Damn cat. I hate cats."

I shot a glance at Putin. He was busy licking his bits and didn't seem the least bit offended, to my relief. I didn't need any more drama.

I gestured toward the bathroom. "Come on. I'll help you clean up." I waved the antiseptic at her and she nodded.

I helped her wash her face and apply the antiseptic. When we were done, she looked a lot better.

She grabbed my shirt. I flinched. "We should take a look at where you got shot."

I relaxed and carefully removed my shirt. She let out a little moan of appreciation at the sight of my chest. I have to admit I found that a tiny bit pleasing, even if it wasn't really *my* chest she was admiring.

She helped me wipe away the blood and we determined that no bullet had entered my flesh, just grazed it. Messy, but not serious. She bandaged my wound in a matter-of-fact way that bordered on the clinical. She had a nice, confident touch.

"My older brothers were always getting into trouble," she informed me. "I've been doing this kind of shit for years."

I refrained from asking what kind of trouble her brothers got into that they needed frequent bandaging. Did I really want to go down that road?

"I'm hungry," she announced when we finished and cleaned up. "Let's order a pizza."

I was fine with that. I wasn't in any condition to go out and I didn't want to leave Art.

She flipped television channels while we waited for the pizza to come, finally getting absorbed in one of those reality shows. That gave me a chance to study Art.

He had lapsed into a fetal position, all calm and cozy. I half expected to find him with his thumb in his mouth. At least he had finally dropped that stupid potato chip.

I poked, prodded and, at one point, pummeled, but he didn't so much as quiver.

"This isn't good, buddy," I said into his ear. "What am I supposed to do now?"

I thought, once again, about walking out the door, getting into the Lexus, and disappearing. Then reality raised its hand and inquired: Where would I go? What would I do? And then there was the little matter of something in Leroy Jefferson's possession that could prevent world-wide destruction, although at that moment, it was low on my list of priorities. I know, I know. Call me selfish.

Being tired and hungry and having been shot will do that to a person, you know.

And there was also the possibility that Art was full of shit and pulling my leg and lying through his pearly pink teeth.

In fact, I was pretty sure that was exactly what he was doing. Or rather, had done. He was a demon, after all. Isn't that what demons did? Lie through their pearly pink teeth?

Then again, what if he wasn't?

That's the problem with demons: you never know when they're telling the truth.

I admit I did wonder if the world was worth saving. Maybe semi-total annihilation wouldn't be such a bad thing. You know, give the earth a chance to reboot. Maybe pick another dominant species that wasn't so self-destructive. Like raccoons. Raccoons are smart. They have hands. Sort of. They have potential. They could easily replace us in a million years or so. By then, the earth might have recovered from the Age of Humanoids.

It was a thought.

In record time, the pizza arrived. It was hot and cheesy and overall delicious. We ate steadily, pausing only to open a couple of cans of Coke.

I thought for sure the smell would rouse Art. When it didn't, I truly began to worry. I was in this spot because of him. He had to snap out of whatever state he was in or I was going to be in deep trouble real soon.

Oh, wait—I was pretty sure I was already there.

"What's your name?" Felicia reached for another slice of pizza. I was glad I ordered a large. I think it was her fourth slice. I admired her stamina. I was only on my second.

I had to think about it. What was my name? And who the hell was I? Finally, I said, "Leroy Jefferson. That guy on the bed is Art. Art … something. I don't know his last name." Maybe demons didn't have last names. It's not like they needed one to collect social security or to vote.

"Leroy Jefferson? *The* Leroy Jefferson?" I must have really impressed her with the blank look on my face. "Oh, come on, man. Don't play dumb. I know all about you."

"Enlighten me." It came out as a challenge.

"You're a lawyer now. I seen you on court TV. And you work

for that crazy preacher, don't you? What's his name? Peter Knutson? I seen that video of you and him and that creepy senator, Charles Hunter, golfing with the president last week." She laughed gleefully. "I can imagine the look on all them white faces when your ass turned up at that exclusive golf club! Good thing you was with the Prez or you'd never gotten in." Her eyes narrowed as if she was considering whether that was a good thing or not. "You like that asshole?"

My eyes spun backward as I tried to keep up with her. "Wait—Charles Hunter is a senator?"

"Are you kidding me? Yeah. He whacked his wife and now he's on the run. Great guy, eh? Where the hell have you been? In a cave? It's all over the news. The president doesn't think Hunter did it. He's blaming the whole mess on the Canadians. He's calling it a smear campaign on a great American." She tilted back her head and let out a deep, long cackle. "Yeah, right."

I swore under my breath.

"So, do you like him?"

"Who?"

"The president," she said.

"I think he's an asshole," I said, hardly paying attention to her, still trying to wrap my head around *Senator* Charles Hunter. Why had Art kept that from me? What else had he kept from me?

"So, why are you hanging out with him?"

I glanced at her, trying to focus. "Business. If you want to know your enemy, you play golf with him."

That made her smile, a slow smile that lit up her face. She reached for another piece of pizza and settled back to enjoy it. "You used to play football for the New Jersey Devils back in the day, right?"

I nodded noncommittally. Did I?

"You went to high school with my father. He says you were a nasty bastard back then."

Her father? My eyes narrowed again as I tried to do some math. "How old are you?" I asked again.

"Relax. I'm over 18. My daddy got started young." She was proud of her daddy, that was for sure.

I wanted to believe her. Really, I did. "Who is your dad?"

"Pearson Wainwright. The third."

I nodded, trying to look as though I was placing him, but I

had never heard of him.

"He says if it wasn't for you, he'd be in jail."

"Oh?"

"You stopped him from doing something really stupid."

"Glad to hear it." I was, too.

"You don't remember him, do you?" She sighed. "I'm not surprised. My daddy says you and him were best friends. My mother says you never gave my daddy the time of day."

"Then how did I stop him from ending up in jail?"

"He says you talked him out of joining a gang."

"Really?" I was impressed. Maybe Leroy wasn't such a bad guy, after all.

"He says you talked him out of joining the *wrong* gang."

I nodded sagely as if I understood what the hell she was talking about. "What's your dad doing now?"

"Ten to twenty in Attica."

I blinked, probably more than once. "You're kidding."

She laughed. "Yeah. He teaches shop at Kensington High School. He got out of that gang as soon as he realized they were crazy."

"I'm surprised it was that easy."

"He says gangs were different back then. And he was kind of a klutz. They were happy to let him go. He goes bowling with some of the guys every Thursday. Seems like a bunch of them were klutzes."

Bowling. The cross-cultural activity for all ages. "Where did you go wrong?"

She stiffened at that. "What do you mean?"

"Didn't you rob that auto parts store?"

"Well, yeah."

"So, who pissed in your corn flakes?"

"What are you talking about? I don't even like corn flakes."

"Why did you rob the store?" Keep it simple, I told myself. S-I-M-P-L-E.

"I told you—I needed the money."

"Ever try getting a job?"

"Ha, ha." She crossed her arms tightly over her chest. "I need a lot of money in a hurry. It was either rob the stupid store or sell my body. Which do you think I should do?"

"I have no opinion on what you should or shouldn't do. You're an adult." I narrowed my gaze. "You are, aren't you? An adult, I mean."

Major eye roll. Like I was an idiot. Or old.

"I chose the one that was the safest."

"Safest? You could have been shot."

"How? I had the gun."

This was over my head. I eyed the last piece of pizza. "You going to eat that?"

She shook her head and I grabbed it. I thought about leaving it for Art if he ever woke up, but, screw Art, I was stress eating now.

"That Knutson guy?"

"Yeah?"

"He's weird as fuck. You should watch out for him."

"You know him?"

She shrugged. "I heard him preach not too long ago. Lordy, he is one crazy-ass bastard. You know what he says?"

"What?"

"He says the world's gonna end real soon, like next week, and he's gonna make it happen 'cause God told him to. He's got him a whole bunch of crazy-ass followers, too. But not me, I'm too smart to fall for that shit."

"Lots of crackpots have predicted the end of the world. It hasn't happened yet." But I was thinking of Art and his own prediction and his remarkably similar timeline. I suddenly wasn't hungry anymore and I let the pizza fall through my fingers.

"Yeah, but this guy's crazy enough to make it happen. And him and Waterman are as tight as virgin assholes. You know what that means—" She paused, giving me *the look*.

"What?"

"Jeez-Louise, are you dumb, or what? I gotta spell it out for you, Leroy? Waterman's already got one finger on THE BUTTON. Won't take much for him to press it, him being so fucking crazy and all."

"He wouldn't. And even if he wanted to, someone would stop him."

"Ha! Like who? Knutson? He *wants* him to press it. So do half the guys Waterman's got advising him." She gave me an epic glare, followed by a rousing finger-wagging, and then her eyes widened.

"You're not one of them, are you?"

"One what?"

"One of Knutson's followers. You don't believe his shit, do you?"

I shook my head. "Hell, no. I'm just his lawyer." A safe bet, I thought.

She considered that. "Man, now that's fucked."

Truer words were never spoken.

"I'm tired," Felicia announced, followed by a mammoth yawn. "Mind if I lay down?"

"You have your own room," I reminded her.

She looked me over with narrowed eyes and a deep frown. "Are you really gay?"

"Yes." Sort of. *Hector* was still gay. Leroy was straight. A bit of a player. I could feel that part of him burning in the background, flaring each time he, or *I*, glanced a little too long at Felicia. No, not burning. Simmering. A slow rolling simmer on the back burner. Tough titties, Leroy. I'm in charge.

She sighed. "Well, if you change your mind—"

"It doesn't work that way."

She stretched out on the bed and turned her back to me. "Well, I guess I'm glad because I don't want to be alone right now but I ain't in the mood for no messing around."

I opened my mouth to insist she go to her room and then closed it. I supposed I could use the room instead, but I wasn't tired and, to be honest, I didn't want to be alone either. Art didn't count, given his current lack of responsiveness.

Putin rubbed against my legs. I jumped and let out a little squeal. He ran to the door, which I opened for him. "Hurry up. I don't need to worry about you, too."

I closed the door and surveyed the room. A girl who may or may not be of legal age sprawled on one bed while a comatose demon occupied the other. Fun times, let me tell you.

I sank into a chair and turned on the television. Against my better judgement, I switched to the news.

*"... tensions mount as the US team negotiating with the Canadian government fails to secure a deal on Canadian oil."*

Cut to video of President Stanley Morris Waterman on the golf course, talking to reporters: *"We want to continue negotiating with the Canadians, but they aren't playing fair. They want to charge us an exorbitant price for their oil. That's not very neighborly. We're not going to let them hold us over a barrel.* (Wait—did Waterman make a pun? As in *"over a barrel"* of oil? I groaned. Maybe Art had a point: the man needed to go.) *No, sir. Not as long as I'm president. If the Canadians aren't willing to give us their oil, we may have to take further action."*

*"What about the rumor that the Canadians took out Senator Hunter's wife?"*

Waterman shrugged dramatically. *"Well, we're investigating, but who knows? Maybe they did. Maybe they didn't."*

An unseen voice called out: *"What do you think, Mr. President? Did the Canucks do it?"*

Another mammoth shrug. (I'm surprised the guy didn't lose his shoulders.) *"If I were a betting man—which I'm not—I'd say they're the odds-on favorite. And if they did, you can be guaranteed we will take further action."*

They cut back to the anchor, a preppy-looking guy with too-long sideburns wearing the most gawd-awful plaid jacket I had ever seen, in or out of a thrift shop. *"The President declined to elaborate on what he meant by 'further action', but sources at the Pentagon indicate that military action has not been ruled out ..."*

Military action? Against Canada? Seriously?

Then they did this person-on-the-street thing: *"What do you think about relations between the US and Canada?"*

Bearded stoner: *"Who cares, man? As long as they use protection."*

Middle-aged woman with cat-eyeglasses: *"I always knew Canadians were too nice to be real. It's an act, you know. Well, they can't fool us! Not no more."*

Fat guy flashing the victory sign: *"Ban Canadian bacon."*

Some guys behind him starting chanting, *"Down with Poutine!"*

*"Nuke the bastards,"* chimed in an elderly lady with a maniacal grin and lacquered bleached blond hair that took up half the block.

I sighed. At the rate things were going, Art could be right. The world was going to end in a flash and a bang real soon. He still hadn't moved a muscle. He'd picked a fine time to decompensate.

Then my attention zipped back to the television because there I was as Hector Gonzales, the mad bomber/terrorist AND as Charles Hunter, the dead senator.

The *dead* senator? I swore loudly.

I sat up sharply as video rolled showing Charles with his wife at some fancy function "... *Senator Charles Hunter, a longtime critic of President Waterman, was found dead late this evening from an apparent gunshot wound, two days after his wife's murder. Suspected Cuban American terrorist Hector Gonzales*—they flashed my picture—*is wanted for questioning, although officials refuse to speculate if there is a Cuban connection. The White House also refuses to speculate on a possible Cuban-Canadian connection, but sources say the possibility is being considered, given the current unrest.*"

Felicia sat up at the mention of Charles Hunter. "Well, I'll be horsewhipped and hogtied. This just gets better and better, don't it?"

I assured her that it did, indeed.

"That Hector Gonzales guy—he didn't do nothing," she said.

"Oh? What makes you say that?"

"He's too stupid looking. It's probably a set up by Waterman. Wouldn't take nothing for the president to order Hunter killed, would it? Not that president, anyway."

"But why?"

Felicia shrugged. "Politics can get nasty."

She had a point.

Then the local news came on and a picture of Felicia popped up. Nice picture, I thought. Very flattering. Much better than mine.

Felicia thought differently. "Where the hell did they get *that*? I look fat."

"Security camera?" I offered.

"Oh, shit." She collapsed face first into a pillow. At least, the news confirmed that she was over 18. One less thing to worry about.

Whoopee do-da-day.

~20~

When Felicia finally fell asleep, I grabbed the duffel bag and the briefcase and slipped into the adjacent room. Putin scratched at the door and I let him in. He claimed a place in the middle of the bed and then proceeded to scrutinize every move I made, complete with critique.

I decided to check out the briefcase, which was, of course, locked.

*Meeooww.*

I thumped it a couple of times, looked around for something sharp to jab it with, and then, finally, remembered I still had Charles' keys.

Okay, okay, so a genius I am not.

*Meeeooowwww.*

I tiptoed back into the other room. Sure enough. There they were, neatly laid out on the dresser alongside Leroy's keys, a little pile of spare change, Leroy's wallet, and my pocketknife. And there it was, a little brass key dangling on Charles' keyring. I swear it winked at me.

I popped open the briefcase and then nearly had a coronary. It was filled with more cash, a bundle of checks, a program from a Sunday service at the Restored Missionary Evangelical Gospel Church of the Sacred Order of Anarchy and underneath it all, several bricks of plastic explosives with detonators attached. Not that I am in any way familiar with such devices beyond the occasional James Bond movie, but it would take a complete toadworm not to figure this one out.

*MeeeeoooOWwww.*

I glared at Putin. "Your sarcasm is noted and not appreciated."

You would be amazed at how calm I remained. You would be amazed at how coolly I removed everything but the explosives from the briefcase and then closed it up and locked it. Then I slipped out the door and placed the briefcase in the garbage bin behind the motel. You would also be amazed that I did this without (a) shitting myself and/or (b) blowing myself up.

I still marvel at that.

Back in the room, heartbeat returning to normal, I counted the cash: $14,853. A relatively modest haul. The checks were in a neat bundle, wrapped in a strip of paper with the words "Bank of Solar Resources" printed in block letters. I didn't bother adding them up exactly, but I quickly estimated there was at least half a million. That kind of took my breath away.

What the hell had Charles been up to?

I put the cash and checks in the duffel bag and then laid down, convinced I would be awake all night, but Putin curled up beside me, his paws curved protectively around my arm, and purred me to sleep.

Damn cat. Just when you want to strangle him.

~21~

When I woke up, I swore I could smell bacon. On the other hand, it could have been air pollution.

Whatever.

I stretched gingerly—my shoulder where the bullet grazed me felt stiff. I had no idea of the time. It was too dark to read the watch on my arm. I randomly pushed a couple of buttons until the dial lit up: 6:30. Much too early. I rolled over with the intention of going back to sleep, but my bladder had another suggestion.

I dragged myself out of bed, pushing aside the drapes to let in a bit of dull light while mumbling a few choice curse words about the stupidity of anatomical needs, and staggered to the bathroom. On the way back, I checked the other room. Art laid there in the same position he had occupied the previous night, still motionless.

Putin stretched, yawned and sauntered to the door. I opened it, as commanded, and he slid out on stealthy cat paws.

The gray dawn light crackled at the horizon, promising another day of heat, although at the moment the desert air felt cool and refreshing. I stood in the doorway, drinking in the stillness.

It took a moment. Maybe two.

Then it hit me—more like it slapped me up-side the head and took me out to lunch: the Lexus was missing.

I stepped outside to survey the parking lot. Maybe I'd just forgotten where I'd parked.

But no, I hadn't.

It was gone. Definitely. Completely.

Poof!

Vanished.

I ran back into the room and flung open the drapes and turned on the lights. Felicia was also gone.

So was Leroy's wallet, the pile of change, and the keys. There was no sign of my suitcase, although my Boy Scout knife was still on the dresser.

Maybe she'd taken the car to get coffee and donuts. Or Starbucks. Surely, there was a Starbucks close by.

And then I remembered the duffel bag.

I rushed back into the other room.

It was gone.

That's when I punched Art in the stomach. I mean, I wound up my arm and I really nailed him. Wham! Right in the solar plexus.

His body folded, and he gave a little *th-rump* and a shudder. Then he coughed and his eyes snapped open. He bolted upright. I let out a sharp, very shrill scream.

"Really, Hector, what's your problem?"

I couldn't speak. All I could do was flap my gums. Finally, I managed to croak, "I thought you were dead."

"Honestly, Hector. Sometimes you're too much."

"No. Really. You haven't moved for—" I glanced at my watch. "Eighteen hours."

His eyes narrowed and then he frowned. "Are you serious?"

"What's the last thing you remember?"

He gave it some thought. "Stopping at the gas station and buying ..." He looked around. "How did we get here? And, where are we?"

I filled him in. It took a while because I kept leaving parts out or messing up the order. I have never been very good at telling stories.

"So, where is this Felicia? She sounds like my kind of woman."

"She's gone. She took everything. All the money and the car." I gave the room another sweep. "My clothes! She took my clothes." All of them. I had nothing but the pair of boxers I was currently wearing.

"Wow," was all he could say after a long pause. "She really is my kind of woman."

~22~

"What do we do now?"

Art stood in the doorway, sniffing the air. "We go after her."

"Go after her? How?"

At that moment, a cab pulled up and we got in. Even Putin, the sneaky little bastard. The driver, a cheerful sort, didn't seem to notice I was only in my underwear. But then, we were in Vegas. Maybe he was desensitized.

Art told him to head to the Strip and we briskly set off.

We drove two blocks. "Stop here," Art said, and the driver obligingly pulled to the side of the road. "Wait, please."

"Oh, yes, sir, I would be happy to do so." The driver pulled out a cell phone and proceeded to shoot aliens. He left the meter running.

A few feet ahead of us was the Lexus. To my surprise, Felicia sat in the driver's seat, sleeping soundly.

Art knocked on the window. She jumped and let out a little shriek. She banged on the door in a panic. She couldn't, or wouldn't, open it. She tried to scramble to the other side of the car, but she couldn't get out of her seatbelt.

Art calmly opened the door as Felicia frantically attacked the seatbelt. "What the hell?" she screamed. She looked at Art and then at me. "Get away from me."

"Car problems?" Art asked, so solicitously I half expected her to collapse from a sugar overdose.

"Fuck you," she screamed. Felicia was good at screaming. I

would say it was her number one talent.

Art took her gently by the arm and she immediately calmed down. "Now, Felicia, my dear. You shouldn't carry on so. It's not good for your heart."

She nodded dully.

He coolly leaned across her and unbuckled her seatbelt. "Come with me, dear." And Art led her back to the cab. "This is Mr. Sethi, Felicia, dear, he's going to take you on a little drive."

Mr. Sethi gave her a little nod and a bright smile.

"All right," Felicia said blandly, and she got into the cab.

Art reached into his pocket and pulled out a wad of bills. He peeled off a few and stuffed them into her fist. Then he peeled off a few more and handed them to Mr. Sethi. "Take her to Salt Lake City. The downtown Sheraton. Don't stop until you get there."

Mr. Sethi took the bills and grinned broadly. "Oh, yes, sir. I am happy to do this for you, sir."

Art gave Mr. Sethi a little wave and watched them drive away. Then he turned back to me. "Don't look so sad, Hector. You'll see her again."

"I don't want to see her again. She's crazy."

He shrugged. "All the better. Now get in the car, Hector, before you cause an accident."

Art announced he would drive. Whatever. I did a quick search of the car and found, to my relief, Leroy's wallet and keys, along with the duffel bag, still stuffed with money, but my suitcase was nowhere in sight. "Where are my clothes?"

"How should I know?" Art said. "You really need to keep better track of your stuff."

"I looked. They're gone."

"Well, maybe you didn't look hard enough." He turned the car around. "We'll have to go back and check."

"Fine with me." I fastened my seatbelt, doing my best not to snag anything of bodily importance in the straps. "Can you turn the heat on? I'm freezing."

Instead of saying, "Be my guest," or turning a knob, he began to glow. By glow, I mean he turned fluorescent orange and cranked out enough heat to roast a tyrannosaurus.

"Whoa, that's enough." I was now glowing a bit myself, as well as dripping in sweat.

He shut himself down. "Sorry. I get a little excited when someone asks for heat."

"Your 'instant on' feature is quite something." I rolled down a window and let in some cool air. Immediately, a cloud formed inside the car and little lightning bolts lit up inside the cloud, followed by tiny booms. Then it began to rain. Inside the car.

*Híjole!*

It rained for a solid minute, although it felt longer. When the cloud had dissipated, I went back to being cold and now I was wet, which made me colder, but I kept my mouth closed lest Art invoke a hurricane.

We'd gone a block when Art glanced at me. "You look ridiculous. You can't go around like that, even in Vegas, you know. People will complain."

I sighed. Well, at least he was catching up. "Felicia did something with my clothes. I didn't know what, but I was sure she did something." I spoke slowly, as if he were three, not … whatever.

"She stuffed them under the mattress."

"Oh. Why?"

"Who knows? Perhaps she did it to slow you down. Or piss you off."

"Are you sure Salt Lake City is far enough away? Couldn't you have sent her to Baltimore or Cleveland?"

"Not part of the plan, Hector, my friend."

"Plan? What plan?"

He cut loose with a derisive little sneer. "You don't think I'm winging it, do you? Really, Hector—you might give me a little more credit than that."

I opened my mouth and then closed it. What was the point?

A few minutes later, he pulled up in front of our room and handed me a room key.

"Aren't you coming in?"

"Nope. No time. Grab your clothes and make sure you don't leave anything. And hurry. We don't have time to linger."

"Why? Is the world ending or something?" I know, I know. Sarcasm is not my strong suit.

"Or something." He made that annoying shooing motion with which I was becoming all too familiar. "Go. Quickly."

I got into the room, found my now very wrinkled clothes

under the mattress and got into them as quickly as I could. I couldn't find my socks. I did a quick check of the room and then looked under the bed again.

As I reached under the bed to grab a sock, a loud blast shook the room so badly that the bedside lamps fell to the floor, narrowly missing my head. I swore rather significantly, latched onto the sock, grabbed my shoes in one panicked swoop, and scrambled out the door as another blast hit.

This time, the windows broke, and glass sprayed everywhere as I dove into the backseat of the Lexus. Art took off, brakes squealing, gravel flying, and my legs dangling out the car door.

I pulled myself in and turned my head up in time to see a ball of voluminous fire where the Wayward Inn had stood a few minutes ago. Shades of Iggy's alley. I nearly crapped myself.

"Holy fucking hell."

Art let out a roar of maniacal laughter and slapped the steering wheel with evangelical zeal. "Halleluiah and amen, brother!"

I lay on the backseat, staring at the roof of the car for several long minutes, too stunned to do more than blink. I had flashbacks, back to when I was Hector in body and soul, back when life was simple and boring. I saw my grandmother, shaking her wooden spoon at me. My mother, dressed in a pale pink dress, her hair dyed Viking red, a bouquet of carnations in one hand and a flask in the other, kissing the top of my shaggy head. Iggy, grinning gleefully at a fucked-up carburetor, dollar signs radiating out of his eye sockets.

I missed Hector. Okay, yeah, he might have been a wimpy little dude, but he *fit*, if you know what I mean.

"I want my body back." It came out in a pouty huff.

"Which one?"

Which *one*? What was he talking about? "Hector's."

"Sure. But not right now." He sounded sharp but then he softened his tone. "I mean, I wouldn't advise it right now."

"Why not?"

"Because the guys that investigate things that go boom are going to discover that the explosives used to destroy the Wayward Inn are the same kind of plastic explosives that blew up Iggy's garage. And by 'same kind,' I mean they were put together using the same materials and in the same manner, by the same person. And they've already decided that Hector had ties with Charles Hunter's murder.

Of course, blowing up the Wayward Inn was a brilliant move—it'll confuse the hell out of them." He giggled like a little boy with a dirty secret.

"I didn't do it on purpose."

"Oh, Hector, my friend. You didn't do it at all. Not that anyone's going to believe that. That's the fun part. Although, I must say tossing those plastic bricks in the dumpster was brilliant. Couldn't have done better myself."

"Then what does it have to do with me?" Okay, so I was being stubborn. Maybe even a little pissy. I knew exactly what it meant: Hector's picture was soon going to be plastered on every "Most Wanted" board in every post office in the country. Fortunately, I reminded myself, I wasn't "Hector."

"Hector, Hector, you really are a moron, aren't you?"

"I suppose I could tell you to go to hell, but you'd like that, wouldn't you?"

"Put your socks on, Hector. And shut up."

A wave of futility and doom washed over me. I might as well put on my socks, but I couldn't bend far enough to get them past my toes in the confines of the backseat. And I only had one sock.

~23~

When I woke up, it was dark. I sat in the passenger seat with no recollection of how I got there. My head and my shoulder ached. "Where are we?" The words came out cracked. My mouth was dry as dust. So was my brain.

"We're about ten miles from Santa Barbara, California."

That didn't mean much. I rubbed the sleep from my eyes and looked out the window. Lights everywhere. Little twinkling lights above us. Bright headlights flying toward us. Masses of little red lights in front of us. Quite hypnotic, in a spaced-out, freaky kind of way. I stared into my lap until my head cleared.

Art pulled a Diet Coke out of the pack sitting between us, wrapped his fingers around it for a few seconds, and then handed it to me. "Drink this."

The icy liquid was a balm to my parched throat. "How did you do that?"

"Do what?'

"Make it cold."

"I have magic fingers." He waggled his eyebrows.

I didn't say anything. I drank the Diet Coke, not even minding the "diet" part, but I really could have used a ProPower Energy Drink.

"We'll be in San Francisco in a couple of hours, give or take."

It took longer than that. Traffic remained heavy all the way from Santa Barbara to San Jose. Even Art couldn't maneuver around that.

"I could use breakfast," I finally said once it was light again.

We found a Denny's on the outskirts of San Jose, and I ordered banana pancakes with bacon *and* sausages, which is as decadent as I get at breakfast. Our waitress was a fresh-faced girl—woman, excuse me—probably still in her teens, or just out of them, a little on the rotund side. (Okay—a lot on the rotund side.) She wore her blondish hair slicked back into a tight bun. Little licks of hair stood straight out here and there. She had naturally rosy cheeks, clear gray eyes, and a bright guileless smile. Her apron rested right below her rather ample bosom. Her legs were thick, her ankles puffy, her fingers were short and stubby. She was the kind of person you wouldn't give a second glance if you passed her in the street.

Too bad for you.

She was hilarious. She even had Art laughing within minutes of handing us our menus. She brought me an extra dish of whipped cream for my pancakes. (You haven't lived until you've had bananas and whipped cream on thick, fluffy pancakes.) She told us about the cook and a busboy named Sam and how they were so busy trying to grope each other without anyone seeing them that they nearly burned the place down, but not to worry. That was last week, and neither was working today. She kept the coffee coming, and never stopped smiling.

The place was busy. Nearly every table was full. The middle-aged couple across from us never spoke to one another; the woman was on her cell phone; the man was reading the San Jose *Mercury*. The man had bacon and scrambled eggs. The woman had cottage cheese and fruit.

There were a number of solo diners; men in suits, women in suits, yapping on their cell phones, texting; checking the stock market, plotting international espionage, making secret pacts with the devil. Whatever. It was certainly entertaining.

Next to the silent couple sat a group of four: two men, two women. Friends? Couples? College students? Co-workers? They were loud. Like Friday night at the bar loud. And demanding. ("What do you mean you don't have almond milk?" "When I say I want my eggs over easy, I mean EASY." "Make sure you pat the extra fat off my bacon. And please warm the plates.")

I ignored them as best I could, which wasn't easy. I watched our waitress juggle tables with mind-bending grace. Her name tag said her name was "Betsy." It fit, I thought. She was, indeed, a Betsy, the kind of woman that didn't make me want to hide, the kind I wouldn't mind as a friend.

It all fell apart when she brought the table of four their breakfast. "This bacon is too crisp," said one of the women, a skinny redhead with a voice so loud and shrill I wanted to stuff cotton in my ears. "I specifically asked for you to make sure the bacon wasn't too crisp. And look at all that grease! Eww." She shoved the plate toward Betsy so hard, it fell to the floor and shattered, sending shards of cheap pottery and strips of bacon flying.

Suddenly, the restaurant became very, very quiet.

The foursome snickered. Loudly, of course, if not a bit uncomfortably. "Well, I guess you can't charge us for that shit now, can you?" the woman snapped.

"I'll get you another order," Betsy said, with far more dignity than I would have been capable of displaying.

As Betsy walked hurriedly toward the kitchen, one of the men called out, "Hey, fatty, are you gonna clean up this mess, or what?" He was youngish; close-clipped blondish hair, which he was already losing (badly), medium build, hard brown eyes, broad forehead, narrow chin. He had the look and tone of someone used to throwing his weight around, literally and figuratively. Plus, he reeked of expensive aftershave; I could smell it two tables away.

Betsy didn't answer; didn't turn around, but I could see her. Her lips were quivering.

"Hey, you. Fatty Patty. Or is it Betsy-wetsy? I'm talking to you." He got to his feet, knocking over his coffee. "Hey, you. Bitch. Turn around and answer me." The women at his table twittered; the other guy grinned stupidly, silently egging him on.

I stood up. No, *Leroy* stood up. Hector would have hidden under the table. I looked at the bozo-wannabe-bully. I stared at him, letting the rage making my skin tingle shine through. I might have been seven feet tall. I towered over him in so many ways. Me and Leroy.

His chin jerked upward as he caught my movement, interpreting it immediately as threatening. "You got a problem?" Like most bullies, he didn't know he was already beaten.

Bless his heart.

~24~

"I'm not the one with the problem." My voice got so deep, I expected to vibrate a hole right through the floor. My chest expanded. A cold heat raced through my body. This bully was going down.

"So why don't you mind your own business." He paused, breath half-in, half out.

The Word perched precariously on the tip of his tongue.

He didn't say it, but he thought it. That *word*. You know the one. The one that pops up regarding people of African descent when someone with shit for brains wants to broadcast their IQ or lack thereof. It sat fat and heavy on his snarling lips. It pulsed in his head. It flashed in his eyes. Right here in Silicon Valley, the heart of liberalism and kumbaya. *Híjole!*

I kept my calm. "It's my business when you disturb my breakfast and insult someone. Someone who is doing her damnedest to help you. I think you and your friends need to shut up, eat your breakfast, and get the hell out of here. And, oh yeah, apologize to Betsy."

"Betsy? Who the hell is Betsy?"

"Your waitress."

He snorted. "Fuck you—" There was that word again. Right there, unspoken but oh-so implied.

I held his gaze. The stubborn bastard wasn't going to back down. Maybe he didn't know how. Maybe it was time he learned because I wasn't going to back down either. Leroy and me. What a pair! Besides, I had better backup than he did.

"Well, she should have brought me the right bacon in the first place," the redhead whined. I ignored her. My eyes locked on Mr. Shit-For-Brains.

A middle-aged Latino with a tiny mustache and thinning hair came rushing toward us. His name tag read "Roberto" and MANAGER. "What seems to be the problem?" He radiated a can't-we-all-just-get-along-for-the-love-of-God-and-for-the-sake-of-my-job nervousness.

Mr. Shit-for-Brains gave him a cold once-over. "Hell, aren't there any Americans left in this fucking country?"

Leroy and I gave him our best sarcastic snort. "You're really something, aren't you? And here I thought everybody in California was a doped up liberal, all full of peace, love, and bean sprouts, and here we walk into a breakfast meeting of the junior KKK, Golden State chapter."

Mr. Shit-for-Brains pointed a perfectly manicured finger at me. "Look, you. *Boy.*" His last word hung in the air like a mushroom cloud. Not *the* word, but close enough.

And the air got very, very cold as everyone waited. His buddy looked away, a stricken look on his face. *It's all fun and games until someone finally crosses the line* ... and the women stared at me, ready to take cover. In the heavy quiet that lingered, even Mr. Shit-for-Brains realized he'd stepped over the line, but then he tried to shrug it off, as if it was all a silly misunderstanding.

I could have let him off the hook. Or I could have bitten off his finger; instead, I crossed my arms over my well-inflated chest. "I want you to listen to me very carefully." I/Leroy took pains to articulate each syllable very clearly. "You and your friends are going to get up and walk out, calmly and quietly, without another word, because every second that you delay is going to cause that man ..." I gestured over my shoulder to Art—"to make really bad things happen to each and every one of you."

Shit-for-Brains rolled his eyes. The other guy laughed; the women giggled nervously. *As if.*

Then someone's cellphone rang. It was the redhead's. She glanced at the screen and rose to her feet immediately. "We have to get back to the office," she said, a note of panic in her voice.

She grabbed her purse, shoved her way out of the booth,

leaving behind a trail of spilled coffee dripping onto the floor.

She turned to her companions. "Come *on*. Mr. Iwase wants to see us right now." Mr. Iwase must have been important because she looked like she was about to piss herself.

And then, so did the rest of them. Classic deer-in-headlights look. It was priceless.

We watched them trip over themselves getting to the parking lot. We watched them scramble to get into a brand-new BMW and tear out of the parking lot. The BMW swerved to miss an oncoming car and ran up the curb. Even from inside the restaurant, you could hear metal scraping. I cringed. That was going to cost someone a lot of money to fix. Company car? Wasn't Mr. Iwase going to be pleased about that.

I turned to Roberto. "We'll pay their bill."

Roberto was smiling brightly. "You don't have to—"

"No, we want to. It's not your fault or Betsy's. People can be such assholes, can't they?" He gave me a slow, conspiratorial nod. Oh, yeah. He knew. He was a member of the club. He probably even had the tee-shirt. "*Lo siento mucho*," I whispered. I meant it, too. I was sorry, very sorry that the world contained so many assholes.

"I should give you your meal for no charge, for the inconvenience."

But I wouldn't hear of it. He never did bring us our bill, but I left more than enough to cover our table, the other table, and leave Betsy a nice, healthy tip.

I was amazingly lighthearted. "That was fun."

Art shrugged as if it were no big deal, but a tiny grin teased his upper lip. "Too bad we won't be there when Mr. Iwase fires their sorry asses. Now, that would be fun. Slackers, the lot of them. Not only is he going to fire them, but he is also going to toss them out on their well-heeled ears, publicly humiliate them, and make sure they never work for another company in the Valley of Silicon. And they haven't even started to make a dent in their student loans. They might have to sell their fancy cars because I'm pretty sure they won't be able to make the payments. They will have to give up their apartments and cut up their credit cards. Well, I suppose they can always go back home to mom and dad." He grinned mercilessly. "Oh, dear. Well, that's not going to work, now is it? What a coincidence! All their parents just sold their houses for fabulously high prices and are moving to Belize. Guess they'll have to figure it out on their own. Too bad they have the survival skills of gnats."

That seemed a little harsh. "I love karma as much as the next guy, but do you really think you need to go that far? I'm sure they've learned their lesson."

Art shook his head. "Hector, Hector, you are so naïve. I don't have to do anything to them. They've done it all to themselves. I haven't had to lift a finger."

I felt pretty good when we left. Like I'd stood up for something. For someone. And on some level, for myself. I'd had my share of name-calling, put-downs, trash talk over the years, even from my own family. (*Be a man, Hector. Toughen up, Hector. You a girl, Hector? Hey, cake-boy. Hey, you four-eyed pansy. Hey, faggy butt, man up....*)

I'd had more moments of fear, humiliation, helplessness while someone bigger and stronger called me names and dared me to do something about it than I cared to count. Or pushed me around. Or beat the crap out of me. Or simply made me feel less than human.

And in return, all I had was anger. So much anger. Anger I couldn't do anything with. Anger that turned to depression, self-hate, hopelessness, and helplessness. Yeah, I knew all about that. Well, fuck it. And fuck *them*.

We almost got to the car when Betsy came loping toward us. I had hoped we could get out of there without her realizing we had left her such a generous tip. I didn't want her thanks.

Good thing because that's not what I got.

She caught up to me and thrust the money at me. "Here. Take it back. I don't want it."

"But—"

She shook her head vigorously. "Thanks for standing up for me, but I don't want your money."

"It's no big deal. I'm very rich." It rolled off my tongue with amazing ease, although it left a sour taste in my mouth.

She was still shaking her head. "I'm not a whore."

I stared at her, unable to comprehend. "A whore? That's the last thing I think you are."

She shook her head vigorously, her bun bobbing on the back of her head, her face flushed bright red, right down her neck. "I can't take that kind of money from you. Especially from someone like you."

"Someone like me?"

"I'm not a whore."

"Yes, I know. I never said—"

"If I take that money, I'm a whore. I'm not. I'm not. Please." She pushed the money at me and when I wouldn't take it, she let it fall and backed away. "I can't owe you." Then she turned and hobbled back to the restaurant.

I watched her retreat, looked at Art, then looked at the money, now blowing across the parking lot. A couple of homeless people popped up from nowhere and scrambled after the bills. I made no move to stop them.

"What was that about?"

Art sighed. "Think about it, Hector. You'll figure it out."

I just stared at him. "I don't think so."

"Get in the car. I'll try and explain."

We got ourselves back on the 101, and drove about ten minutes, heading north. I was still clueless.

"The problem is you're still thinking like you're Hector, the myopic, gay loser of Cuban ancestry. But that's not who you are at the moment. You're Leroy Jefferson, a strong, imposing black man. You're the kind of guy white folks call the cops on for walking your dog in your own neighborhood, or worse, shoot on sight."

"Yeah." That much I got, at least on a superficial level, because even as Hector I'd had moments. "What's that got to do with Betsy?"

"Betsy thinks she is a good person. Betsy thinks she treats everyone equally and with respect. I mean, she really does try, which is more than I can say for a lot of people. She believes in helping the poor, being kind, donating to worthy causes, not that she has a lot of money to give away, but if she did, she's sure she would."

"Where are you going with this?"

"She doesn't think she's a racist, either. In fact, she'd probably be shocked if anyone thought that about her."

"I'm not following you."

He sighed heavily. "I guess I have to spell this out for you."

"Please do." My head was starting to hurt. I was wishing we had never started this conversation.

"Betsy is white. You're black. You stood up for her. On one hand, she's grateful. On the other hand, she's embarrassed. Maybe a little scared."

"Scared? Of me?"

Another sigh. "Yes, Hector. Of you. But not you—Leroy. A big, strange black man who showed kindness to an overweight, not very attractive white girl. No one has ever stood up for her before. She doesn't understand why you would do it. She can't help but wonder if there's an ulterior motive. She's never in her life been able to trust anyone, not even her own family. Everyone she's ever known has wanted something from her. How can she possibly understand you might be different? Consequently, if you were walking your dog in her neighborhood, she'd be the first one to call the cops on you."

"No—"

"Yes. Oh, she'd never admit it. She'd deny with every fiber of her being that she would do such a thing, even to herself, until she's confronted with something that doesn't quite fit in the neat little box she's constructed, the one that keeps her safe in her very own special world, of which you have no part."

"But—" What the hell? How do you wrap your head around that?

"You know what humanity's greatest failing is?"

I shook my head, too befuddled to even postulate an answer.

"Ambivalence. In particular, moral ambivalence. Being confused by all those shades of gray, all those variations on a theme. Most people can't just say, 'Leroy is nice.' They have to qualify it. 'Leroy is a nice *man*.' 'Leroy's a nice *black* man.' Or, 'Yes, Leroy is nice—for a *black man*.' All those shades of meaning, of understanding, of interpretation, misinterpretation—they can really fuck people up. People like Betsy, who want to do the right thing, provided you stick to her expectations, stay in your proper place, and don't surprise her."

I was starting to get it. "Like standing up for her in public against other white people or walking my dog in her neighborhood. Or giving her a pile of money she doesn't think she deserves."

"Yeah. Like that."

~25~

Leroy lived in a condo in Pacific Heights. Everything about his place said *class*—furniture, artwork, books, clothes, paint color, wallpaper, kitchen appliances. And shoes. He had really nice shoes.

I constructed a first-class meal, if I do say so, from Leroy's well stocked fridge. Cooking relaxed me. Or maybe it was all that food. In any case, I slept better that I had in days in the most comfortable bed I had ever occupied. *Hijole*, I liked being rich!

Fully charged, I got up early and made breakfast: cheese omelets with truffle sauce. Be still, my heart!

I dressed and got ready to do business. We were here to get something important, right? So where was it? What was it? "What are we looking for?" I asked Art, once I had had my second cup of coffee.

"It's not here. I spent the night looking while you indulged in your sleep cycle." Art lounged in a reclining chair, his eyes fixed on some artwork attached to the ceiling. I'd never seen artwork on the ceiling before. It was, I must admit, quite mesmerizing.

"But you said—"

"Yeah. I know. I was wrong." Art twitched as if someone had attached electrodes to his muscles. He'd given up Diet Coke after discovering ProPower. ("Bad stuff," I told him. "You'll be sorry." But he didn't listen to me. No surprise there.)

"Where, then?" I asked.

"First, his office."

"Great. Let's go." I wanted to get this *thing*—whatever it

was—done because then I'd be free to get back to my life as Hector. Oh, I know—such naïveté. Such foolishness. Such is the nature of hope.

Okay, so I wouldn't be particularly attractive anymore. And I'd have to wear glasses.

And I couldn't go back to Florida or anywhere near Iggy. But I'd figure it out. Besides, I now possessed buckets of cash. Which made me wonder—could there be more?

"How does Leroy have the money for this?" I did a panoramic gesture of the condo. All those floor-to-ceiling windows. The view. The upholstery. The real Grecian urns. The genuine Picasso over the fireplace. (They had to be real. Leroy didn't strike me as the kind of guy who faked anything.)

"You don't think all that money we've been hauling around actually goes to the Restored Missionary Evangelical Gospel Church of the Sacred Order of Anarchy, do you?"

"Beats me." The important part was that it was mine now. All mine. Was I supposed to even care? And if there was more—

"He takes a cut. A really big cut. Plus, he launders money for a drug cartel out of some South American country. It pays very well. And he's particularly good at hacking social media. The Russians appreciate that about him. So do the Chinese, come to think of it."

"So?"

"You think Waterman got elected President of the United States because of his stellar leadership qualities?"

I considered the ramifications, but abandoned attempts at comprehension because Art began to pace. "Why does he do it?" I asked.

"Who?"

"Leroy."

Art repeated my panoramic gesture. "For the view, of course."

"Even though he could get caught and lose everything?" Including his life.

"Go hard or go home," Art said, smiling. "It's his motto."

"Sounds stupid to me."

"Yes, Hector, I imagine it would. Pity."

Enough of that. "So, are we looking for proof of Leroy's connection to the cartel or the Russians?"

"Nope. Don't care about either. It's his involvement in the Restored Missionary Evangelical Gospel Church of the Sacred Order of Anarchy that interests us. And the Canadians."

"What's the connection with the Canadians?" My head reeled. Couldn't it be a tad less complicated?

"Haven't you been paying attention to anything that's going on?" He gave me a scowl before sprinting toward the kitchen. "I'm hungry."

He riffled through the cupboards until he found a bag of corn chips and salsa. He considered them and then put them back. Then he started going through the freezer.

"What exactly are we looking for?" I imagined more cash, secret documents, incriminating photos. Something tangible. Silly me.

"Ice cream!" Art exclaimed, as he pulled a gallon of ice cream and a block of ice from the freezer. He tossed the ice block to me. "Melt this."

I jumped when it hit me. Ice is heavy, you know. And cold. I took it to the sink and turned the hot water on and let it run. In the meantime, Art found a spoon and settled at the kitchen table with the carton of ice cream.

"Aren't you going to put that in a bowl?" Only godless pagans ate directly out of the carton, according to my grandmother.

"Nope. I hate washing dishes, don't you?"

I did indeed, and since I figured I was damned regardless of how I ate ice cream, I grabbed a spoon and joined him.

Raspberry ripple. Made with real cream. And real raspberries.

"You should probably turn off the water now," Art said after we'd hunkered around the ice cream carton long enough to scrape bottom. "Unless you want to flood the place."

I got to the sink just in time to prevent an overflow.

From the watery mess, I retrieved a well-sealed plastic bag that contained a couple of credit cards, passports, and drivers' licenses with Leroy's picture but issued in various names, and a wad of cash. Plus, a safety deposit key.

Art regarded the safety deposit key with interest. "Maybe we don't have to go to his office. Maybe all we have to do is check out the Bank of Solar Resources."

"It's Saturday. Won't the bank be closed?"

"We're in the big city, Hector. Lots of banks are open on

Saturday."

"The Bank of Solar Resources? Is that even a real bank?"

"Real enough. Bring the checks. We'll make a deposit while we're at it."

I put the checks and the cash into the Bottega Veneta briefcase (classic leather weave, bright blue) I found next to the front door. I grabbed a nice leather bomber jacket from the hall tree. San Francisco can be chilly even in summer. I read that somewhere. Then I followed Art out the door.

In for a penny, in for a pound.

~26~


The Bank of Solar Resources turned out to be housed in a dicey storefront on Turk Street, nestled between two sex shops, which was appropriate since I was pretty sure Leroy and I were about to be screwed. Me, anyway.

We got to the bank slightly after noon. A little bell tinkled when Art opened the door. I expected to see an old woman with a pointy hat and a wart on the end of her nose when we stepped inside, but all we found was a grimy counter in the center of an empty, dusty space that smelled of dead spiders and stale candy corn.

I eyed a long vertical crack in the wall. "Is this where the wall suddenly flips and there's a bunch of gremlins manning a switchboard?"

Art laughed. "You do have an imagination, don't you?"

Actually, I'm about the most unimaginative person I know. But I know a trope when I see it. Well, if the wall didn't flip, maybe the floor would open and I'd find myself plunging into an underground cavern of some sort. I braced myself.

Art glanced at his watch, a sleek Hublot. A demon with a watch? Yeah, I know. Weird. Who wears watches these days? Especially one so fancy it doesn't have numbers on the face. I mean, you'd think for a cool million they could put numbers on the darn thing. Then I recognized it: it had been Charles Hunter's. "We're a little early," he announced.

I stayed close to the door. A noise on the street caught my attention and I turned to watch out the dingy window as some guy in a gorilla suit toppled off of a unicycle. No one stopped to help him. People walked around him as if he were a concrete barrier. I poised to render him aid but he jumped up and cycled out of sight before I could get the door opened.

Art cleared his throat. I jumped. Someone—or some*thing*—stood behind the counter. I can't describe him.

Or her.

I don't remember anything about them. I can't tell you if they were young or old, male or female, dead or alive. I don't know if they were tall or short, or thin or fat, or white, black, brown or purple. Or human.

Except I do remember they had the most intensely blue eyes I have ever seen. Tropical ocean on a sunny day blue. Two little electric blue beacons shining through a dark cloud.

To this day, when I close my eyes, I can see those two blue dots staring at me, cutting through the fog in my brain.

"Welcome." The voice had a mechanical twang to it. Pleasant, but flat. "Hello, Art. Good to see you again."

Art pointed to me. "New recruit."

"Well, isn't that peachy," Blue Eyes said. "The last one didn't work out so well, did they? What makes you think this one will be different?"

"I got a hunch." Art gave me a friendly slap on the back. "This one's got balls aplenty."

I opened my mouth to say *Leroy* had balls aplenty; Hector, not so much, but instead, I grinned stupidly and gave a bobble-headed nod.

The cashier smiled warmly. "Business or pleasure?"

"Business, I'm afraid." Art motioned me up to the counter. "First, my friend here would like to make a deposit."

I handed the cashier the stack of checks. They thumbed through them and then wrote something down on a deposit slip, which they then passed to me. I read the slip and gasped: $472,900.

"Sign it," they said. So, I did. As Leroy. He had a nice signature. Strong, with the right amount of flourish to make it interesting. "Do you want it put in your account or do you want the cash?"

I looked at Art. "Cash," he said.

"Are you sure that's a good idea?" We were already carrying a large amount of cash. The thought of more cash made me nervous.

Art shrugged, and said, "Large bills."

The cashier nodded and a moment later handed me a large briefcase. "It's all there. You can count it if you want."

I shook my head. "No, I'm sure it's fine." This briefcase was strictly utilitarian, but more practical than the Bottega Veneta. Pity. I'd grown rather attached to it in the short time I'd been carrying it.

Then Art held up the safety deposit box key we'd retrieved from Leroy's freezer. The cashier's blue eyes widened to saucer-size, and they pushed a button under the counter. It gave a satisfying little click.

The wall behind the counter slid open, revealing a cavernous enclave of twisted metal scaffolding, walkways, and over-sized gears resembling the inside of an old-fashioned pocket watch. It seemed to stretch on forever. The sheer complexity of the twisting wires, shiny gears, and whirling thing-a-ma-bobs made my head hurt with the marvel of it all. That being said, at least there were no gremlins, space aliens, or trained monkeys hanging from the structure.

Blue Eyes led the way. Art took ahold of my arm. "You're going to love this," he whispered. His words were like a splash of cold water across my wonder-struck pencil brain. Yeah. Right. About as much as I love liver and onions. And Disney World during Spring break.

I needed a little coaxing to get me over the threshold.

"Come on, Hector. It's sink-or-swim time," Art cooed. "Youth or beauty. Mickey or Donald. Rice or beans. Chevy or Ford. Democrat or Republican."

I stared at him. "What are you talking about?"

"Decision-making time, Hector, my friend. "Rent or own. Paper or Plastic. CNN or Fox. Elevator or escalator. Capitalism or Socialism." He pinched my arm and breathed hotly into my ear. "You know you want to."

No, I didn't. I stared into the maze of twisted metal and whirling gears. They didn't seem quite as shiny as they had a moment ago. I thought of a million places I would rather be. Like at home watching *Wheel of Fortune* or in Iggy's garage rotating tires.

"That ship has sailed, Hector, my boy. It's now or never. Boom or bust. Backseat or front. Wash or dry. Chess or checkers. Tap or ballet. Fire or flood. Foreign or domestic—"

Yeah, yeah. I got the message. Put up or shut up. I stepped over the threshold.

Three things happened at the same time: (1) Blue Eyes disappeared. Vanished. Melted. Dematerialized. Whatever; (2) the door closed behind us with a thud; and (3) the infinity of twisted metal and gears vanished, leaving us in a narrow room lit only by a yellowish light bulb, swinging from a cord. It rapped me on the back of my head, and I yelped.

"See? That wasn't so bad. You can make a decision."

I rubbed the back of my head. "What the fuck, Art? You trying to make me crazy?"

He grinned. "Too late for that, my boy."

"Don't call me *boy*." That was Leroy on automatic coming through; Hector didn't give a damn. Hector mostly wanted to punch him.

"Yeah, yeah. Whatever. Come on."

There was yet another door. I didn't see it until Art opened it and then bounced through the opening without so much as a backward glance to see if I was following him.

"Move it, Hector. You're in too deep now to back out."

I stepped forward. (Like you thought I'd do anything else?) There was no other option. Remember: lack of free will is a hallmark of the demon set. Besides, when you're at the top of the roller coaster, it's too late to debate if you should have bought the ticket. The best you can do is hold on and hope you don't upchuck your popcorn on the way down.

The room was small, and the walls were lined with little boxes with metal doors. Safety deposit boxes, I realized. Running down the center of the space, was a thick table bolted to the floor. (Like, who would steal a table that heavy? You couldn't even get it through the door.)

Art was scrutinizing the boxes while I pretended to do the same. "Do you know which one belongs to Leroy?"

He shook his head. "Not a clue."

"Does that mean we have to try every box?" There had to be hundreds. We could be here for a long time. I do not do well in closed spaces. Already I was sweating.

"Not *we*. You. I can't. It won't work for me. Has to be you. It's a union thing." He handed me the key. "I'd start over there," he said, pointing.

I went to the opposite wall and stared for a long time, hoping for inspiration. Or something. A vision, maybe. At the very least, a small *sign*. Or a big one.

Laugh if you want, but it worked.

The key grew warm in my hand. I didn't notice until the heat jacked up to red-hot and it burned my palm. I let out a sharp cry while flinging it across the room. "What the hell—"

"Don't swear," Art said automatically as if I were an oft

offending child.

I swore some more and rubbed my palm. When I checked the damage, I saw numbers burned into my flesh: *275.*

Well, I can take a hint. Yes, sir. I can indeed figure out a sign when one is placed before me, especially when it involves pain.

In no time, I found box number 275. I let out a little gasp of pleasure and turned to Art, grinning broadly. "This is it, I think."

Art showed no expression, except for a faint eye roll that might have signaled distain. "So, open it."

The door swung open with surprising ease. Inside, was a small spiral bound notebook, a roadmap for Utah-Idaho-Montana, a chocolate bar, a two-for-one coupon for a restaurant on Fisherman's Wharf, a bottle cap, and a book of matches from a diner in Jackknife, Montana, wherever the hell that was.

"It's not in hell," Art said, "although it's close." (It really irritates me when he does that.) "Although, it's actually closer to Alberta. That's in Canada."

As. If. I. Didn't. Know. My momentary good humor was fading. "Now what?" I picked through the booty again, wondering if there was a point to any of it.

Art wiggled his fingers over the items. "Grab them. They might prove useful."

"In what universe?" I mumbled, but I put the stuff into my jacket pocket, except for the two-for-one dinner coupon and the chocolate bar, which Art grabbed out of my hands. He stuck the coupon in his pocket and then handed me half of the chocolate bar.

I was hungry, so I ate it.

Just in case you're wondering—the road to hell is not paved with good intentions; it's paved in chocolate. Milk chocolate, to be exact. With toasted almonds. Washed down with ProPower. And two-for-one coupons.

We utilized the coupon and had lunch on Fisherman's Wharf. Art spent a lot of time examining the menu and checking under the tablecloth. And frowning. He frowned a lot, stared into space, checked under the table again. And again.

"Are you looking for spies?" I was sure he was losing it. "Secret passages? Hidden messages?"

He never did answer. A moment later, he was looking at me with an expression of glee. "You still have the bottle cap? And the matches?"

I fumbled in my pocket and held them out to show him. He snapped them out of my hand. "Come on." He took off, nearly running out of the restaurant and I dutifully followed.

Just for the record, there's a lot of nasty hills in San Francisco. It's not a city for the faint of heart, weak-kneed, or those prone to shortness of breath. Or for someone carrying a case full of very heavy cash.

Art, of course, was invincible, and Leroy was in pretty good shape, but even Leroy had his limits. Hector found the whole thing mentally exhausting.

By the time we got back to the apartment, I needed a nap. I didn't get it, of course.

Art spread out the map we'd found in the safety deposit box while I made ham sandwiches—all that walking made me hungry again. I dug out some beer I found at the back of the fridge. He studied the map thoughtfully, pausing to frown while casually twirling the bottle cap between his fingers. He wrote a few things down, consulted the notebook we'd also retrieved, and ignored me.

I watched him until I couldn't stand it anymore. "What are you doing?"

He looked up and smiled coyly. "Nothing you need to worry about, although this map is a little out of date. That might be a problem."

"A problem?"

"Nothing you need to worry about. Yet." He continued to roll the bottle cap between his fingers as if taunting me.

I took the bait. "What's with the bottle cap?"

He stopped and regarded it. "This?" He shrugged. "Nothing much."

"Bullshit." I was catching on to his tricks.

"Well, okay, if you must know—" He leaned forward as if sharing a major confidence. "There's a list of every member of the Restored Missionary Evangelical Gospel Church of the Sacred Order of Anarchy on a microchip, tucked under the lining. Worth a pretty penny, it is. In fact, I dare say, some would kill for it. You might be surprised who's on the list. A whole bunch of Congressmen, a few senators, some governors, a whack of highly placed judges, a Certain World Leader. And a whole bunch of Hollywood biggies."

He stuck the bottle cap into his pocket, along with the matches, the notebook, and the map. Then he settled back to watch *Wheel of Fortune*, leaving me flapping in the breeze as usual. Putin sat beside Art, enjoying the bits of shrimp I'd saved for him from our lunch. It was downright homey.

After *Wheel of Fortune*, the news came on, but I wasn't paying a lot of attention to the television.

I almost missed the piece about Charles Hunter. *"... police initially considered Hunter a suspect in his wife's death; however, they now believe that Hunter died before his wife was murdered."*

"Huh?" was the best I could manage.

"Just wait. It gets better," Art said.

A picture of me—Hector—popped up on the screen alongside a crisp, professional headshot of a smiling Leroy. *"Witnesses report seeing noted lawyer Leroy Jefferson and suspected terrorist Hector Gonzales in Hunter's neighborhood around the time the senator and his wife are believed to have been murdered. Police refuse to speculate publicly about Jefferson's role in the double murder or his involvement with Gonzales, the Cubans, or the Canadians; however, both men are wanted for questioning and are considered extremely dangerous."*

I responded with a low, guttural moan, too freaked for words. Art was thoroughly disinterested. He had the remote pointed at the television. I knocked it out of his hand.

"Holy fucking shit hole." I am not very eloquent when freaked out.

"Relax," was Art's response.

"You told me Charles Hunter killed his wife. I thought—" What exactly had I thought?

Art shrugged, then grinned. "I was just messing with you."

I balled up my fist and punched him.

If smarted like hell, but it felt damn good.

He rubbed his jaw, and then sighed. "That hurt."

"Good."

Back to Leroy. "How long is it going to take before they come after him—me?" I gestured at the television. I was now screwed on two counts. The panic rose and fizzed around my eye sockets.

He glanced at Charles Hunter's watch. "You might have time to finish your beer."

"Do I have time to pee?"

"If you hurry."

I was being sarcastic, but something in his tone made me drop my beer and head to the bathroom.

While I was there, I brushed my teeth.

When I got back to the living room, Art was standing in the entryway holding the duffel bag and the case full of our newly gained cash assets. Putin was pacing, his tail puffed and snapping with static. "Are we going somewhere?"

"Yes," he said, fairly bouncing. "We have things to do. Places to go. People to see. Mayhem to create. We're finally going to have some fun."

A sense of dread washed over me. You'd think by now I'd have gotten used to it. You'd think.

When Art opened the front door, Putin booked it.

That was the last thing I remembered until I woke up the next morning.

In the hospital.

Handcuffed to the bed.

~28~

I don't know what kind of drugs they shot into my veins, but it was good stuff. Like yeah, I was handcuffed and all, and I think I was in pain, but really, I didn't give a flying chicken.

I drifted in and out of sleep, waking up occasionally to look into the beady eyes of some guy in a suit who didn't look even remotely pleased with his life.

It occurred to me in these waking moments that perhaps everything that happened to me hadn't happened at all. I imagined waking up in my own bed, in my own body, late for work as usual, and realizing "it was all a dream."

Now, wouldn't that just cut the mustard?

Well, in case you can't wait until I get to the end of this missive to find out if it's all been a cheat, let me reassure you: that ain't going to happen. I am not/was not dreaming. The truth is that strange things do happen. Impossible things, even. Like the US adopting the metric system. And you can strike a deal with the devil whether you are black, white, brown, male, female, young, old, queer or straight. Or none or all of the above. Trust me on this. I speak from experience. I did learn something.

At some point, the effect of the drugs wore off enough that I could open my eyes and hold them open for more than three seconds. My first view was of someone's armpit, followed by a pair of dark brown eyes, up close and personal. "Hi, ya," I managed to squeak out.

There was a tiny rush of air, followed by a shriek. A

woman—a nurse?—jumped away from me, knocking something metallic to the floor, sending a jolting wave of sound vibrating through my bruised brain.

"Sorry," she mumbled as she dropped to her knees. "How are you feeling?"

I blinked. "Feeling? I dunno. How should I be feeling?" She stepped out of my line of sight and enthusiastically fiddled with a dial on another machine. "What happened?"

"You were in an accident."

I rattled the handcuffs. "I think it must have been more than an accident."

"You'll have to talk to the police. I don't know the details."

*Liar.*

"My cat. What happened to my cat?"

"Cat?" She continued to fiddle with dials.

"Yeah, a big, hairy gray thing. Answers to Putin."

"Putin?" She moved away from the dials, toward the door, her back to me.

"Putin-on-the-Ritz."

"I'll check. Maybe somebody knows," she called over her shoulder as she put her hand on the door. She hadn't even tried to fluff my pillow.

Why was I worried about the stupid cat? He had far more resources than I did. Then I remembered Art. Where was he? Had he abandoned me? It would be just like him. "One more thing—"

The nurse hesitated.

"Do you have a mirror?" I asked this because I had no idea if I was still Leroy or back to being Hector or if I was someone else entirely. My arms were covered and shackled in place, so I couldn't check for skin color. Not that that would have been conclusive. No, I needed to see my face.

"I'll see what I can do." She bolted from the room as if I were about to shoot her. Really? I must have done something good.

A different nurse returned a moment later with a small makeup mirror. (She didn't fluff my pillow either.) She held it in front of me and I twisted my head around to get a good look.

I was still Leroy. A little worse for wear, I might add, but still very definitely Leroy.

I wasn't sure if that was a good thing or a bad thing.

Then the suit I had glimpsed earlier returned. The suit's owner was a stocky guy with bushy eyebrows.

"You're awake." He was a cop, I realized, given his brilliant use of deductive reasoning, and his suit. It was cheap and ill-fitting. Also, he flashed a badge.

"So it would seem." I did a repeat of the rattling of my chains. "What did I do?"

He flipped open a notebook. "Well, for starters, you tried to blow up the Transamerica building."

"Did I succeed?"

"You did not."

"What else?"

"You robbed a convenience store."

"Was that before or after I tried to blow up the Transamerica?"

"After."

"What did I take?"

"Several bottles of ProPower and some cat food."

"Hardly a capital offence." Then, again, this was California. "What else?"

"You tried to set fire to a couple of buildings on Market Street."

"Was I successful?"

"Not particularly."

Hardly surprising. "How did I get hurt?"

"You resisted arrest." He looked up from his notebook. "You ever play football?"

I let that pass. "I don't suppose you noticed a big, gray cat hanging around while you were busy subduing my resistance, did you?"

He tapped his notebook with his pen. "No, I did not."

"Or a short thin guy with a receding chin?"

"Your accomplice?"

I could not lie. "Possibly."

"This guy got a name?"

"Art-something. I don't know his last name." The cop's eyes narrowed. Perhaps he didn't believe me. Whatever. "Anyone get hurt? Other than me, I mean."

"One of my officers has a broken nose."

"Did I punch him?"

"No." He actually smiled a little. "He tripped on a bit of cracked pavement while he was chasing you."

"Well, I hope he makes a miraculous recovery."

The cop used the tip of his pen to scratch his ear. "You don't remember anything, do you?"

"Nope."

"Are you denying any of this?"

"I can't deny what I don't remember, can I?"

I was fairly certain he didn't realize I was the Leroy Jefferson being sought in the murder of Charles and Doris Hunter. I wondered when he'd make the connection. His number one concern now was if I was crazy.

"Quite possibly," I responded amiably, answering his unspoken question—Art was rubbing off on me. "My new best friend is a demon who drinks Diet Coke, although, against my advice, he's switched to energy drinks. Those things are poison, by the way. So, you tell me—am I crazy?"

"Is this by any chance the 'Art' you mentioned earlier?"

My face must have given him the answer he was looking for because the psychiatrist showed up an hour later. I was oriented to time and place, although I had a little trouble when he asked me my name, age, occupation, and current address, and if I had ever been committed to a psychiatric institution or ever suffered from memory loss. "If I had ever suffered from memory loss, would I remember?"

He determined I was as mentally fit as one might expect a black man to be under the circumstances. What circumstances? You mean, being black? Or male? Or being a black male who had recently been beaten up by the cops? And was now in handcuffs? Was that a trick question, or was I missing something? Of course, he didn't have enough junk in his white ass trunk to actually tell me any of this to my face, which was a good thing because I was feeling a little stabby.

I had a deep longing for my old body, the skinny, myopic one, and wondered if I'd ever occupy it again. I missed my sad, pathetic little life; my dead-end, greasy life; my boring, never-gonna-get-better life. I even missed Iggy. I missed Florida. I missed my bed, my pillow, my cast iron fry pan. I missed the smell of curry and chili peppers and smoldering cigarette smoke, and the sound of Mr. Hasselbacker's snores drifting through my window in the middle of the night.

    I wanted to go home, damn it. Home, sweet, home. Oh, yeah.

~29~

I dozed, lulled to sleep by sweet, sweet pharmaceuticals or some demonic charm. Six of one, half dozen—blah, blah, blah. I woke up and found Art sitting by my side.

"You—" I tried to wave my hand limply in his general direction, but I was still handcuffed to the bed. To my surprise, I was happy to see him. "Get me out of here."

"Sure thing." He touched the handcuffs and they fell away as if made of paper. "In fact, we need to leave right now."

"Fine by me." I pushed myself into a sitting position, although I had a persistent lean to the left. My head felt like it was the size of a watermelon on steroids.

I swung my leg over the end of the bed. The floor was a long way down. Miles, even. I teetered, but Art caught me. "Clothes?"

"No time."

I was on my feet and halfway out the door before I was aware of anything else.

At the doorway, I turned around. I could have sworn I was still in the bed. Someone was in the bed. I pointed and wiggled my fingers. "What gives? Who's that?"

Art gave me a push. "Never mind. Come on. We have to get out of here *now*."

There was no point in resisting. Hell, I had given up resisting. Yep, that ship had sailed days ago. I let him push me into the hallway and down the corridor. I was having trouble walking. Walking. Standing. Talking. Thinking. "I want to go home."

"No can do, buddy-boy."

I stopped. "Then I'm not taking another step." I swayed precariously, a loose boulder on top of a pinnacle of a moral vicissitude.

"Suit yourself." Art kept walking. "But the hospital is about to explode. If you want to be divided into a million separate molecules, that's fine by me."

The floor rumbled and the walls vibrated, causing me to lurch forward. "Wait. What do you mean?"

The ground shook a little harder. The beams creaked. "Boom-boom time, buddy. Gotta run." With that he sprinted down the hallway and into the stairwell.

Who was I kidding? It was inevitable.

I scuttled after him.

~30~

I got into the car—a snappy little Fiat—just as Art was gunning the engine.

"Do you have a never-ending supply of explosives, or what?" And cars. Where was he getting all these cars?

"What do you mean?"

"I hear we wreaked a little havoc in the City. Why is that?"

"A diversion." Then he grinned. "Guess I got a little carried away. Sorry about that."

"So why can't I remember it?"

"Do you want to?"

He had me there. "Not really." I know, I know. I should have asked more questions. I didn't see the point. Being around a demon can get pretty mind-numbing after a while. Finally, I asked, "Why did we need a diversion?"

"Ah, Hector. Let's just say your presence in the City was noted by certain unfriendly forces. I needed to buy us a little time, so I created a mostly successful distraction."

I let it sink in. It wouldn't sink. It just sat there, like a grease spot on my best shirt. Finally, I asked, "Where are we going?"

"As far away from here as we can get."

Fine by me.

~31~

The next thing I knew, we were out of the city and heading north. I came to this conclusion because the setting sun was to my left.

My stomach was settled. My head was clear, and nothing hurt. Hell, I wasn't even hungry. But I was full of pointless questions.

"Where's Putin?"

"Don't worry about the damn cat."

I couldn't help but worry. We had bonded, that cat and I. Soul brothers. Kindred spirits. Two of a kind. Trauma-bonding at its finest.

I raised my hand and studied it. It looked kind of translucent, like it might have been there, or it might not have been.

"Who am I now?" I assumed that Leroy was now a thing of the past. Pity. I liked Leroy. Except for the part about him killing people. There was no excuse for that.

"Some guy named Stan. Not my first choice, but we were in a hurry."

I pulled down the visor and looked in the little mirror. White skin—possibly. Brown, bloodshot eyes. Stan needed a shave. And a bath. Several, in fact. "How do you do that anyway? Do you stick my spirit in a dead guy and animate them, or do you use some kind of shapeshifting spell?"

"I'm not a witch, Hector. I'm a demon. I don't do shapeshifting or spells."

"But you do something, don't you? Something you control?"

He shrugged as if bored by the conversation. "It's complicated."

I bet.

We continued north on Scenic Highway 1.

Here's a word of advice: never let a demon drive on a winding coastal road unless you have a death wish, or a very strong stomach, especially if he's in a hurry.

I spent a lot of time with my eyes closed, trying to keep from spilling Stan's alcohol infused guts, which was a shame because this was my first time on the West Coast and I'm pretty sure I missed a lot of very fine scenery.

When we finally stopped, it was late. The sun was below the horizon, leaving things cast in pink and gray. All we could find was some little roadside motel that hadn't been updated since 1956. There was only one room left. The other rooms were occupied by a lusty group of motorcyclists. Not Hell's Angels, the clerk at the front desk was very clear to point out. More like Hell's Cherubs. Art shrugged. Like he gave a fig.

"It's all relative," I said, and then laughed. The clerk didn't get it. I didn't take the time to explain.

The room was cramped and smelled of mothballs, and the air conditioner rattled so loudly I had to stuff toilet paper in my ears to keep from screaming into my pillow.

"I want to go home," I said. It was one in the morning. A backfiring motorcycle woke me up. Art was watching television, a rerun of *Emergency*, the classic 1970s show about a couple of sappy, albeit kind of hot, LA paramedics.

Art glanced at me and then pointed to the door. "Happy trails, pilgrim."

I fumbled in the drawer next to my bed and chucked the ubiquitous Gideon Society offering at him, narrowing missing his head. It bounced off the wall, resulting in a hiss and plume of gaseous smoke that did nothing for the ambiance in the room.

Art glared at me, looking down the long edge of his finely crafted Roman nose. "Fine," he said, sighing mightily. "Go home. Go back to your fucked-up life. See what being Hector will get you."

~32~

I jerked awake to a loud buzzing beside my head. I put my hands over my ears, rolled over, and fell out of bed, landing hard on my knees, tangled in the sheets. I flopped around until I fought my way out of my shroud. All that flopping and flapping stirred up a load of dust and I sneezed seventeen times in a row. When the sneezing finally stopped, I waved my arm around vigorously, trying to locate my glasses.

My glasses?

I checked my arm. To my delight, I was back in Hector's skin—I recognized the mole on my forearm.

I lapsed into a fit of deliciously effeminate giggles, punctuated by a few more sneezes.

I was back! In all my screwball, fucked up, blessedly queer glory, I was back. Amen and hallelujah.

If I could just find my glasses and turn off that damn alarm.

I batted at the nightstand until I found the clock. When I couldn't get it to shut off, I picked it up and hurled it against the wall, lapsing into another fit of giggles when it exploded into a billion pieces. I can't begin to tell you how good that felt—wish fulfillment at its finest.

I found my glasses behind my nightstand, a common landing place after a night of restless thrashing.

I put on clothes—*my* clothes—and skipped to the kitchen— yes, I *skipped*. There was my high-tech coffeemaker! My lovely pink four-slice toaster! My fridge with the automatic ice maker and hot-

and-cold water dispenser! My lovely six-burner gas stove! My 1950's cherry red kitchen table with its matching set of red vinyl and chrome chairs!

I opened the fridge and sniffed the milk. It was still good.

I got the coffee going and flipped on the stereo, and then proceeded to dance around the kitchen as I fried bacon and scrambled eggs. A gray cat leaped onto the counter and meowed. I petted it automatically.

A cat? Where did the cat come from? I didn't have a cat. But there was a dish on the floor filled with cat crunchies and a litter box somewhere. I could faintly smell it. Ugh. Still, he was pleasant enough. I gave him a few more pats and he lifted his chin, which I rubbed. He responded by purring loudly. The cat had a name. What was it again?

Chekov? Rasputin? Gorbachev?

Something was nagging at me. A memory? Maybe part of a dream.

Not something, I realized. Someone. But who? I could almost recall a face, a voice, but then it vanished. My head began to ache. How much had I had to drink the night before?

Wait—what day was it?

For that matter, what month was it?

Year?

Was I supposed to be at work?

Did I have a job to go to?

For that matter, what about Iggy? Was he dead?

Dead? Iggy?

Something about an explosion.

I froze, spatula in one hand, my head cocked to the side as if that might separate dreams from reality like wheat from chafe. I stared at the cat, now crouched on the counter. Its gold eyes caught the light and glowed.

Someone commenced pounding on my door. It made the entire apartment shake. What the hell?

I raced to the door, the spatula still in my raised hand. I barely touched the knob when the door burst open and there was Iggy, looking as though he was prepared to wrestle a water buffalo.

"Iggy!" I was unusually happy to see him. I moved to hug him. He shoved me away.

"Where the hell have you been? Why haven't you been answering your phone? And what are you still doing here?"

I sputtered. "What—?"

"You packed?"

"Packed?"

"For fuck's sake, Hector! You got your head permanently stuck up your ass, or what? If you weren't my cousin, I swear to God I'd leave you here to rot. Come on. We gotta go."

"Where? Why?"

"Just come on." He grabbed my arm and tried to pull me to the door, but I resisted.

"I haven't had my coffee yet," I said, waving the spatula in his face to illustrate how serious I was about having my coffee. "And I have to turn off the stove."

Then his fist was flying at me, aimed right between my eyes. *Don't break my glasses,* was my last conscious thought.

I woke up, hanging upside down over his shoulder, my glasses dangling off one ear. He tossed me in the back of a flatbed truck and then he got into the driver's side of the cab. I landed in the lap of a woman who squealed and tried pushing me off, but there was nowhere to go. The bed of the truck was filled with people.

Nasty, hysterical, angry people, judging by the weeping and wailing and gnashing of teeth. The truck took off with a start that sent me sprawling again.

I pulled myself into as tight a ball as I could manage and somehow wiggled my way to the front of the truck, where I ended up between a kid of maybe twelve and a woman crying into a balled-up sweater.

"What's going on?" I addressed the kid since he seemed the more rational choice.

He regarded me with a full load of disdain, drenched in incredulity.

"Come on," I begged. "Fill me in. I haven't a clue."

"You been living under a bush or something?"

"Or something. I just woke up from a diabetic coma. Too much sugar. Come on. Please."

Fortunately, I do clueless really well and he relented. "We have to get to the fallout shelter before the bombs hit."

"What bombs?" What fallout shelter?

"The ones the Russians are going to launch."

"The Russians?" I laughed. His face tightened. "What kind of bombs are we talking about?"

"The bad kind."

"But why?"

"He was aiming for Canada and missed. The bomb landed in Moscow. The Russians are pissed."

"He?"

"Waterman. What an asshat he turned out to be."

"Waterman? The president? What did he do?"

The kid looked at me with a mixture of pity and disbelief. "You can't be that stupid, can you?"

"Trust me," I said. "I can."

"He tried to bomb Canada. Something about Manifest Destiny and oil reserves. Or water. Or possibility revenge because they killed that senator. And burned down the White House. Maybe all of that. I dunno."

Water? Oil? Senator? "Why?"

"Because the Canadians are greedy bastards and won't share," said the woman, lifting her head out of her sweater.

"And they burned down the White House," another woman sitting across from us said. "Don't forget about that!"

"They did?" How long had I been asleep? "When?"

"In 1814," someone called out. "Idiot. It wasn't even the Canadians. It was the British. And now we're all going to die." The woman beside me let out a piercing wail and buried her head into her sweater again.

"Whatever," the kid said. "My dad says Waterman's been looking for an excuse to blow up the world."

"Why?" I was missing something, that much I figured out quickly enough.

"'Cause he's gonna speed up the return of Jesus," someone in the back called out. "Bless him. Amen. We is goin' to glory!" That was followed by a chorus of "fuck you," and then the sound of a body being hoisted and tossed overboard. There was a loud scream and then a thud.

No one even glanced in the direction of the ejected body. "Waterman really is crazy. That's what CNN is reporting," said a young man.

"Yeah, and we know how reliable CNN is," came a woman's snappish voice.

"Fox is reporting it, too," said a man behind me.

There was a moment of silence and then someone said, "Holy catfish, we're all screwed."

A low flying jet streaked overhead. The truck swerved wildly, and people screamed as they grabbed for anything they could. Two people flew off the back end just as someone's fingers tightened around my arm.

The jet flew on, and the truck straightened out and picked up speed again. Whoever was gripping my arm let go.

We were back on the bumpy road, headed to Armageddon and Glory. Amen and hallelujah. *Híjole!*

Where were we going, anyway? There are no bomb shelters anymore. They went the way of hula hoops, saddle shoes, five-cent chocolate bars, and "I Like Ike" buttons.

As it turned out, we ended up at the Restored Missionary Evangelical Gospel Church of the Sacred Order of Anarchy of Greater Miami.

Wait—why did that sound familiar?

It looked more like a bunker than a church, which seemed to suggest that they might have had prior knowledge of our present predicament. I didn't find that comforting.

We piled out of the truck and ducked through a heavy door. Over the door a sign advised us we were entering The Ark.

We were herded down several flights of stairs and then crammed into an area the size of basketball court. I was jammed between the woman sobbing into her sweater and some pudgy guy in a faded Hawaiian shirt who reeked of stale tacos.

We hadn't been there long until some guy dressed in a flowing canary yellow caftan came around to shake our hands and spout words of canned comfort. Someone said he was Peter Knutson, and we were indeed blessed to be in his shelter. ("We might even survive this," someone whispered, "with him around.")

He didn't look particularly god-like, so I took those words with a grain of salt. He was a short, roly-poly white guy with snow-white hair, sharp black crow-like eyes, and an expression frozen into a state of permanent admonishment, framed by a healthy set of jowls. Hardly the savior-type.

We sat huddled on a cold concrete floor for what seemed like hours. Much weeping and wailing ensued, along with some loud entreaties for forgiveness for a whole host of sins from adultery to stealing cable signals.

Pastor Knutson out wept-and-wailed the best of them, occasionally shouting out a heart-felt, "Hallelujah!" "Amen." And every five minutes: "Repent, sinners, before the fires of hell roast your soul."

Hardly the comforting words one might expect at a time like this.

Finally, I'd had enough. I got up and headed toward the stairs. Iggy saw me and sprinted after me. "Where do you think you're going?"

"You don't really think the Russians are going to blow us up, do you?"

"Of course, they are. Haven't you been paying attention? The bombs are on the way, Hector. The Russians, the Chinese, the North Koreans, the Canadians—they're all sending us their bombs, air express." The fear in his eyes was real. He truly believed the world was about to end.

But seriously—the Canadians? It was all I could do not to laugh. The Canadians didn't have bombs. I was pretty sure they didn't even have an air force. A couple of biplanes, maybe. But an honest-to-God air force? Hardly!

As for the Chinese and North Koreans—the last I heard they could barely get a rocket lit, let alone fly one halfway around the world.

The Russians, however, I had to admit, might be a problem. But they weren't stupid. I'd met one or two Russians. Not stupid at all. Cagey, perhaps. Maybe even devious, but not stupid. They might bomb us all right, but they had to know they wouldn't escape the consequences of nuclear fallout.

"And then what?" I asked. "If anyone really did drop a bomb or two, we'd probably all end up dead sooner rather than later, even if we did survive the initial bombing."

Iggy got a look in his eyes, a kind of far away, mystic, foggy look. "Then Jesus will come."

I opened my mouth and then closed it. I was about to ask, "Who would be left to greet Him?" but thought better of it. Around me came another refrain of heartfelt "amens" and "hallelujahs." I swear the mood turned to excitement, in a blood thirsty kind of way.

The urge to run was accelerating. And I really needed coffee.

"Catch you later, Ig." I ran up the stairs, jerked open the door, and collided headlong into a new group of desperate people who would have trampled me in their haste to reach safety had I not been agile enough to slip through them.

The door clanged shut behind me, leaving me to stand alone in the sunlight and blessedly fresh air.

~33~

There was no one on the street. I mean, NO ONE.

I walked for several blocks before I found a Starbuck's and dashed inside. The coffee was still hot, still relatively fresh. I poured a big cup, loaded it with cream and sugar, and grabbed a scone.

I sat outside at one of those little tables I'm never lucky enough to get during regular business hours, which gave me a great view of the city, right down to the ocean. The sun sparkled on the water, making it dance. I thought I even heard a couple of birds chirping. It couldn't have been more pleasant.

This, I decided, was a much better way to wait for the world to end than in a bunker listening to some cockeyed preacher lamenting the Wages of Sin and anticipating the Coming of Glory.

I sipped my coffee and picked at the scone. It was blueberry and very fresh. It probably had been baked that morning, before people got their shorts in a knot about the world ending.

Out of nowhere, a gray cat appeared. He hopped up on the chair across from me and rested his paws on the table, giving me a woefully intense stare with massive gold, unblinking eyes.

I knew that cat from somewhere, but it was fuzzy. "Putin?"

Was that his name?

The cat meowed in the affirmative. I passed him a few crumbs. He batted them with his paw and then sucked them up. I fed him a few more bits. Finally, I passed the whole thing to him. I had lost my appetite.

"Do you think the world is really going to end?"

He eyed me dispassionately, and then finished the scone, carefully nibbling around the blueberries.

Then he leaped onto the table, walked across it, and nudged his way into my lap. I let him settle, glad for his company. I sipped my coffee and stroked his fur, which turned out to be surprisingly soft. He hummed with heart-felt appreciation.

I closed my eyes for a second, feeling the air around me, the warmth of the cat in my lap, the metal of the chair poking me in the back. I was alive and well. For the moment. Who had the right to ask for more?

"You really are something," came a deep voice. I opened my eyes. There was a guy sitting across from me. A strange looking guy, with thick, slicked-back black hair, a classically curved nose, with perfect teeth that appeared a little on the pink side, and a slightly receding chin. It took me a moment to place him.

Oh yeah.

Art. Good ol' Art what's-his-name.

How could I have forgotten?

"Not sure why it would matter to you," I said, "if the world is about to end. You're already dead."

He snorted derisively at that, as if I said something ludicrous. "You confuse death with oblivion. A common mistake."

"Whatever."

"And you're just going to let it happen, aren't' you?"

I shrugged. "What can I do against the forces of Armageddon?"

His eyes widened. "You realize, of course, that this is all your fault."

I laughed. "Don't be ridiculous. Who am I to cause the end of the world?"

"You are Hector Gonzales, a gay American of mostly Cuban descent who was given the opportunity to save humanity and elected to drink coffee instead."

"Mostly?"

"Focus, Hector."

"What do you mean 'mostly'?"

"Let me rephrase that. You are a stupid, gay, nearsighted American of, yes, *mostly* Cuban ancestry who was given the opportunity to save humanity and help a demon regain his rightful place in hell, but who elected to drink coffee, sit on his ass, and turn his back on all of creation, including one poor, homeless gray cat."

I stared at him. "I'm pretty sure I am completely Cuban on both sides of my family—"

He glanced at his watch. "You have fifteen seconds to change your mind."

I took another sip of my coffee. It was cold. I put the cup down on the table. "What if I don't want to? What if I think the world is about to get what it deserves? What if I think the world would be better off if humanity was wiped from the face of the earth? What if I think the world would be better off coming up a different dominant species? Like dolphins." Yeah. Dolphins. Cute. Clever. Smart. Peaceful. They would do. Better than raccoons. Not as sneaky.

"Hector, you idiot, it won't only be humans who get the ax."

The cat stirred in my lap and sunk his teeth into the fleshy part of my hand. I yelped. And something inside me broke, and I wailed, "I can't save anyone. I can't even save myself. If you're so eager to save the world, go find someone who can actually do it."

"I thought I had."

"Well, you blew that, didn't you?"

He looked up. Way up. I could hear a whine, a thin whistle, coming toward us. The air grew very, very still.

"Did I, Hector? Did I really?"

"I hate you," I said, at the tail end of a deep, deep sigh.

"So you've said."

And then the world vanished in a white-hot flash.

The flash only lasted a second, if that long. Then it faded, leaving everything looking fuzzy and overexposed, bleached of color, and devoid of detail. I blinked a few times, rubbed my eyes, checked my glasses for smudges.

I was still sitting at the little table at Starbuck's. That much I was able to figure out, but I was alone. No Art. No Putin. I looked around, turning to look over my shoulder. When I turned back, *he* was there.

Not Art.

Some other guy. Some guy with thick, wavy silver hair, and clear watery eyes that sparkled like diamonds. He appeared translucent and glowed a cool white light.

"What the—" He put his fingers to his lips and gave me a reproachful look. "—heck?"

His expression was pleasant; warm, but not overly friendly. "Hello, Hector."

That voice … it wrapped itself around me and through me like a velvet kiss.

It scared the crap out of me.

"Are you God?"

He shook his head. "Not even close."

"You're not the Prince, are you? Lucifer, I mean."

Again, he shook his head, but this time, he added a sigh. "I am not God. I am not the Devil."

"Then who are you? What are you?"

"I am the Ghost of Christmas Past." He waited a beat, and then he started to laugh. "Hector! You should see the look on your face."

And with that, the fear was gone. In its place was annoyance, quickly accelerating to anger. Not God. Or Jesus. Or Lucifer. Or an angel. Not even a genie who was going to grant me three wishes.

Just another smart mouth, lying demon.

"What's wrong? Art's plan not working the way it's supposed to? Has he recruited you to have a go at me? What I don't understand is why me? I'm nothing special. I'm not all that smart. I'm not even all that good looking."

The silver-haired demon gave me a crooked smile. "Well, actually, Hector, you are very handsome, in an earthly kind of way."

I stood up. "I'm out of here."

"No, Hector, I'm afraid you're not." His tone was serious now. "There's nowhere for you to go. You can only be *here*."

I looked around me. There was nothing but thick, swirling mist. And the little table and two chairs. And me. And him.

I sat down. "What do you want?"

"How about a night on the town?"

I glared at him.

"A cozy weekend in Atlantic City?"

I continued to glare.

"A cruise down Mexico way?"

I upped the glare to a scowl.

"Fine. You're not nearly as much fun as Art led me to

believe." He leaned across the table until we were practically eyeball to eyeball. His eyes had little flecks of gold the shape of anvils floating in them. "I want you to ditch Art."

"Ditch him? Why?" Nothing about this demon made me want to trust him.

"He's going to get you killed, you know."

"Isn't it a little late for that?"

"It's never too late, Hector." He grinned invitingly. Was he trying to seduce me? If he was, he was doing a piss-poor job. "For redemption."

"*Vete pa la puñeta.*" The phrase rolled off my lips like I'd been saying it my entire life. Which I had. Go to hell. Although, perhaps I should have said go *back* to hell.

He stopped grinning and put on his serious face. "Fine. But you could at least listen to my offer."

I crossed my arms over my chest. "I'm listening."

"You're wrong about one thing—none of this has happened yet. This is merely a little taste of what could happen."

"Let me guess—You're the Time Lord and you have mastery over time and space and little things that go bump in the night, and you can make this all go away if I'll bend over and kiss your … feet."

The little gold anvils in his eyes crashed into each other. "Will you shut up for one minute and listen!"

I was getting tired of this. "Fine. I'm all ears." He glowered magnificently. "Go on. Tempt me. I dare you."

"This *will* happen and very soon. I would give you a chance to go out in style. Unlike Art, who's going to use and abuse you and then toss you out on your ass."

"Right. And what do you want me to do?"

"Nothing. I want you to do nothing. I want you to walk away from Art. No, not walk. Run. I want you to let nature take its course. Let the bombs go off. Let the world end, as it should."

"And then what?"

He spread his hands wide and shrugged as if he had no idea what would happen next. He was a worse liar than Art. "This world isn't meant to last forever. Time to end it, don't you think? Or if not end it, at least shake it up. This isn't the only world, you know. I can make sure you get sent to a much better one. Or if you prefer, you can have a nice cushy spot, right next to me. For Eternity." His grin turned savage. It made my stomach churn in an unpleasant and potentially explosive way.

"And if I say no?"

His expression darkened. His eyes went black. His face morphed into ice. "You have no idea what I can do to you."

I was beyond intimidation. "So, let me get this straight. You want the world to end? You want to see it destroyed? You want life to end?"

"Oh, yes." He closed his eyes and lifted his face upward. "Destruction is perfection. Chaos is heaven. Death is life." Then his gaze turned on me. "You can't stop what is coming."

"Maybe. Maybe not. But God—"

He swiftly put up a hand. "—doesn't give a sorry ass fig. He's washed His hands of this world. It's ours now. He's moved on. It's a great big universe out there and He has new worlds to create. This world was for practice. A real patchwork of creative fails, if you ask me. Dinosaurs. Neanderthal. Cro-Magnon. Homo sapiens. Doomed from the start. Flawed design. Amateur stuff. You'd think a god could at least get it right the first time. None of this, including humanity, was meant to last more than a millennium or two. And now your time is up. Can't keep pouring resources into a dead world. Chin up, Hector. It's not all bad news. We can use a clever, willing foil like you."

"No."

He laughed, a dark, snaky laugh that made the mist shiver. "You can't say 'no,' Hector."

"I can and I just did. I'd rather take oblivion, thank you very much. I'm done being a pawn." I tightened my arms over my chest. I was done, all right. Double done.

The demon let out a long, sulfur-infused sigh, uttering something about, "Stupid, free agency. Whose brilliant idea was that? That's why the universe is falling apart."

Liar. He was lying. I could see it in his anvil-infused eyes, hear it in his voice, read it on the undulating transparency of his dull skin. Art had taught me something, after all. Was that fear lurking at the back of his eyes? Desperation? *Que lastima.* I didn't care. Let the world end.

Out of nowhere I thought of Iggy—yes, Iggy. And the father I'd never known but hoped to meet someday. And a peculiar gray cat who against all odds had wormed his way into my affections. In that instant I wanted to scream, "Stop!" I didn't want the world to end. Hell, no. But *save* the world? Who, me? Maybe I could. Maybe I couldn't. But I could try. I could sure as hell try. For them.

Then I got up and walked away. Theoretically, at any rate.

~34~

"I still don't get it. If you're trying to earn your way back into hell, wouldn't a nuclear war cinch it?" I asked for about the tenth time. "What could be more evil than that?"

"It lacks subtlety," Art said. "It ranks a big, fat zero on the finesse scale. Really, Hector—anyone can set off a bomb. It takes no imagination and even fewer brain cells. It's too easy."

"Too easy?" I had no comeback for that. None. Nada. Maybe in a week it would come to me. If we had a week.

We were heading east, through the Nevada desert, but at that moment, we were waiting in line for gas at a station a few miles outside of Elko. The line was long, it was hot, and they were out of bottled water, Diet Coke, and ProPower. Also, Pepsi, Dr. Pepper, and root beer, all varieties. We'd been waiting for about forty minutes for our allotment of fuel, which wouldn't even fill the tank of our late model midnight blue pickup truck half-way. So far, we'd witnessed two fistfights, one robbery attempt, four domestic meltdowns, and a kid about three whip out his who-who dilly and pee in the parking lot.

"They're going to run out of gas before we get to the pump," I said.

Art didn't seem concerned. Not about the gas or if we'd get where we were going, wherever that was.

"Aren't we in a hurry?" I asked. "Weren't you the one who said we were on a schedule?"

"Don't worry. We'll get there in plenty of time."

"Get *where?*" I asked, also for the tenth time. Did he know? I had serious doubts. I ached for a soft bed. Also, I was craving steak and beer. It didn't help that my head was killing me, my stomach was jumping all over the place, and I was dizzy as hell.

A side effect of time travel, Art told me. "Alternate universe time travel," he amended. "It's the worst for side effects. You'll be back to normal in a day or two."

If we had a day or two. "So, what was that, anyway?" Alternate universe time travel, my skinny Cuban ass.

"A taste of your potential future if I hadn't come along and saved you."

"Saved me?" I didn't feel saved. In fact, I felt like I was floundering in the deep end of the pool with bricks tied around my ankles.

"Well, maybe 'saved' is taking it a bit too far. One never knows about these things. Let's say I've given you another option, one with at least some hope for survival. No need to thank me." He opened the last can of ProPower. "You got any more pretzels?"

I reached into a grocery bag at my feet and pulled out the pretzels. He took a swig of the energy drink, put the can in the beverage holder, scooped up a handful of the pretzels and jammed them into his mouth.

"Besides, that's not how it works." He coughed and sprayed the steering wheel with pretzel crumbs.

"How what works?"

"The nuclear war thing as an instrument of ultimate evil." He was back to my initial question about war being a good thing for him. Sometimes I had trouble following him; his thoughts bounced around like a helium balloon in a wind tunnel.

"Oh, yeah. Explain that to me one more time." Okay, so I was being difficult. He deserved it.

He brushed the crumbs off the steering wheel briskly. "Well, for one thing, if the world blows up, we'd all be out of a job."

"By 'we,' I assume you mean you and your fellow demons?"

"Yes, of course. Job security is one of the benefits of demonology. I thought you understood that. If the world ends, we get sent to hell for good. I mean, we'd get stuck there. No more side trips. No more Diet Coke. Or ProPower. Or chocolate cake. Or pretzels. No more walks along the beach at sunset. No more poking, prodding or provoking humanity into lovely, self-destructive activities. Our punishment would be eternal boredom and eventually mass oblivion. No, our goal should be to prolong life on earth. Twist it, pervert it, derail it, absolutely. Heap suffering on the masses. Make the lies believable. Seduce the innocent. Wreak havoc by perverting good intentions. Grease the slippery slope. Whatever it takes to make life miserable, but ultimately to put off The End of the World for as long as possible." He was working himself up into a fine lather. "How is that so hard to understand? How many times do I have to explain it?"

"Okay. Fine. But how could they cast you out for not being evil enough? You seem plenty evil to me. I mean, look how you've screwed up my life."

"Thanks! But that's not enough. I gotta screw up a whole lot of lives before I can get my position back."

"What about Charles Hunter and Doris? Didn't you screw up their lives? And Leroy Jefferson's? Not to mention, all the others."

By "others" I was referring to the parade of entities I'd inhabited since we left Leroy back in that hospital room in San Francisco. In the last few days, I'd been a homeless guy named Stan, an 18-year-old Asian kid named Frankie, a shoe salesman named Manuel, an overly tattooed biker named Percy and, briefly, a seriously fucked up suicidal crossdressing model whose name I think was Teddy.

Currently, I was sporting the body of a middle-aged Samoan guy by the name of Willie Potts. I didn't like Willie. He was mean and would have murdered the guy standing next to him rather than give him the time of day. I could feel his homicidal proclivities itching under his skin, trying to scratch their way to the surface. I hoped Willie would be short-lived, but all this body-hopping was exhausting and more than a little nerve wracking.

"Small potatoes," Art said. "Little drops in a very big bucket. And I really didn't do that much. They did most of the work all by themselves. I merely capitalized on their own frailty."

"Did you kill them?" This was a question that had been bothering me a lot, although it may have had something to do with Willie Potts' influence. Still, it was a valid question.

Art laughed. "You ascribe to me far more evil than I possess."

"I doubt that," I replied. I stared into his red-rimmed black eyes. "Well? Did you?"

"I am not a murderer," he said, with a touch of sincerity I found disconcerting. I could almost believe him. "A demon cannot commit murder."

"But you can suggest it? Whisper into someone's ear? Give someone the idea?"

He gave me a coquettish shrug. "Theoretically."

"It wouldn't take much to tip Willie Potts over the edge."

He nodded. "True enough. But that's not part of the plan."

I shivered. "I don't like this body."

"I know," he said. "I'll get you out of it as soon as a suitable one becomes available."

I was relieved to hear it. "But back to the Hunters—if you didn't kill them, who did?"

"Leroy, of course."

I could feel confusion stopping up my brain. "But you made me think I killed Doris."

"Not you. Charles."

"So, he didn't?"

"Of course not. He was already dead."

I cradled my head in my puffy hands. The damn demon was hell-bent on driving me crazy. "Leroy did it?"

"Yes. Leroy."

"While I was in the shower?"

"Yes."

"But you made me think … why did you do that?"

He grinned. "Because it was fun. You should have seen your face." He lapsed in a series of little hiccup-giggles. "If I had told you it was Leroy upfront, you wouldn't have enjoyed his body nearly as much. And you did enjoy it, didn't you?" *Wink, wink. Nudge, nudge.*

I clutched my fist—Willie's fist. I raised it and took a swing at him.

I missed him by a mile and slammed my fist into the dashboard. I yelped. Art laughed.

"Hector, Hector—when will you learn?"

I shook my fist—Willie's fist. There was now a nice crack in the dash, a jagged line five or six inches long. "Why would Leroy kill them? He didn't seem the type."

"You're so naïve, Hector! I think that's one of my favorite things about you."

"Whatever. So, why?"

"Because Peter Knutson told him to."

"Peter Knutson?" I blinked in confusion—and pain. I was going to have a nasty bruise on my hand—Willie's hand.

Art sat primly with his hands folded in his lap. "Okay, Hector, let me explain this to you as simply as I can. Knutson and Waterman are as tight as a pair of new patent leather shoes. Knutson provides spiritual guidance to Waterman, and Waterman uses Knutson to get rid of his critics."

"So, what's the connection with Charles and Leroy?"

"It's a little complicated, but I think you'll appreciate this. First, Charles and Leroy worked for Knutson, but they were robbing him blind. Knutson found out and it didn't make him happy. You with me so far?"

I nodded.

"Okay. To continue: Charles was a senator, remember? Charles was about to announce that he was going to challenge Waterman for the nomination for president in the next election. He might have gotten it, too, since he was a bigger asshole than Waterman. Possibly a little smarter, but definitely a bigger asshole. Waterman found out what he was planning and turned to his spiritual advisor for a little advising."

"And?"

"Well, what do you think? Knutson advised him to get rid of Charles. And even agreed to take care of it. All part of his patriotic duty and spiritual service. For a price, of course." He sighed. "There's always a price, isn't there, Hector? No one ever does anything anymore simply for the sake of doing a good turn."

I took a swig of the ProPower to clear my throat. "In other words, Knutson got Waterman to pay him to get rid of Charles, which was something he was going to do anyway because Charles was skimming the assets."

Art beamed. "You got it!"

"What about Leroy?"

"Knutson ordered Leroy to kill Charles and Doris. It wasn't the first time he'd used Leroy to get rid of people who proved troublesome. Anyway, Leroy wasn't very happy about having to whack Doris and threatened to spill the beans if Knutson didn't give him a lot more money. Since that wasn't something Knutson felt like doing, he went after Leroy, once Leroy had taken care of the Hunters. Knutson thought that by ordering Leroy to blow up the Transamerica building, he'd get himself killed, either in the explosion or while running from the cops. When that didn't happen, Knutson sent someone to blow up the hospital. It wasn't necessary. Leroy died because someone at the hospital gave him a little too much of something. Not quite sure who. Maybe the nurse. She looked a little fishy, don't you think?"

Come to think of it, the nurse looked a little like…what was her name?

Felicia.

Not possible, I decided. The damn demon was messing with me. I shook the thought out of my head. "So, why are we going to Montana? That part's still not clear."

"Because Knutson's headquarters is in Montana, although I didn't know where exactly until a few days ago."

I sat up sharply. "You know where we're going? There's a final destination? Where? Why didn't you tell me sooner?"

The demon sighed. "Because it's not important."

"But—does that mean there'll be an end to *this*?" I swept my hand across the horizon to indicate Nevada, traveling, body snatching, and the heat (among other things).

"Of course, Hector. You didn't think *this* was going to go on forever, did you?"

"But—"

"Like I said—I didn't know for certain where we were going until a few days ago."

"And now you do?"

"Yes."

"Where?"

"No place you've ever heard of. Relax. I'll let you know when you need to know. As for now, just enjoy the ride."

I flexed my left fist. It was tempting. Oh, so tempting.

Art seemed oblivious to my distress and resumed his nattering as if I'd never interrupted. "As a bonus, we have to stop Knutson from spewing any more of his end of the world crap. A lot of people, not just Waterman, believe that shit, you know."

"But isn't that a good thing? Wouldn't making people believe that the end of the world was coming at a certain time screw them up when it didn't happen?" Wait—what?

Art sighed and then explained with utmost patience: "The problem is that a few people—like Waterman—feel they need to personally see the prediction fulfilled. And there's nothing like the promise of glory to turn even the most mild-mannered believer into a gung-ho soldier of the Apocalypse. Especially if someone like Knutson is standing behind them egging them on. Waterman is particularly dangerous because he has access to some really big guns, but if we don't put the kibosh on Knutson, getting rid of Waterman will only make way for the next heaven-bound, trigger-happy bozo. The thing is, timing is going to be tricky."

A fight broke out between two truckers. Art watched, mesmerized, a smile fixed on his thin face. Dark thoughts pounded my Willie-infected brain. *Kill, kill, kill* ....

"Art? Art!" I gave him a nudge. "Do I have to kill Knutson? Is that part of your plan?"

"It wasn't in the beginning," he said, "but that's only because I didn't know where to find his headquarters."

"And now you do?" The Willie-brain was rooting for death and destruction. Lots and lots of death and destruction. I needed to get out of this body soon.

A slow, smoldering smile spread across Art's face, revealing teeth glowing a thermonuclear orange. "Well, no, you don't have to kill him, but we do have to put a stop to his nonsense."

"How are we supposed to do that?"

"Don't know yet," he said cheerfully.

I thought about that for far too long. "You're making this up as you go, aren't you? You have no grand strategy, no sure-fire plan of attack, do you?" I massaged my fist, wishing I hadn't already bruised it. I lapsed into a big-boy sulk. It felt damn good.

"Oh, come on, Hector. Have a little faith!"

I harrumphed stubbornly. At least five minutes passed. We moved up two car lengths. Then something occurred to me. "If we stop Knutson, do I still have to kill Waterman?" That, I realized, was what had been bothering me. Yes, he was an asshole, but I really didn't like the idea of killing him. (Willie called me a wimp. *Yes, Willie, I am. So, sue me.*)

"The only way to stop the bombs with any certainty is to kill him, Hector."

Now, my sigh was deep and heavy. I'd heard enough. "So, tell me this—am I getting out of this alive?"

He patted my beefy arm and grinned. "Of course, Hector. I promise you. You'll survive."

Lucky me.

"So, now what?" I yawned. Art had one thing right: time travel was exhausting, and the heat made me sleepy. I wanted a nap.

"This is going to work. Don't worry."

"I'm not worried." I yawned again. *Liar.* I really needed to sleep. And a beer. Or better yet, a double shot of whiskey, and a Bowie knife.

*All the better to dice you into pieces, my dear.*

~35~

"So why are you so bad at being bad?"

Art sighed and opened another ProPower. We were now sitting on a bench in some little park in Helena, Montana. The sun was warm on my back and there was a bank of fluffy clouds floating toward us. Thunderclouds, I guessed. You know, the big, billowing ones that hide imaginary kingdoms.

Don't ask me how we got there. I couldn't tell you. All I know is I went to sleep in Elko and woke up in Helena. Fine by me.

It was mid-day but which day I had no idea. It could have been next Tuesday or last Thursday or maybe even some Wednesday ten years from now.

I was in a new body. Early 40s. Tall. Strong. Nice set of pecs. Perfect vision, which was a plus. White, with a pinkish glow to the skin. Red hair, with lots of the requisite freckles. Two triangles of facial hair that itched on either side of my chin. Receding hairline. And tattoos. Lots and lots of tattoos, up and down toned arms. I was dressed in worn jeans and a soft cambric shirt with the sleeves rolled up, steel-toed work boots, and sporting a newsboy cap. And cheap, drug store sunglasses. The kind with mirror lenses.

This body, like Charles and Leroy, was straight, and yet, under the surface I could feel the familiar rumblings of my gayness doing its best to exert itself. I stretched and re-crossed my legs. With a flourish, I brushed away a leaf that had landed on my shoulder. I liked this body. It had potential.

Art guzzled half the can of ProPower before he came up for

a breath. "I'm not bad at being bad. I'm actually pretty good at it."

"Oh?"

"I made a mistake. It happens, you know. No one's perfect."

"What kind of a mistake?"

"It's not important."

It probably was but since he wasn't going to tell me, I changed the subject. "So, does this body have a name?" I patted my well-nourished belly.

"Elliot Matheson."

I cringed. "Sounds like a wuss."

Art shrugged. "Don't be so judgmental."

I held out an arm and checked out the tattoos. "I'm not liking this." I missed Leroy. Leroy had had style as well as muscle tone. "Why this one?"

"I know what I'm doing, Hector. Trust me."

Trust him? Yeah, right.

"For one thing, you have a lot in common with Elliot."

"Oh?"

"For one thing, his mother was also Irish."

"My mother wasn't—" I sighed. Whatever.

"And, he too, once dreamed of being a chef but, alas, life interfered, as it is wont to do."

I reached into Elliot's head and poked around tentatively. After Willie Potts, I was careful how hard I poked. Elliot wasn't a bad sort. Maybe a little rough around the edges, but essentially a good sort. I poked some more, and discovered, to my delight, that he had a weakness for Crème Brule and a genius for combining unusual ingredients on pizza. Another reason to like this body.

After our little chat in Elko, I felt a bit better about things. Not much, mind you. Still, it helped calm some of my anxiety.

Art tossed his empty can into the trash and opened another one. His fourth. I wanted to suggest he lay off the ProPower because he was starting to vibrate, but I held my tongue. After all, it's not like it would kill him.

"What about dinner? I'm getting hungry." That was an understatement. I was starving. Like I hadn't eaten in a week. Like I could eat a horse, a cow, several pigs, and a whole flock of chickens.

He shrugged. "You go without me. I'll wait here."

"Are you off food again?"

Another shrug. "I'm not hungry. And I've got some thinking to do."

"Fine. I'll be over there—" I pointed at the McDonald's. I had a craving for a Big Mac and fries. I checked my back pocket and pulled out a wallet. I had $40 and a couple of credit cards. I checked the driver's license. Elliot was 42. It was his birthday in a week. There was a school picture of a stout blond kid about six tucked behind the credit cards. I held it out for Art to see. "Cute."

He shrugged. "His son. His name is Connor. He hasn't seen him in 15 years."

That struck me as sad. Fifteen years was a long time in the life of a kid.

I thought of my own father. If I had known where he was and who he was, I sure wouldn't have gone 15 years without seeing him.

I did a little calculation. If my father was alive, he'd be about 50, give or take a year or two. Not so old, I thought. There was a big hole in my life where my father should have been. I didn't even know what he looked like. Or his name. My mother refused to tell me. Of course, it's possible she didn't know.

It's a sad thing to spend your entire life feeling as though your father was nothing but shadow and smoke. I wondered if my father even knew I existed. Maybe he didn't. That might explain why he had never tried to get in touch. I could almost forgive him for that.

Almost.

I ended up ordering three Big Macs, two large fries, and a chocolate milkshake. I was still hungry, so I topped off my order with a quarter pounder and three apple pies. I came back half an hour later and Art was, as promised, still there. "So? Solve any existential crises?" I asked as I joined him on the bench.

"You're a riot, Hector."

A man the size of Paul Bunyan walked by, sporting a cowboy hat bigger than Texas and a pair of pristine boots. He glanced at us and made some comment that made his female companion lapse into a fit of high-pitched chortles.

I reddened by old habit and muttered something about him being a poseur. The clean boots were a giveaway. I must have said it louder than I intended because he stopped and then got into my face.

"You say something to me?"

I shook my head.

"Speak up."

I didn't say anything. I gave him an off-handed shrug. He wasn't worth the effort.

That, apparently, was the wrong thing to do.

He looked from me to Art and then back to me. "A couple of fucking pansies, aren't you? Just what we need. You're both going to hell, you know that. Yeah. When the world ends, which it's going to do real soon, you're going to burn." He came at me, hell bent on knocking the "fucking pansy" out of me. I mean, seriously—was it that obvious? Was I walking around with a big sign on my forehead that read "Fucking Pansy"? Or was the guy just a dickhead, out looking for someone to punch because, well, why the hell not?

He missed me by a mile and a half. It didn't faze him. He leaned close, breathing stale beer and yesterday's tacos into my face. "Unless, of course, you repent." It struck me he had no wish for me to repent of anything. Because if I did, he wouldn't have a reason to shove his fist up my nose.

Turned out that once on my feet I was taller than my would-be attacker. I puffed up my chest, blew him down, and gave him a swift kick. I must have kicked him damn hard because he doubled over and then dropped to the ground as if I'd cut off his balls instead of merely nudging them.

"See?" Art said later, when we'd gotten far, far away. "Not turning the other cheek can be a whole lot of fun, can't it?"

I had to admit that he was, for once, very, very right. For once in my life, I stood up for myself. Hell, yeah! Hear me roar!

Okay, so the feeling was short-lived. But it was indeed fun.

Not just fun—it was intoxicating. It was something I could get to enjoy, heaven help me. For the first time since this whole thing started, a little surge of excitement burned in my gut.

"What's next?" I rubbed my hands together in gleeful anticipation.

Art glanced at me, his eyes flashing red, and shrugged. "I'm not sure."

"Not sure? I thought you had a plan."

"Plan? Oh, yeah. The plan ... I need to work out the details. I need some time to think."

Think? Art? Was he sick? "Whatever happened to 'don't think—do'?"

He shrugged and took a little hop-skip move that nearly sent him sprawling. He shook off my attempts to steady him. "I can't 'do' right now. The voices in my head are running amok. Jabber, jabber, *jabber* ... I can't ... I can't ... think. I can't *do*."

He raised a shaky hand to push back a lock of his jet-black hair that had fallen into his eyes. Given his hair was always plastered to his head and never moved, even in the fiercest wind, this should have been a clue that all was not well. Then a little wisp of smoke trailed over his head. Another clue that failed to catch my attention. "I need another ProPower."

We stopped at a 7-11 and he bypassed the cans and went straight for the two-liter bottles. "Hey, look at that, two for one."

I treated the glee in his glowing eyes as nothing more than another symptom of demonology. I grabbed a bag of chips and a Dr. Pepper and followed him out the door.

We wandered for a while, arm and arm, swilling pop, munching on chips, looking into store windows. Like regular folk.

Ain't life grand?

We got a few stares/glares, a few smiles, all par for the course. One old lady hissed at us. I hissed back. She jaywalked to get away from us and nearly got hit by a bus. That made Art smile for the first time in several hours.

We were, I suppose, quite the pair: skinny Art, with his sleek black hair and receding chin, and me, Elliot, a three-hundred-pound Titan of ribald muscle-bound tattoos.

We walked in circles until the sun went down. Finally, I had had enough. "Shouldn't we get a motel or something?"

"Motel? You mean, to sleep? I don't understand how you can sleep all the time. You miss so much of life with all that sleeping."

"Can't help it. Biological imperative. If I don't get enough sleep, I turn into a zombie."

"No such thing," he said. "Good idea, though. Zombies, I mean. Much better than vampires. Those guys are scary. Besides, sleep is a waste of time."

"Metaphorically, speaking."

"What?"

"Not sleep. Sleep is a not metaphor. Sleep is real. I was referring to the part where I turn into a zombie." I gave him my best zombie swag.

"Fine. Whatever. We'll get you a motel."

"And dinner?"

"Dinner?" he wrinkled his nose. "Didn't you eat already?"

"I had a couple of Big Macs and some fries four hours ago. It's worn off."

"Okay, fine. You can eat, too."

"Don't you want anything?"

"Not hungry." He drained the first bottle of ProPower. He tossed the bottle aside, smiling as it hit the sidewalk and rolled. I retrieved it and carried it to a recycling bin. He snarled at me. "Well, aren't you Mister ... Mister ... Something." His voice had a slight tremor in it, kind of like he was drunk. He even staggered a bit.

"How much of that stuff have you had today?"

He shrugged. "How the hell should I know? It's damn good. Yum." He grinned at me, showing off his perfectly aligned, slightly pink teeth, which were now more orange than pink. He twisted the cap off the second bottle.

"Maybe you should lay off that stuff for a while." I didn't like the way his eyes were glowing a radioactive green.

"Fuck that. Mind your own business." He took a few halting steps, and then let out a cry.

"What's wrong?"

One hand was over his eyes, rubbing, poking. "Holy crap—I can't see."

"What do you mean?"

"I mean, you weedy pig-boar, *I can't see*. I'm blind. I can't see a damn thing." He tugged at his eyes, gave his head a shake, and let out a long, low-pitched wail, and then walked into a telephone pole as if he needed to prove his point.

~37~

I grabbed him to keep him from stumbling into traffic. "Hold still! Let me look at you." I forced his hands from his face and took a good look. On a positive note, running into the telephone pole had done more damage to the telephone pole than his face. His eyes, however, had faded to a sick minty green. White specks shaped like little fluffy ducks floated in them.

"Come on." I gave him a firm tug. "Let's get out of here and find a motel."

He gave a half-hearted nod and let me lead him down the street. We didn't get far when he came to an abrupt stop and clutched his head. "I have to sit down." I maneuvered him to a bench and then sat beside him, holding on to his arm. If I let go, he flopped like a fish out of water and let out these little high-pitched squeals. "What the hell did I run into?"

"A telephone pole."

"What was it doing in the middle of the street? Those things are dangerous."

A few people passed us; some stared; some rolled their eyes. One or two crossed the street so they wouldn't have to pass us, which made me grip his hand a little harder.

"I think I'm going to be sick." Sick? Art? Was that even possible? His breathing turned fast and shallow, and his face grew paler by the second.

"Take slow deep breaths or you're going to pass out."

He teetered on the brink, bobbing precariously.

"A little drunk, is he?" some guy said. He was dressed all in black, except for a red tie. He came right up to us, leering, his own breath none too fresh. "Hey, honey, maybe you should lay off the booze. A little goes a long way when you're a lightweight. Frickin pansy-ass." He dissolved into a fit of knee-slapping guffaws, which ended abruptly when he was attacked by a flying mass of gray fur.

Ah, Putin. You gotta love a cat with good timing. (Cat? Was that all he was? I was beginning to wonder.)

The man sputtered and spit, but Putin held on like a champ, and I realized he'd gone easy on Felicia, back in that parking lot in Vegas. This guy was getting his face ripped to shreds. The blood was flying, along with strips of skin.

Finally, the man got himself free. "Little piece of shit. I hate cats. I'm gonna kill you."

He lunged for Putin, but I got between them. "You touch that cat and I will personally see you to hell. And trust me, I can do it. I have connections."

He tried to push past me, but I held my ground. He was five-eight to my six-three and I out-weighed him by a hundred pounds. He couldn't budge me. He couldn't get around me. He couldn't push me away. He couldn't get over me. Oh, yeah. I was the frickin Rock of Gibraltar and the Great Wall of China, all in one. Best of all, every time he tried to touch me, these little sparks of white-hot electricity shot out from my body and made him shriek. He obviously wasn't very bright because he kept coming at me, and I kept zapping him.

Holy hell, but that felt good!

Finally, he crumpled into a saggy lump. All the hot air, all the bravado hissed out of him, leaving him ... well, flaccid. He flopped wildly, bouncing from one edge of the sidewalk to the other, causing more than one person to utter threats and give him a good shove, which sent him sputtering, drooling and farting, until he finally turned the corner.

In the meantime, Putin curled up in Art's lap. Art had a lost-in-the-ozone smile on his face while he gently stroked the thick, gray fur. "Well, looked who showed up!" he said when I sat down next to them. "And you were worried. I told you he could take care of himself."

I reached my hand out to give Putin a congratulatory pat. Carefully, mind you. But he gave me an affectionate nudge with his head and let me pat him, as was his due. And then he jumped off Art's lap and strolled down the sidewalk, tail at full mast, waving it as if he owned the world.

Which come to think of it, he probably did.

In a few moments, Art recovered enough that we could continue. He still couldn't see, and he was as jittery as a rat in a snake pit, but at least he stopped falling over every few steps. I maneuvered him to the Lexus. No, wait. SUV. No—what were we driving? I scanned the street. Oh, yeah. A new pickup. Silver, this time. Extended cab. Cloth seats. Nice stereo.

Oddly, Art didn't say much. He didn't bemoan his condition, question his existence, or swear vengeance on whatever god/goddess or demon lord had rendered him sightless. He meekly let me push him around without so much as a huff or puff.

Yeah, I know. Pathetic.

We found a motel a few miles down the highway that offered free breakfast and had one of those vibrating thingys attached to the bed, which Art usually found amusing.

I left him happily vibrating at full speed, TV remote in hand, while I went to find food.

I ended up at a restaurant across the street. I ordered the special—meatloaf and scalloped potatoes, plus a salad, and two pieces of apple pie, one of which I had the waitress pack up for Art. (And if he didn't want it, I would have a midnight snack.)

I took my time. I was still pretty shaken. The restaurant wasn't busy, and I enjoyed the relative quiet and unhurried pace.

My waitress was a woman of imprecise middle-age by the name of "Kristy", according to her name tag. She looked like she had lived a hard life, but she smiled a lot, and didn't rush me. It felt good to be around someone who was both pleasant and normal. It restored my faith in humanity. Perhaps if I had to save the world, I'd save it for people like Kristy—good, hardworking people who'd give you the shirt off their back, if you needed it. I left a hundred-dollar bill tucked under my plate. Then I thought of Betsy, the waitress in San Jose who had thrown my money back in my face. I picked up the hundred-dollar bill. Then I put it back under my plate and left quickly.

When I got back to the motel, Putin was squatting in front of our door. He got up when I approached and let out a plaintive *meow*.

I greeted him as he rubbed against my legs and bent over to pet him. His mouth looked funny. I looked a little closer: he had the remnants of something small, gray, and furry, plus a little blood smeared across his mouth.

"You really are Satan's little helper, aren't' you?"

*Meow.*

"Well, you can't come in like that." I made him drop his package, which I discreetly disposed of in the nearest trash can. Then I pulled a tissue out of my pocket and wiped his mouth. He only protested a little, gave an indignant swish of his tail when I finished, and moseyed into the room as if he were God's own anointed avenging angel.

It occurred to me that if anyone could play on both teams, it would be Putin. All the more reason to be wary.

The cat immediately hopped up on the bed and gave Art a headbutt, which Art responded to with enthusiasm. "Putin, you old flap dragon! How have you been?"

Pretty good, apparently, because after a few more friendly headbutts, he planted himself in Art's lap and proceeded to purr so loudly, he drowned out the television.

As it turned out, Art wasn't interested in the apple pie; however, Putin devoured it with relish.

"So, now what?" I asked when it became apparent that Art wasn't going to talk about his current condition willingly.

"What?"

"You're blind, Art. In case you haven't noticed."

"Of course, I noticed. What do you think I am? Stupid?" He groped for the remote and began flipping through channels. "Nothing I can do about it." He went by the food channel twice before I finally grabbed the remote out of his hand.

"Art! What the hell is wrong with you? You're *blind*, for God's sake. Doesn't that mean anything to you?"

"Don't swear," he snapped. "At least, I won't have to look at your ugly face anymore."

I responded by throwing a pillow at him, which hit him squarely on the end of his pointy nose. "Jerk."

He turned on his side away from me and covered his head with the blanket. Putin perched himself on the crest of Art's hips. He wasn't fooling me. He never slept. Fine by me if he wanted to pout.

He could pout from now until next Wednesday for all I cared. Let the world end. Hell couldn't be much worse than this.

I took a shower and took a good look at my new-to-me body. It was passable, I supposed. A little worse for wear but maybe that was a good thing.

With nothing better to do, I went to bed. "We're going to have a heart-to-heart tomorrow, Art. I mean it."

Not that I was going to bet on it. Demons can be stubborn bastards.

~38~

I woke up to Putin kneading my chest furiously. When I wouldn't open my eyes, he gave me a rousing headbutt. And then another. And another. Then he bit me. Not hard, mind you. Just enough to make me open my eyes.

The clock on the bedside table read 6:14. I hauled myself out of bed, opened the door and watched the cat rush out, clearly on a mission. It was too early for missions, so I climbed back into bed, pulled the covers over my head, wiggled back into my happy place, and rubbed the palm of my hand where the beast had bitten me.

"I need a ProPower," came Art's voice, shamelessly whiny.

I ignored him. (Note: word of advice: never ignore a whiny demon. There's no pretending you're not home when it comes to demons on the whine. They simply up the whine.)

"Hector, please. My head is killing me."

"So, go get one yourself." Did he seriously think I was going to wait on him?

"I can't. I'm blind, remember?"

I sighed. "It's too early in the morning." Now I was on the whine.

"Please, Hector." He proceeded to issue a groan so full of angst and pathos that he truly deserved an Oscar. Or a slap upside the head.

It was clear I wasn't going to win this one, so I got up, got dressed, and went in search of a vending machine, if for no other reason than to shut him up so I could go back to sleep for a few more hours.

Yeah, like that was going to happen.

I was back in the room in five minutes. No ProPower. He had to settle for Diet Coke, but I bought two with the last of my change. He grunted, but downed the first one in one long gulp, and then opened the second one.

He perked up as I watched him. A bit of color returned to his face, his twitching slowed, his face relaxed.

"Holy Hannah, you're addicted to caffeine." I know, I know—no big surprise there. I should have figured that out sooner, but I was a little preoccupied.

"Am not." He glared at me. Or tried to. His eyes crossed, which made him look even more demented than usual. "Demons don't get addicted to stuff. I could use all the drugs on the planet and not get addicted."

I tried to imagine Art high as a kite. With that image now firmly, indelibly lodged in my beleaguered brain, I said. "They also aren't supposed to drink or eat or feel pain, but you've been doing all three, haven't you?"

He mumbled into his Coke can.

"Well, haven't you?"

He shrugged. "Did you only get two?"

"You are *so* addicted. No wonder your head hurts. You have to lay off the caffeine."

He glared at me with his sightless eyes, only he was off about thirty degrees, which made the whole thing seem like something out of a Monty Python movie. "I am not addicted. I can't be."

"Bullshit. How much of that stuff did you drink yesterday?"

"I don't know."

I did some mental calculations. He'd downed at least a dozen ProPowers and several large bottles of Diet Coke. And that was just yesterday. "You've overdosed on caffeine, you butthead. No wonder your head hurts. That's probably why you've gone blind, too."

"Caffeine doesn't make you blind."

"No, it wouldn't make *me* blind, but do you really know the effects of large doses of caffeine on your system?"

He waved me off. "I feel like shit. I haven't felt like this in—" He used his fingers to count. "In three hundred years. Not since I was tarred and feathered."

That brought me up short. "You were tarred and feathered? What for?"

He shrugged petulantly. "The usual. I think there was a woman involved. Or maybe two."

I decided I didn't want to hear about it. "Okay, look, you need to get that stuff out of your system before you kill yourself."

That made him laugh.

"Don't be an asshole. You know what I mean."

"Yeah, fine." He sat up, groaning with every movement. "What's the date?"

"I don't know. I've lost track." That little throw-back trip home had really messed me up. I hadn't been the same since I'd come back. Plus, I had gone through at least half a dozen bodies. That alone was enough to cause some serious temporal distortion. Had I gained a couple of days or lost them? I'd been counting on Art to keep track of things. It was his circus, after all.

"What day is it? Do you know that much?"

"I'm not sure."

"Figure it out," he said. "It's kind of important."

I ended up turning on the television. According to the program schedule, it was Friday.

"That's not good." Art got out of bed. "Help me get dressed. We have to get going." Under his breath, I heard him mumble, "Maybe I can buy us an extra day or two …."

"Where are we going?"

"Does it matter?"

He looked so innocent as he posed that question; innocent enough that it gave me pause. I recovered quickly. "Back in Nevada, you said you knew. Was that a lie? Do you have any idea what you're doing or are you just winging it?"

"Winging it?"

"Yeah, you know—improvising? Making it up as you go along? Faking it?"

He snorted. "I never fake it. You have to trust me, Hector."

"Trust you? You're a demon. Why should I trust you?"

"You have so far."

"No, I haven't. You got your hooks into me in Florida and you've been dragging me along ever since for some fool reason that nobody in their right mind would ever believe."

He cocked his head to the side, clasped his hands together, striking the pose of an overly patient kindergarten teacher. "Then I guess it's a good thing you're not in your right mind."

I sighed. I know, I know—I walked right into that one, didn't I? "I hate you, you know."

He grinned. "So you've said. More than once. It's getting a little tiresome, you know." He drained the second can of Coke and wiped his hand across his mouth and let out a lengthy belch. "Look, Hector, there are more important things at stake than your ego."

"My ego?" My gums flapped. I couldn't think of a response that didn't involve punching him in the face.

"Yes, Hector. Your ego. You keep thinking this has something to do with you. It doesn't. You're merely a tool."

No kidding. "That's supposed to make me feel better?'

"Frankly, Hector, I don't give a rat's ass how you *feel.*" He waved his hand in my general direction in a dismissive gesture. "It's what you *do* that matters. And not just to me, Hector. To the whole world."

"Oh, please—"

"You already had one demonstration on the consequences of your inaction. Would you like to see another?"

That brought me up short. "No," I said softly, trying to still the sudden twitching in my leg. "No more demonstrations."

"I didn't think so."

"Could you at least tell me if I'm ever going to get my life back? Am I ever going to go back to being just Hector Gonzales, second-rate mechanic?"

"I told you, once this is over—"

"Yeah, I know." I picked at a spot on my sleeve, trying not to cry. I wanted to go home, back to my plain, boring, stupid life. I could have used a hug right then. Not that I wanted a hug from Art. I thought about Lawrence, my last boyfriend. He had been a good hugger. An asshat, true. But a damn good hugger. I wondered what he was doing right now, if he missed me. Or at least my cooking.

I jumped. Art was beside me, his hand on my arm. "You can't go back to being Hector right now." His voice was surprisingly gentle. "Have you forgotten? Hector's wanted for murdering Doris and Charles Hunter, along with a host of other things."

I ran my hand across my eyes. "But I didn't do any of it."

"I know," Art said, "but the police are still looking for you. They think you murdered the Hunters, blew up Iggy's garage, and tried to blow up half of San Francisco. Face it, Hector's screwed. You're a lot better off being Elliot Mathison."

It couldn't be that easy. There had to be a catch. "Yeah? And what do the police want Elliot for?"

"Nothing," Art said cheerfully. "At the moment." I stiffened, and Art laughed. "Gotcha!"

I rubbed my temples, trying to ease the pain that was creeping into my head. "Could you at least tell me what we're going to do next?"

"That's easy. You're going to buy a diner."

"A diner? What diner? Where?"

Art fumbled in his pocket and pulled out a matchbook and tossed it to me. I recognized it immediately. It was the matchbook we'd retrieved from Leroy's safety deposit box. "Richard's Diner," it read. "Jackknife, Montana: *Home of the bacon bison burger.*"

Great. But I still didn't get it. "Why am I buying a diner? To be specific, why am I buying *this* diner?" Was this his grand plan? Seemed a bit of a letdown after all the hype and secrecy.

Art pressed his hand against his sightless eyes and gave his head a woeful little shake as if lamenting my inherent stupidity. "Well, how else are you going to save the world?"

Putin was waiting for us when we got to the pickup, perched on the hood like a furry ornament. He looked quite pleased with himself. King of the hill, and all that.

He jumped down, tail twitching, and waited for me to open the door so he could ascend into his carriage. All very proper, you know.

I stopped to get gas. This took a while. The lineups continued to be a problem, which was one of the reasons we ended up in Helena for longer than expected. The city had run out of gas until this morning. Now, we were competing with a dozen big trucks and a long line of cars.

I heard more than one person mumble, "Damn Canadians. Bunch of greedy, socialist bastards."

I opened my mouth to say that if Waterman hadn't ticked off the entire Middle East and most of South America, as well as the Canadians, we wouldn't be in this predicament. And if he wasn't such an asshole. And if he had a brain. And—but Art gave me a walloping kick in the skins before I could inhale enough breath to carry on. I acquiesced to his superior wisdom, which was a good thing because a moment later I watched a couple of cowboys block a pickup with Alberta plates from getting into line.

The Canadian pickup responded by executing a couple of exceptional wheelies before it gunned its engine and sped off, leaving a cloud of thick yellow dust behind them. One of the cowboys leaped into his truck, but his friend stopped him from chasing after the other truck by reminding him he was out of gas. He responded with a scowl, a hardy finger wave, and a few choice expressions even a Canadian would have understood.

Art was still blind, so I gave him a blow-by-blow description of the incident. "This is only the beginning," he said. "US-Canadian relations are going downhill in a hurry. And that's just for a start. It's gonna get real ugly, real fast." Judging by the collective mood, he wasn't kidding.

For now, I wanted to get out of here. "Where are we headed?"

"North."

"Toward Canada?"

"Yeah."

"But not Canada?"

He shook his head. "Not Canada."

Well, at least there was that. "Jackknife?"

"You got it."

"You know where it is?

"More or less."

"Do you know how to get there?" That was, perhaps, the more important question.

"More or less," he said again. He waved the map at me. I took it from him and looked for this town of his.

"Are you sure it's on here?"

"It's there somewhere." Well, if it was, it was hiding under a rock. I tossed the map aside. I'd worry about it later. Right now, we had more important needs: cat food and snacks.

But I didn't want to stick around Helena any longer than necessary, so we got the half tank of gas they allotted us and got out of there.

Halfway between Helena and Great Falls, I pulled into a rundown gas station along an empty stretch of highway. This one wasn't busy, and it had plenty of gas. I filled the tank and went inside.

I grabbed some crunchies for Putin, a bag of chips and a couple of bottles of water at exorbitant prices. "Ten bucks for a bottle of water?"

The clerk shrugged. "Everything's more expensive these days, thanks to that asshole Waterman. If you got empties, feel free to fill them up in the bathroom."

I gave it some thought, but bathroom water didn't appeal to me, so I meekly laid my stuff on the counter, grateful for the thick roll of bills in my pocket.

The clerk was a stout woman, pushing sixty and pushing it hard if you know what I mean, but something about her caught my attention. Maybe it was her eyes—they were hazel with flecks of green and seemed to reach into the deepest regions of my pathetic soul. She looked at me over the top of big, round glasses, down her long, thin nose as she put my purchases into a bag. "You look half dead," she said.

I shrugged. What could I say? I was beginning to fear I was more than "half" dead.

She gave me another long look. "You should eat better. Lay off the junk." Her voice was deep and raspy, a life-long smoker's voice.

I shrugged. "We've been on the road for a while."

"I can tell." I'm not sure why I didn't find this conversation offensive, even though I was almost certain she called me fat. Not my fault, I wanted to tell her: not my body.

"You have that 'if-I-have-to-drive-another-mile-I-might-stab-someone' look. I see it a lot."

I laughed. She hadn't called me fat, just worn out. "Yeah, I bet."

"There's something else though—" She hesitated, and her well-lined, lipstick-stained mouth twitched as if it wanted to speak A Truth but wasn't sure how I would take it.

I was in a rare mood, one wallowing in resignation and wrapped in foregone conclusions, or I never would have said, "What? Tell me."

She adjusted her glasses. Then she took them off and polished the lenses on her apron. When she put them back on, she looked at me squarely, her eyes magnified behind the thick lenses. "You have the mark of the devil."

*Demon*, I wanted to correct her, but I held my tongue. Instead, I asked, "Which mark is that?"

"The usual. It suits you, though. Bet no one messes with you, do they?"

No one. Except the demon whose mark I bore. I changed the subject. "Do you know how to get to a place called Jackknife? I can't seem to find it on the map."

"You probably don't have the right map. It's not on most of them." She dug around under the counter and finally slapped a dog-eared map in front of me. "You'll find it on this one."

"Great. Thanks!" I radiated smiles, cheer, and relief.

She made a face. "What are you going there for?"

"I'm thinking of buying the diner."

That made her laugh. Or choke. "Now, why would you want to do that?"

I didn't want to, that was the problem. I had to. That took the fun out of it. But her expression of thinly veiled distain made something in me snap and I shot back waspishly, "I'm going to turn it into a resort for gays, lesbians, and other assorted queers."

To my surprise, she didn't seem bothered by that at all; in fact, she was thoughtful. "No—you should just open a restaurant. It's what you've always dreamed of doing, isn't it?"

I stared, all slack jaw and stupid. "How do you know that?"

"I have my ways," she said, her expression eerie, if not downright unnerving. "You won't make a lot of money but with the right promotion, you'd do fine." She handed me my change, such as it was, and then my bag.

"I doubt that." But I got to thinking, maybe even fantasizing a little.

"Sure, you would. Assuming the world don't end in the meantime." She wrote down her name and phone number and handed it to me. "When you open, give me a call. I have connections. The good kind."

I took the piece of paper she handed me. *Brenda Mabee*, it read. She'd written her phone number in big block numbers. I stuck it in my wallet. "You're on."

"Keep the food simple. None of that French-Thai-Greek fusion stuff. People around here don't have time for that kind of crap. Now, simple don't mean boring. Take chili, for example. Chili can be boring as white rice or it can be—" Her eyes lit up. "Wait."

Then she dashed out the door, leaving me standing in the middle of the empty gas station, holding the bag, so to speak. I watched her race across the parking lot and enter a dilapidated trailer that stood off to one side.

A moment later, she came flying back to the station, out of

breath, pink-cheeked, and glistening with sweat, revealing something of the girl she had once been in the brightness of her eyes. She thrust a notebook into my hand.

I opened it up to find page after yellowing page of recipes, all handwritten in pale, faded perfect script.

"My grandmother's." Her words came out between gasps. "She was one hell of a cook. A ranch wife. Cooked for dozens of ranch hands, seven sons, and four husbands. She outlasted all four of those husbands and most of the sons. She was known for her chili. The recipe's in there somewhere." She tapped the cover of the notebook.

I didn't know what to say but I was truly touched by her kindness. "Thanks." Was that enough? Should I pay her for the recipes, or at least offer her something in exchange?

She waved me off. "I'll never use them. Who am I going to cook for? I don't have any family to pass them on to. When I die, they'll all go up in flames. Someone might as well have them. Might as well be you. There's more than chili in there, you know. There's an excellent apple cake recipe and one for buttermilk biscuits. You've never had biscuits as good as my Gran's, but you gotta have a light touch. You got a light touch?"

I assured her I did. She grabbed my hand and examined it. "Hmm. You'll have to work on it."

I got half-way to the pickup and then stopped. I looked at the rundown gas station and the rundown trailer, stuck out in the middle of nowhere, and I was struck by the utter futility of life in this place.

I thought about all the money that I had, money that wasn't really mine, that had somehow been acquired through means I didn't want to think about. I could do something with all that money. Even something good.

And I then thought about Brenda Mabee. All alone with nothing and nobody. Would she or her trailer survive another winter? Assuming the world didn't actually end in a few days, of course.

For the first time since this whole thing started, I felt a burst of optimism and a reason to carry on, so I turned around and went back to the station. "Brenda, would you like to run away with me? Help me run a diner?"

She looked up from her magazine, studied my face, and then grinned. "Honey, I thought you'd never ask."

~40~

It took her ten minutes to pack a few items and lock up everything. "I don't own any of this," she told me. "Belongs to some douche bag in Billings."

She didn't clean out the till, although she took enough to cover her wages. "Fair is fair." I had to agree.

I wasn't sure how to explain Art, but she took one look at him and gave her head a shake. "You collect the down-and-out?"

I was about to tell her it was the other way around, but I stopped myself. "It's a hobby of mine."

I introduced her to Putin. He gave her a friendly headbutt; she gave him a little rub behind the ears. "Well, isn't he the cutest thing?" She pulled a bag of cat treats out of her pocket and offered some to him. He was officially hers from that moment on. Little traitor.

All this peace, love, and goodwill was freaking me out. Something was going to happen to screw it all up. It would be my fault, too, because that was how things worked in my little soon-to-be-annihilated world.

As if to mock my doom-and-gloom, Debbie-downer predilection, Brenda immediately proved to be an asset. She knew a shortcut to Jackknife that saved us two hours, not to mention the aggravation of trying to find it on the map. When we'd gone about thirty miles up a narrow, winding mountain road, I said, "I thought you said it was just off the highway."

"This is Montana, honey. It is just off the highway."

I'm not sure why I was in such a hurry. In retrospect, I should have taken my blessed time and gone the long way. Through Finland.

Art continued to lean listlessly against the window, neither talking nor acknowledging anyone's existence.

"What's wrong with him?" Brenda finally asked.

"Caffeine overdose. Too many energy drinks."

"I've never seen caffeine do that to a person. Whiskey, yeah. But not caffeine."

"He has a delicate constitution," I said.

"Shouldn't you take him to a doctor?'

"Can't."

"Oh," she said. "No medical insurance?"

"That's not the problem."

She thought about that. "You boys on the run?"

"Kind of."

She nodded as if she understood perfectly. "No wonder you're headed for Jackknife. Still, he doesn't look very good. He's not going to die, is he?"

"He'll be fine as soon as he gets the caffeine out of his system." I hoped.

A few miles later, we reached a town called Nojuice, population 183. "Stop at the grocery store," Brenda said. "Go to the next block and turn right."

I did as she told me, pulling to a stop in front of a small store with the word "Groceries" stenciled across its window in pretty gold letters. Brenda leaped out and dashed inside. While we waited, I munched on potato chips and Putin climbed on top of the seat to watch out the window.

When she returned, she handed me a sandwich. "You need to eat something."

I took the sandwich reluctantly. Smoked turkey. No mayo. No cheese. Lettuce and tomato. The bread was a little stale, but it still tasted pretty good, to my surprise.

While I ate, feeding bits of turkey to Putin in a fruitless effort to win back his loyalty, Brenda fiddled in the backseat, finally handing me an insulated travel mug. "Here. Give this to your friend. Make him drink it."

"What is it?"

"An antidote to the caffeine poisoning."

I held it to my nose to smell it. I caught a whiff of ginger and something else. Turmeric? "I didn't know there was an antidote."

"One of my grandmother's all-purpose recipes. Hold his nose if you have to. Make him swallow it."

I did as she said. Art dutifully opened his mouth and swallowed it easily. For a few moments, nothing happened.

Then he started coughing.

"You might want to open the door," Brenda said. "He's going to vomit up an ocean any moment."

I jumped out of the pickup and ran around to Art's door, got it opened, and turned him outward just in time.

Well, kind of just in time.

A gush of liquid shot out of his mouth. It missed the interior of the pickup and hit me square in the chest.

He moaned—one of those long, low moans like he was being trampled on by a hundred Pygmy elephants. Then he went limp and nearly toppled out of the truck. I gave him a hardy shove, which sent him sprawling across both seats, his head landing with a thud against the steering wheel.

"Oh, dear," Brenda clucked. "I hope I didn't make it too strong."

"He's a tough ol' demon," I said. "I'm sure he'll be fine." I wasn't sure. Not really. But he was already dead, wasn't he? I mean, how much more damage could anyone do?

We had attracted a bit of an audience by now: a couple of kids on their bicycles; a man with a gold nose ring; a woman pulling one of those metal shopping carts; an old man brandishing a cane.

"Get your bikes off the sidewalk," the old man yelled at the kids. One of them gave him the finger. He growled at him. "I know your father, you little shit."

They scattered, buzzing the old man before they shot out into the street, nearly causing a car to swerve into a couple of parked cars. Much honking and swearing ensued. The kids kept going. You could hear them laughing as they turned the corner.

The old man caught me looking at him. "What are you looking at, asshole? Never seen an old man before?" He shook his cane at me and trudged off.

The woman with the cart just shook her head. "Someone

ought to put that old geezer out of his misery."

"You mean out of your misery," Brenda countered.

The woman laughed. "Yeah. That." She continued down the sidewalk, not giving us another glance.

I turned back to Art. Putin was giving him a thorough face-licking. I mean, he was really going at it. Like he meant to lick his face right down to the bone. He was having such a good time, I hated to put a stop to it, but it struck me as bordering on the indecent. I was about to give him a nudge, but Brenda stopped me.

"Leave him. He knows what he's doing."

Which was more than I could say for myself.

41

Finally, Putin stopped licking Art's face, gave a plaintive meow, which sounded roughly like, "Okay, you can wake up now," and then leaped out the window to take up a position on the sidewalk. He batted at a couple of marauding butterflies and then settled down to watch as Brenda and I attended to Art.

He was moving now, his arms and legs twitching as if he couldn't remember quite how they worked. We managed to haul him upright and hold him in place.

I offered Art a drink of water, which he took, although most of it ended up dribbling down his chin. "Thanks, bud," he said weakly.

"Can you see?" I was anxious as hell.

He blinked a few times. "Yeah. I can see just fine." He gave me an odd look, kind of puzzled. "Who are you?"

"What?"

"Who are you, man? Do I know you?" He looked at Brenda. "Mom?"

She snorted. "Boy, do you have that wrong, buster."

Art blinked and looked from Brenda to me. That's when I noticed his eyes weren't red anymore. Well, not exactly. They were brown but the white parts were reddish. Like he hadn't slept in a month. Or he'd been crying. Or both.

"Come on, Art, that's enough." I was not amused. "Quit joking. It's not funny."

He looked at Brenda, wide-eyed and all innocent. "Joking?"

I swore. I was cranky, I admit. I was wet with ginger-scented demon vomit. I was tired. And I was pissed off at Art for being such a jerk.

"I don't think he's kidding," Brenda said.

"He's kidding. It's what he does."

She shook her head. "No, I don't think so." She said to Art, "What's your name?"

He wrinkled his forehead in thought. "I don't know."

"Where are you from?"

"I don't know."

"Do you know what day it is?"

He shook his head.

"The year?"

"1632?"

"What's the last thing you remember?"

Again, with the wrinkled forehead. "Shooting Lord Winston, the bloody traitor."

Brenda turned to me. "Well, either he's crazy or he really doesn't know who he is."

"Great." What was I supposed to do now? I thought about leaving him right there on that street in Nojuice, Montana, and driving away, but there was Brenda, looking at me as though I was going to solve this and all her problems, too, and Putin was now rubbing himself against my legs, purring licentiously.

And, if that weren't enough, I had this sinking feeling that the balance of the world was now completely in my oh-so clumsy hands.

Art looked about as pathetic as a demon with no memory can possibly look. Like a kid who just learned there was no Santa Claus, the Tooth Fairy was a gremlin, and unicorns don't really fart rainbows.

"Come on," I said to Brenda. "We can't stay here. Let's keep going. Maybe this is only a temporary side effect of the caffeine overdose."

She nodded and got back into the pickup. Putin jumped in after her, and I got Art buckled in.

"We're not that far from Jackknife. It's only a few more miles. Can we make it?"

"We can try," I said, and I put the truck into gear. I was happy to get going.

"I'm thirsty," Art said, in a voice that had been roughed up with sandpaper.

I fished out a bottle of water. He batted it out of my hand. "Suit yourself. That's all we got. It's water or nothing."

He stuck out his bottom lip. I'd like to say it make him look cute, but it didn't. It merely accented the demonic slant of his chin. "Well, I can see you're going to be a bunch of laughs." As usual.

We got back on the road, and once again, I was glad Brenda was with us. I would have missed the turn if she hadn't pointed it out to me.

Art tried the radio, but there was nothing but static. Still, he kept turning the dial and pushing buttons until I finally reached out and slapped his hand. "Knock it off." He pulled his hand back and retreated into a sulk. Fine by me.

"What's with you two?" Brenda asked. "You a couple or something?"

"No." It came out a little more forcibly than I intended. "Business partners." It was the first thing that came out my mouth.

"You're both weird, you know." It didn't sound like that bothered her at all.

"Yeah, I know." The engine caught and sputtered as we trudged up a particularly steep stretch.

"Do you also know that there's not much in Jackknife? It's not quite a ghost town, but it has all the earmarks of a soon-to-be ghost town. I could think of a lot of better places to open a business." For the first time, there was a hint of hesitation in her voice, like maybe this wasn't such a good idea after all.

"I thought you said we could make a bundle."

"No, I said you could do well with the right promotion. But you could certainly do better someplace else, and probably with less effort."

"Art's got his heart set on Jackknife."

"You're not part of that church, are you?" Her tone was casual but tense.

"What church?"

"The Restored Evangelical Sacred Anarchy Gospel Church or something like that."

"Hardly. Why?"

"Their headquarters is in Jackknife."

"Oh?" I tried to sound innocent.

"Bunch of weirdos. The whole town is full of weirdos. But they're the weirdest of the bunch."

"Good to know," I said. "I hope they like chili."

She laughed. "You and your friend will fit right in."

"Because we're weird?"

"Because *they're* weird. But I haven't been up there in years," she said. "I could be wrong."

She wasn't. Not even a little.

42

The sun had disappeared behind the mountains by the time we pulled into Jackknife. The blue sky had faded to a bland gray, which blended into the dull shadows of the town. It was as if we had been deposited inside one of those old black and white TV westerns.

We found Richard's Diner easily enough, neatly tucked in between Linda's Ladies Wear and Clyde's Secondhand Goods Plus Bait and Gun Shop right there on Main Street. It was as faded and worn as every other building in town. I was not encouraged.

Inside, it was a little better. Shabby, but clean. Two guys sat drinking coffee at a corner table. They glanced at us briefly through thickly hooded eyes, then went back to their coffee. One of them said something too low for me to hear; the other one snorted\hiccupped into his cup. When no one rushed to greet us, we took a table in the middle of the room.

We hadn't been there long when a lanky guy with a handlebar mustache and more creases on his face than potatoes in Idaho came out from the back carrying a coffee pot. He stopped short when he saw us. He nodded in our direction, and then continued to the other table, refreshed the men's cups, laughed at someone's joke, scooped up the money one of them plopped down, all the while keeping an eye on us.

Finally, he approached us. Gingerly. Did he think we were ghosts? Canadians? "You folks lost?"

I shook my head. "I don't think so."

He didn't look convinced. He sized us up for a minute longer and we must have passed muster, because he finally said, "Would you folks like a menu? Not that there's much on it."

"Sure," said Brenda, smiling. "And some of that coffee."

"Be right back." The guy hustled off, returning with cups and menus. He handed out the menus, a single typed page in a plastic sheet protector, and poured coffee. "You folks passing through?"

"Maybe," Brenda said. "Maybe not. We heard this place was for sale."

The guy's eyes went wide and he all but tripped over himself. "Could be. If the price is right." He pointed at the menus. "Can I get you anything besides the coffee?"

"A hamburger?" I really needed meat. And some grease.

"You wanna try our famous bacon bison burger?"

I hesitated. "Do you recommend it?"

"Personally, I prefer a plain ol' cheeseburger. The bison burger thing was my brother's big idea." He made a face which suggested that his brother was an idiot.

"The cheeseburger would be fine."

"You got any peach pie?" Brenda asked.

"Sure do." He looked at Art, who was picking his cuticles. "Anything for you, sir?"

Art didn't look up.

"He'll have a piece of pie, too," I said. Which I would eat, if he didn't.

"Sure. I'll be back with your orders and then we can talk."

The men at the other table drained the last of their coffee and stood up. They gave us a good dose of local scrutiny before they left, and then no doubt checked out the strange pickup parked in front.

A few minutes later, we had our food, and the man sat down across from me and introduced himself as Richard Washington. "Welcome to Jackknife," he said. He shook our hands enthusiastically. Except for Art. Art didn't look up, although he did pick up his fork, which he held poised over his pie.

"Is he all right?" Richard asked.

"He doesn't travel well." I let it go at that.

"So, you think you want to buy the diner?" Richard said. "Thing is, I'm not sure I want to sell."

"Oh?" Brenda took a bite of the pie. Her expression changed from politeness to one of ecstasy. "This is good." She shoveled in a few more bites. "Really good!"

Richard flashed her a smile. "I have a knack for pastry."

"I'll say. It's like butter in my mouth."

I took a bite of the hamburger. It was a little dry, but I smiled enthusiastically, taking my cue from Brenda. "Good burger. Really good."

"It's okay," Richard said. "The pie is better. Trust me."

"You like baking pies?' Brenda asked.

Richard nodded. "Yeah. It's my passion. Pies. Cakes. Pastry. But I can't just do desserts."

"Maybe you should open a bakery," Brenda said, licking the back of her fork.

His face lit up and then darkened. "I'm too old to start over."

"Don't be silly," Brenda said.

"Besides, to do that, I'd have to move. Couldn't make a go of just a bakery around here, which is why I opened a restaurant. Not that that was such a good idea either."

Brenda brightened. "I have a great idea. I know the perfect place. It's on the highway about fifty miles from here. It's not much. It's a gas station right now. It doesn't need to be a gas station. Plenty of them around, but there's no bakery for a hundred miles. It comes with a trailer. Nothing fancy, mind you, but it would do. You got a wife?"

Richard shook his head. "No. She left me 15 years ago."

"Then it would be perfect. Plenty of traffic. You'd get lots of business. It would need a little work, but I bet you could get it for cheap." She wrote something on a napkin. "This is the guy who owns it. You tell him you want to buy it. He'll be happy to get it off his hands. But don't let him cheat you. The place isn't worth nearly as much as he's going to ask for it. You hold your line. He'll come around. Especially if you offer him cash."

"Cash? Where am I going to get cash?"

"From selling this place to me," I said. I had finished the burger and took a bite of Art's pie. It was good. Very, very good. I took the plate away from him.

Richard watched my face as I enthusiastically downed his pie. Then he glanced at Brenda. "You really think I could make a go of it?"

"Oh, yeah."

He drummed his fingers on the table. His lips twitched so hard his mustache bounced. Finally, he slapped his hand on the table. "I'll do it." Then he sobered. "How much you gonna give me for this place?"

"How much do you want?" I countered.

He looked heavenward as if the figure might appear on the ceiling. "A hundred thousand."

I coughed, sending bits of pie crust flying. Brenda kicked me. When I stopped coughing, I considered it. I had plenty of money. What did I care? But I didn't want him to know that. If I'd said yes right away, he'd kick himself for the rest of his life, thinking he should have asked for more, so I said, "That's a bit much, don't you think? I'll give you seventy-five."

"Make it eighty-five."

Brenda said, "Do you have a house here?"

Richard nodded. "A pretty nice house, too."

"What's it worth?" Brenda asked.

He gazed ceiling-ward again. "In this town? I dunno. Forty, fifty thousand."

"So, throw in the house and the business and I'll give you $125,000." I was feeling generous.

"Make it $130,000 and you got a deal."

Brenda turned to me. "What do you think, Elliot?"

I sighed. I thought I was being taken big time, but as I said, what did I care? It wasn't my money. "Okay. If you leave the furniture and all the equipment in the diner."

"Sure," Richard said, grinning so broadly the tips of his mustache nearly reached his ears. "But I got a few things in the house that are family heirlooms. Mind if I take those?"

I didn't. "Take whatever you want."

Not my money, I reminded myself. Not my life.

I was on a roll.

~43~

Art and I spent the night camped out in Richard's living room, while Brenda moved right into the guest room.

The next day, Richard gave us the rundown on the diner. Brenda gave him the keys to the trailer and the gas station, and I gave him a whack of cash. He was gone by mid-afternoon, scurrying out of town like a rat off a sinking ship.

"You really think he's going to buy that place?" I asked Brenda.

"Does it matter?"

I thought about it. "No, I suppose not."

Especially if bombs were going to start falling soon. Maybe he'd go to Vegas and have a good time before the world ended. Fine by me. Truthfully, I felt jealous.

Brenda and I sat up half the night making menu plans and ordering supplies. Fortunately, the Internet stretched even to Jackknife, Montana.

Cable TV, however, did not, but we had a satellite dish, which—thankfully—kept Art amused and out of our hair.

"Are you sure he's all right?" Brenda asked. The only part of Art that had moved for three hours was his thumb as he flicked the remote.

"He's fine." Not that I had a clue, but I thought I should keep up the front.

"Where did you find him?" she asked, as if he was a badly behaved but oh-so-loveable stray puppy.

"I found him on my doorstep. One thing led to another, and here we are." It was, sadly, all true.

"He's housebroken, I hope?" A puppy, indeed.

"Completely." More or less.

Brenda went to bed a little after midnight. I was tired, but not looking forward to sleeping in someone else's bed until I had washed all the bedding. And what was I supposed to do with Art? He didn't sleep, even when he was more Artful. What if he got out of the house during the night? Someone might think he was a cougar or a bear and shoot him. Not that it would matter since he was already dead, but people might talk.

Fortunately, he remained happily glued to the television, watching *Wheel of Fortune* reruns in six different time zones, and didn't seem inclined to move.

I slept on the couch.

The next morning, Brenda was up bright and early.

And I mean BRIGHT AND FREAKING EARLY.

She did, however, make damn good coffee, so I forgave her.

Somewhat.

"Come on," she said, practically pulling me out the door. "We have work to do."

"Art—"

Art was still staring at the TV. He looked up briefly, flashed Brenda a mechanical grin, and went back to *The Price is Right*, eastern time zone.

"He'll be fine. Besides, it's not like he can go very far."

Nevertheless, I left him with Putin curled up beside him. Let the cat babysit. He could do as good a job as I could.

The first thing we did was take a tour of the town. It didn't take long.

"There's something weird about this place," Brenda said.

"No kidding."

But she was right. There was something weird about it. Maybe it was the dilapidated condition of the buildings. Or the old-fashioned wooden sidewalks that clattered under our footsteps. Or the way the wind whistled between the buildings, sounding like a demented, love-sick train. Or the odd smell, like grandma's attic, worn and moldy, redolent with the scent of cedar, tinged with a hint of copper.

"You don't suppose they eat their young, do you?" Brenda asked.

We hadn't seen any children, so I gave the thought far more weight than one might expect.

The main street was maybe four blocks long. Businesses included a bar, a grocery store, a drug store, a hardware store, a dry goods store. And, to my surprise, a weekly newspaper: The Jackknife *Oracle*. Published every Wednesday, if God be willing and the creeks don't rise. (It said so, right on the front window.)

Brenda pointed to a mountain range east of town. "I bet there are all kinds of abandoned mines up there just waiting for some enterprising millennial with newfangled equipment to find the mother lode."

"God help them," I muttered, but I had to admit it would be a good place to house an end-of-the-world bunker.

Silhouetted against the mountains was a tall church spire. I insisted we investigate. Brenda sighed mightily. "It's just a church. I'm sure they're a dime a dozen around here."

But they weren't. I hadn't seen any other churches in town. "Come on," I said. "Humor me."

It was a beautiful morning for a walk. The air was crisp, the sun bright and dappled through the foliage. The walk was pleasant, so Brenda relaxed. I, on the other hand, got more anxious the closer we got to the lone church spire.

We walked three blocks through a residential area, consisting of small, mid-century bungalows, separated with the requisite white picket fences, most of which were badly in need of paint and a few nails. The neighborhood was eerily quiet, not even a barking dog to announce our passage. There were no birds. No cats. No squirrels. No people. No moving cars.

The closer we got to the church, the heavier the silence got. We left off our discussion of the lunch menu in mid-sentence and now the only thing to mark our passage was the shuffling of our feet and our breathing.

At some point, Brenda reached out and took my arm, for which I was grateful.

And then we were there, standing in front of *it*.

~44~

*It* stood at the end of the block, at the very edge of town, sitting on an expanse of bare dirt, with nothing around it, not even a tree. At first glance, it looked like any other late-nineteenth-century Protestant church build in the Wild West—a tall, stately wooden structure, painted white, with a graceful roof and a bell tower, culminating in a tall spire.

But there was something odd about this building, this "church." Something dark and heavy. And wrong. I slowed down and approached it with the wariness of prey sensing a predator.

Brenda felt it, too, judging by the pressure she exerted on my arm. Then, as we circled around the building, she let out a little gasp. "There are no windows. Shouldn't there be windows?"

She was right. Where you might have expected a row of arched windows, with or without stained glass, there was nothing. Either they had all been removed and the spaces expertly filled, or they had never existed.

Who builds a church without windows? Or doors.

That was the other thing. There didn't seem to be a way in. Or out.

There was a sign in front of the church, but we had to get up close and personal to read it:

**Restored Missionary Evangelical Gospel Church
of the Sacred Order of Anarchy.
By invitation only.**

## All others be damned.

"I guess missionary work isn't really their forte," Brenda said, suppressing a nervous giggle.

There was more writing on the sign, but I had to get even closer to read it: *Rev. Peter Knutson, Founder and Curator.* "Curator? That's a little odd, don't you think?"

Brenda shrugged. "I guess if you're the founder, you can call yourself anything you want."

At the very bottom of the sign, written in small letters and covered in a layer of dirt, was this final bit of welcome: *Trespassers will be shot.*

"So much for peace and love," Brenda said.

I got up and brushed the dirt off my knees. "Yeah, well, from what I understand of the good Rev, peace and love ain't his style. He's more the doom and gloom and hellfire-be-praised kind of preacher."

"What do you think is really inside that building? I refuse to call it a church." Brenda's usually pleasant face had taken on a stormy countenance.

I had a few thoughts on the subject, but I summed them up as "Nothing good."

I could tell Brenda was thinking about breaking in. I could see it in the way she tightened her jaw and squared her shoulders, the way she narrowed her eyes and tensed her muscles.

I grabbed her hand. "No. We need to walk away. Trust me on this. Besides, there's no way in."

"There has to be." She held her ground.

"I don't think this is all there is."

That gave her pause. "You're right. They have a compound somewhere. Somewhere up in those mountains." We both automatically raised our eyes to scan the peaks behind the church spire. "I've heard rumors about it. I'm not sure I ever believed them to be anything but a bunch of harmless wackos. Until now. This place is too strange."

A breeze sprung up, turning into a gust that stirred the fine dirt around us into tiny tornadoes, and bringing with it, the sickly-sweet smell of decay.

"Brenda, we need to leave." I spoke calmly, although I was

far from feeling calm. I had to swallow hard multiple times to keep from retching. I pulled on her hand gently but firmly until she finally looked away.

"Yes," she said. "We should go."

We walked briskly, poised to run if anything came after us. We didn't slow down until we reached Main Street. A police car pulled alongside us.

"Hey, there," a cop called through the open passenger window. He gestured us to come closer. "You new in town?"

I nodded and introduced myself and Brenda. "We're taking over the diner."

The cop gave us his best welcoming glare. "What happened to Richard?"

"He left town yesterday," I said.

"Kind of sudden," the cop said.

I shrugged. "I made him an offer he couldn't refuse."

The cop didn't laugh. He didn't even crack a smile. He looked as though he was going right down to the courthouse to get a search warrant to make sure we hadn't chopped up good ol' Rich and stuffed him in the freezer. "You got some paperwork to that effect?"

"Sure do," I said, grinning pleasantly. "He sold us his house, too. In case you're wondering."

"Umph," he said. Then he rolled up his window and drove on.

"I'm going to love this town," Brenda said.

I noted her sarcasm and concurred.

$\sim$45$\sim$

In the bright light of early morning, the diner wasn't as bad as I had first thought. Yeah, it needed some work, mostly cleaning, but it was functional. Brenda walked around, poking into corners, and under things—never a good idea, in my opinion—and made copious notes while I checked out the kitchen.

It was in surprisingly good shape, which meant we could be up and running in no time.

By now, it was close to ten and I was starving. "I need food."

Brenda reached into her purse and tossed me a couple of granola bars. I grunted my thanks. "Come on," she said a few minutes later. "Let's get back to the house. We have some more orders to send."

By now, there were people on the street. Not many, mind you. Just a few, here and there.

They stopped in their tracks and took us in, openly staring as if we had two heads each. Their expressions were blank and cold; not quite hostile, more like the look you give the monkeys in the zoo. They responded to our "hi, there" and friendly smiles with expressions bordering on consternation. *("Did you see that, Martha? They spoke to us. In English." "Oh, no, dear. You must be mistaken. Speak? Impossible.")*

"Are we that odd?"

"You certainly are," she countered.

True enough. True enough.

~46~

I don't know what kind of magic Brenda wielded, but by that afternoon the supplies she ordered started to trickle in, one truckload at a time.

I expressed amazement at the quick delivery. "I told you I had connections," Brenda said.

By the end of the day, we had a fully functioning kitchen and the place had been thoroughly cleaned.

Then we got busy in the kitchen. I made up a batch of Brenda's grandmother's chili.

It wasn't all that great.

"I don't understand it,' Brenda said. "She won the chili contest at the state fair six straight years in a row with that recipe. They finally made her retire."

"Needs a dash of chocolate," Art said, out of the blue. He sat in the corner, playing games on Brenda's phone. "Or maybe Dr. Pepper." He looked up and stared at something in the ether. "Yeah. Dr. Pepper. And chocolate. The good kind."

Brenda brightened immediately and headed for the fridge.

"You can't be serious," I said.

"Grandma always hinted there was a secret ingredient. Maybe that was it. She did love her Dr. Pepper."

"And chocolate?"

She shrugged. "Mexicans use chocolate in their cooking, don't they? So why the hell not?"

"I'm not Mexican," I started to say and then shut up. Hector could be a little defensive; Elliot, on the other hand, couldn't give a worm-bitten pignut.

We didn't stop with chili, of course. I added a few of my favorite Cuban dishes—*empanadas, tamales, ropa vieja*, things I had grown up eating in my grandmother's kitchen. Brenda insisted on shepherd's pie, another of her grandmother's recipes, and pork ribs, basted in her grandmother's barbecue sauce, that was so good I wept with pleasure.

Oh, yeah—we were on a roll.

While Brenda and I were having fun in the kitchen, Art sat perched on a stool, sometimes peeling potatoes, sometimes staring blankly into space and grinning stupidly.

"Are you sure he's safe?" Brenda asked.

"Yes," I lied.

Time was running out to save the world. With Art out of commission, I had no idea what to do about it. The spire of the Restored Missionary Church cast a long shadow. Brenda assumed my anxiety was because we were opening our doors the following afternoon, just in time for lunch.

"Either we succeed, or we don't," she said. "If we don't, it won't be the end of the world."

Easy for her to say. She was blessed with ignorance. I was tempted to tell her everything, but the thing was, I liked Brenda. I couldn't do that to her. Besides, what were the chances she'd think I was crazy, and she'd run for the hills? I needed her, especially with Art on the fritz.

"Relax. Don't worry," she said, patting my shoulder. "I've got this covered. I have connections. Remember?"

I nodded vaguely as I pulled a batch of Cuban bread out of the oven with one hand while stirring a batch of *arroz con leche* with the other.

On the other side of the kitchen, Brenda made buttermilk biscuits. We would look up from time to time, catch each other's eye, and lapse into fits of the giggles.

The bread, to my intense pleasure, came out perfectly: golden brown and nicely rounded. My mouth watered at the thought of an honest-to-god Cuban sandwich, piled high with slices of thin ham, a staple of my previous life, followed by a heaping serving of rice pudding. I forgot all about Art and the end of the world for a few moments. At least we'd be well-fed when the end came.

I put the sandwiches together while the *plancha* (which conveniently had arrived that very afternoon) heated, humming to myself while Brenda snapped a few pictures with her phone. Even Art paused in his vacantness and gave me his full attention—for about ten seconds.

I slipped the sandwiches into the heated press and did a little dance while I waited, which made Brenda snort. "You really are something," she said, with a note of fondness I found touching.

"Wait until you taste this," I said. "Then you'll know what something is."

If I could have frozen any moment in time, it would have been the moment I took my first bite, followed by the moment I watched Brenda take her first bite, her eyes wide and bright with pleasure, and Art's first smile in days.

"Where did you learn how to cook all this Cuban food?" Brenda asked.

"You like it?"

"It's amazing."

I beamed with satisfaction. "I grew up in Miami." She nodded, as if that explained everything, including any latent weirdness.

Then I tasted Brenda's rich, tender biscuits, dripping with butter and honey—all I can say is if they don't serve them in heaven, I don't want to go.

Oh yeah. The golden moments of life; fleeting and too few. When you have them, cherish them. Because you never know when all hell is going to break loose.

It didn't take long to garner some attention from the locals, not any of it good.

First, there were the phone calls: "Go home, fag." "We don't want no fags here." "Take a hike, bum lover." "You gonna burn in hell, fag boy, and I'm gonna light the match."

Then there were eggs and tomatoes hurled at the front window. That was more troublesome because we had to clean up the mess.

And then there were the notes slipped under the door, like shiny bits of glitter fluttering down from heaven. "You're dead, fag head" was my favorite because it rhymed, although the meter was a little off.

Apparently, no matter what I looked like on the outside, my fagginess still shined through. I didn't know whether to be pleased or annoyed. Pleased because, well, why shouldn't I be? It's who I am. Annoyed because, well, it was distracting.

"Is it really that obvious?" I asked Brenda when, once again, I was cleaning egg off the front window.

She sucked in a deep breath, gave me a thorough, thoughtful (and frank) appraisal. "Yeah, honey. It is."

"Well, fuck them," I said sharply.

"Amen," Brenda said, a slight smile twitching at her lips. And then, all traces of mirth vanished. "Maybe you should call the police."

That made me snort and roll my eyes. "What do you think Officer Friendly would do?"

She thought about that for a moment and then sighed. "Probably advise you to leave town before things get ugly."

"Well, I'm not going." Screw them. Screw them all. This could be my last stand and I wasn't bailing.

Brenda patted my back. "Good for you. I'm with you all the way, kiddo."

As if to illustrate my resolve to stand my ground, I went into the kitchen and whipped up a batch of brownies. Extra chewy.

Brenda joined me and made more of her killer barbecue sauce.

While we worked, Art sat in the corner, mumbling to himself. Every so often, he'd cut loose with a gale of demonic laughter. It was freaky as hell. Twice, he startled me so badly, I cut myself.

The question is why didn't I run away, head for the hills, go on one final hedonistic fling or, better yet, climb into bed and pull the covers over my head?

Damned if I know.

Maybe I'm one of those fools who never gives up hope of winning until the ref blows the final whistle, or checks the losing lottery ticket twice, just to be sure.

Maybe I was content sailing down Denial River.

Who knows? Maybe I was too worried about the Big Threat to worry about the little ones.

Truthfully, I was having fun. I didn't want to go anywhere, so there I stayed, cooking my puny heart out as though I had to get everything I could baked, steamed, boiled, broiled, sautéed, stewed, poached, roasted, fried, creamed, and fricasseed before THE END came. In case there was a party and people actually came.

Being in the kitchen, cranking out one dish after the other, made me happier than I had been in years. For once, I wasn't thinking about the life I'd left behind. Screw Hector. He was a nobody.

While we were busy in the kitchen, Putin was busy reducing the local mice and rat population. The only problem with that was he'd drop his catch as offerings at the back door. We found the latest when we left that afternoon: a nice plump rat with shiny black eyes. I did a little dance while Brenda calmly picked it up by the tail and studied it.

"That's strange." She dangled it in my face while I stuffed my fingers in my mouth to keep from shrieking.

"What?"

"It looks like it's got eggshell stuck in its fur."

"So, it got into some eggs. That's not so strange."

"Hmm—" She eyed Putin, who was giving himself a nonchalant touch-up licking, as innocent as pie. "Just what kind of cat are you, anyway?"

Putin paused mid-lick and looked at her, his gold eyes bright and steady. Then, I kid you not, he winked at her.

"Why, you little devil," she said.

Oh, lord, I thought—not you, too?

~48~

That night, I couldn't sleep. I couldn't even stay in bed. I got up and paced in the tiny bedroom, finally tromping into the living room where Art sat staring dully at the television. Putin sprawled beside him, one paw resting protectively on Art's leg.

I got some milk and a handful of Oreos from the kitchen and then sat down across from Art. "What are you watching?"

His eyes flickered vaguely in my direction, but he didn't answer. I studied the television. Some old black and white courtroom drama with over the top dramatic background music.

"We need to talk." I offered him a cookie. He glanced at me as though I had offered him a slug. I snatched it back. "Sorry," I mumbled. I forgot he was off food. "But seriously. We need to talk."

I gently took the remote from his hand and turned off the television. That got a reaction. A sharp intake of breath and a glare.

Progress.

"Art—" I cupped his face, so he had to look at me. "We really need to talk."

He blinked a few times. "So, talk."

I jumped. "Art?"

"What? Hurry up. I'm going to miss the ending. I think Perry's really up a creek this time."

"Art?" I studied him carefully. His eyes glowed a soft red. Was he coming back? "What's going on?"

"What do you mean?"

"Is the world still going to end?"

"Of course."

"When?"

His eyes rolled upward and then popped back into place. "Four days."

I considered questioning his math, but then thought better of it. Four days was more than I expected. I'd take it. "Unless we can stop it."

Again, with the upward eye-roll. "Yes."

"Can we stop it?"

"The odds are about fifty-fifty, but you don't need me. You got this covered." His eyes lost their red glare and his face went slack. Then he took the remote from me and turned the television back on.

Putin stood up and stretched, made a complete circle and settled down again, his back to me.

"A lot of help you are," I mumbled, stuffing the last cookie in my mouth. Putin dismissed me with a sharp flick of his tail. Like he gave a rat's ass.

While my conversation with Art had been brief and not very helpful, it did give me hope that he hadn't completely lost his mind. That, plus a stomach full of Oreos and milk, and I was finally able to fall asleep.

It was a weird sleep, though, filled with all kinds of strange rattles and rumblings, eerie hums and unearthly groans. But no dreams. None that I could remember, anyway.

I awoke at 5:30 to hear Brenda rattling around in the kitchen. She handed me coffee as I staggered out of my room. I drank two cups before I went to get Art. He was ready for me, dressed in a clean shirt and pants. And he wore a tie, which made him look more like the dapper demon I had first encountered. When was that? Two weeks ago? Three? Four? I didn't know anymore. I had lost the ability to measure time, although I was well aware of its current weight pressing against me, driving me into a future I did not want.

I was pleased to see no one had egged the restaurant overnight. Everything was the way we left it. I took that as a good omen.

I got to work in the kitchen, prepping for the lunch crowd. Crowd? Who was I kidding?

"You'll need more than that," Brenda said, surveying the lettuce I had torn up for salads.

"Your optimism is appreciated, Brenda, but you don't really

think that many people are going to show up, do you?"

She shrugged and gave me a tiny smile. "I got connections, remember?" And then she sauntered off to do ... something.

I tore up another head of lettuce. Just one. All I could think about was the cost if it was all for nothing.

By eleven, Brenda was bouncing with excitement. Even Art was perkier than usual. I was so nervous I thought I was going to throw up. My hands shook continuously.

Brenda gave me a once-over when she came into the kitchen. "Take a break. You look like you could use one."

"And do what? Pace? Staying busy is better, believe me."

"Go into the dining room and take a look out the window." She was grinning, full Cheshire-cat mode. So, I washed my hands, took off my apron, and traipsed through the dining room.

I paused to look around. Brenda had done a fine job of making it look nice; comfortable, homey; even—dare I use the word? Pretty.

The woman was a gift from God (yes, I noted the irony and smiled). I couldn't have gotten this far without her. I made a mental note to give her a bonus.

Then I got close enough to the window to see outside, and gasped. There was a line of people standing along the sidewalk. A long line of people. All chatting and laughing and looking eager.

What were they doing out there?

Then I got it.

Oh, yeah. I got it.

I nearly hyperventilated myself into a dead faint.

"Breathe," Brenda said, catching up to me and grasping me by the shoulders. "Nice and slow."

"I should have cut up more lettuce. Maybe I should—"

She held me in place. "Too late. It's almost 11:30. Shall we open the door and let in our customers?"

Hell, yes.

~49~

I had never been so busy, or so blissfully happy, or so run off my feet. It was agonizing and amazing, and probably the best day of my life.

The food was a hit. People raved about the chili, the ribs, the *ropa vieja*. Especially the chili. They couldn't seem to get enough. We had to make several more batches to keep up with the demand. They even liked the rice pudding. They asked for seconds of the brownies and ice cream. They sang our praises, kept calling me out of the kitchen so they could take my picture and shake my hand and pat me on the back.

And then, as quickly as they had come, they were gone, and we were alone.

I sat down for the first time in hours. "How did you do it?" I asked Brenda. I had no doubt this had been her doing. More people had come through our doors that afternoon than lived in the town of Jackknife, possibly the entire county. Maybe even the entire state of Montana.

She shrugged. "I told you I had connections."

She offered no further explanations, being the consummate woman of mystery, as I was coming to see her. I was too content to press her.

But what if that was it? What if that was all there was? "Will they be back tomorrow?"

"In spades," she replied. "You might want to think about hiring some help."

Hire help? I glanced around the kitchen. Art was happily doing dishes, but the place was looking far less pristine than it had a few hours earlier. "Good idea. Should I put a sign in the window?"

"Don't bother. I already hired two people, one for the kitchen and one to wait on tables. We'll probably need more but it's a start."

I gazed at her in amazement. "Brenda, I think I love you."

She tilted back her head and laughed. "Oh, honey, that's the sweetest thing anyone's said to me in years." Then she pinched my cheeks and ruffled what was left of my hair. "I love you, too, baby cakes."

It was a fine, fine moment. All that love and goodwill.

We were only open for lunch, which meant we were closed by three. That gave us plenty of time to get ready for the next day and not kill ourselves in the process.

When the last of the dishes were done, and the prep for the next day completed, we lingered over a pot of tea and leftover scones.

Art stood up abruptly. "I'm going for a walk."

I was too tired and too full of blackberry scones—Brenda's contribution—to do more than wave at him. "Don't get lost." As if he could.

By the time we left, the sun was down, but the twilight lingered. It was still and warm and so quiet I was tempted to make a little noise just to take the edge off. "Were there any locals here today?"

Brenda wrinkled her face. "Locals?"

"Yeah. You know, people from the town."

"I don't know. Does it matter? We had an amazing first day." she said. "Anyway, it's kind of hard to know for sure."

True. We'd hadn't been in town long enough to know a lot of people, but we'd been tramping up and down the street, passing people on the way to the hardware store and the market. "Did you see anyone you recognized from the town?"

"No," she said after a moment. "I don't think I did. Maybe they'll come tomorrow."

I wasn't so sure. "So, where did all those people come from?"

She shrugged. "I put the word out. I told you—"

"You have connections. Yeah, I know." I wanted to believe

her, just like I wanted to believe everything was going to be okay, but I was nervous. Not the nervousness of opening the restaurant, but something else; something vaguely disquieting I couldn't put my finger on. Like this was all too good to be true kind of nervousness.

She took me by the arm. "Don't worry, Elliot. Everything's going to be fine."

I wanted to believe her, so I smiled and tossed my head with firm resolution. "Of course, it is."

I gave her a quick hug. "Thanks for your help, Brenda. You're an angel, you know."

"Well, I wouldn't go that far," she said, laughing.

Art wasn't in the house when we got home, but Putin was there, hovering over his food dish with an entitled air of expectation.

"You are the bossiest cat I have ever known," I told him, as I scooped food into his dish.

*Meow.*

"How did you ever get along without me?"

*Meee-owww.* He nudged my hand and I gave him an extra helping.

Brenda went to her room, so I turned on the television, even though I wasn't interested in watching it. I needed some noise and something to distract me. I felt oddly deflated, like Christmas morning had come and gone, and I'd opened all my presents. I had my very own restaurant. Dreams do come true. So why was I so glum?

*Because the world is going to end in three days, you idiot.*

Well, yes, there was that.

~50~

I fell asleep in front of the television. I woke up at midnight with a start when Putin jumped on me and proceeded to lick my face. I tried to fend him off, but he wasn't easily deterred. "What's wrong with you?"

He let out a long, plaintive meow, ending it with a slight rise that made it sound like a question. "Do you want out?"

*Meow.* Strong emphasis on the *ow*. I opened the door and he zoomed out, furry little lightening-beast that he was. I stepped out on the porch and took in the night air—clean, pure, a hint of moisture, scented with pine and roses. For a moment, a single, tiny heartbeat of a moment, I let the universe wrap itself around me and hold me.

A word of advice: treasure those moments; they are all too fleeting.

Then it occurred to me—Art had not returned.

I made a quick tour of the house. Brenda was in her room, sleeping; I could hear her snoring. Everything was calm and in its place, but there was no trace of Art.

Had he buggered off and left me? Had he had a change of plans? Had I imagined him? Or had he simply wandered off and gotten lost? I grabbed a flashlight and went looking for him.

I met up with Putin, who paused in his pursuit of small furry things to regard me with a sharp, impatient snap of his tail. "Do you know where he is?"

*Meow.* He took off and I followed.

He led me to the end of the block, around the corner, across

212

several lawns, past a rusted pickup and an abandoned refrigerator, and then over a broken chain-link fence, and finally into a field of tall grass, at which point my flashlight sputtered and died, leaving me in breath-stealing darkness. "Fuck." I stumbled over a rock. "Fuckity-fuck-fuck."

"Don't swear," came a voice out of the grass.

"Art?"

"Who else would it be?"

I stumbled forward until I fell over him, landing face-first in a pile of cut grass. I sneezed. "What are you doing out here?"

"Shut up. Shut up and look up."

I rolled onto my back and gazed upward. I gasped at the sight of an entire sky crowded with little flickering suns—little portals into ancient history, worlds upon worlds, kingdoms come and gone. "Wow."

"Yeah," Art said. "Wow."

"You okay, Art?"

"No. Not really. I'm not sure it's possible for me to be okay."

A shooting star streaked across the sky, leaving trails of sharp little sparks. "What's wrong?" Something was wrong. I could feel it.

It was a minute or two before he answered. "You have any regrets, Hector?"

I choked back surprise. Art, introspective? "Of course. Doesn't everyone?"

"What? What do you regret?"

The question brought me up short. His tone suggested he was serious. He really wanted to know, so I dug deep. "I regret never knowing my father. My grandmother said he was an asshole, and maybe he was, but I wish I could know for myself."

"Would you like to meet him? I could arrange it."

That brought me up short. "He's dead."

"No, he's not. He's very much alive. He owns a used car dealership in Battle Mountain, Nevada. Otto's Auto Barn."

"My grandmother and mother told me he was dead."

"They lied."

I let that sink in. "Why?"

"Why does anyone lie about things like that?"

Why, indeed? "You can really introduce me?"

"Just say the word."

I struggled to wrap my head about the revelation that a man I had always assumed dead was, in fact, alive and breathing and living in Nevada, of all places. What would I say to him? Would I shake his hand or punch him in the nose?

"I don't know. Let me think about it."

"Your call, but you're running out of time, so don't think about it too much," he said. "What else? That can't be your only regret."

It wasn't. "I regret that my mother was crazy. It kind of messed me up. I regret that I will probably never be a father, not that that's the end of the world." I let out a sharp laugh at that. "But I think I would have been a damn good one."

"Times are changing, Hector. It's not outside the realm of possibility."

"I suppose." I wasn't convinced, but I was on a roll now. "I never finished reading the Harry Potter books. And I've never been to Italy. Or France." Or anywhere, for that matter, until Art showed up. "I've always wanted to travel."

"It's overrated."

"Maybe." But I didn't think so. "Mostly, I regret never falling in love."

"Ah, that." We shared a long, collective sigh over that one.

"What about you, Art? What do you regret?"

"Don't get me started." He let out a sharp bark of laughter. Then he sighed. "I regret doing evil things to good people. Evil things to evil people—not a problem. That's fun. But bad things to good people … it gets to you after a while."

"So, stop."

"Can't. I signed a contract. I'm in it for the long haul."

"Contracts can be renegotiated. Maybe there's a loophole."

"Not in this one. Trust me, I've tried. It's airtight."

For a while, we laid side by side, staring up at the stars. Then the cold started to seep in, so I sat up, shaking stray bits of grass from my shoulders. "Do I still have to kill Waterman?"

"Pretty much."

"How? I mean, it's not like he's going show up on my doorstep …" I laughed, but my laughter quickly trailed off. "Is he?"

Art said nothing.

I stood up quickly. "I'm going home. It's late. I need to sleep.

You coming?"

"In a little while. You go ahead."

I gave my flashlight a shake and it flickered and then lit, making me blink at the sudden brightness. "If you're sure."

"Yeah, I'm sure. I'll be fine." And then, "Hector?"

"Yeah?"

"You're a good guy, you know. One of the best."

How does one take a compliment from a demon? I looked for irony, for sarcasm, for a hidden meaning. For the lie. I found none of those things. "Thanks," I said, and I pointed the beam toward town and started walking. I didn't look back.

As I walked toward the house, I sensed movement all around me: the rustling of leaves; the scurrying of small creatures; heavy breathing.

By the time I turned the corner to our house, I was in a half-run. Home. I had to get home.

And then I hit a wall.

I came up short, nearly toppling to the ground as I struggled for balance.

My flashlight caught the glow of two malevolent eyes.

Someone screamed.

Okay, I screamed.

It was me. I admit it.

The eyes blinked. It was the blink of exasperation.

It was only Putin, crouched on top of the mailbox in front of our little house.

He jumped off, assured of my attention, and walked up to the front door, which was standing wide open. *Hello, world. Come on in.* I took in a sharp breath. I was certain I had closed the door when I left.

I paused, listening for sounds that an intruder was present. Nothing. "Brenda?"

She answered with a low, guttural moan and I shot through the doorway, into the living room, frantically searching the darkness with the flashlight.

I found her in the opening between the living room and the kitchen, sprawled face down on the floor. I fought back the cold rush of panic and scrambled to find the light switch.

I dropped beside her, checking her pulse. She shuttered when

I touched her. "Brenda, it's me. You're going to be all right. I got you."

She groaned again, but there was more substance, more force. "Elliot ...." She struggled to raise her head.

"Hold still. Don't move." I put my hand on her back to comfort her, to hold her in place.

Think. Think. *Think.*

I couldn't lift her. She out-weighed me by at least fifty pounds, which was saying something, given my current configuration. Was there a doctor in town? An ambulance? Anything? Anyone who could help?

*Breathe, you moon-maggot ....*

"I have to get help." I spoke right into her ear as if that would make her understand why I had to leave her. "I'll be right back. Don't try to move."

There were three houses in a neat row across the street that looked like they might be occupied.

My foot crashed through a step at the first house. Still, I knocked. I pounded. I tried the door. Locked.

At the second house, I thought I heard voices. And the cocking of a gun. I backed away.

By the time I got to the third house, I was hyperventilating.

I pounded on the door. "Please," I called out. "I need help. My friend's been hurt."

"Nobody lives there," came a voice from behind me. I jumped and let out a little scream as I turned. Standing in the middle of the street was a kid, maybe 12 or 13, leaning on a bicycle.

"I need help. Do you know anyone who could help me? My friend fell and hurt herself. I can't move her."

He came to the sidewalk, walking his bike. His movements were slow and easy. Calming. "I can help you."

"She's a big woman."

The kid weighed next to nothing. "I'm pretty strong."

"Don't you know anyone else? Your dad, maybe?"

"My dad's busy. Come on. Show me."

Reluctantly, I led him to Brenda. When we got to her, she had pulled herself into a half-sitting position.

I reached out to her. "I told you not to move."

She waved my concern away with a jerky sweep of her hand.

"I'm fine. Just a little dizzy. Help me up, will you?"

Between us, the kid and I managed to get her standing and then led her into the bedroom and helped her onto the bed. "Thanks," she mumbled. She closed her eyes and let out a long, slow groan.

"You should keep an eye on her." The kid didn't look as though he trusted me to have much common sense. "In case she has a concussion."

I assured him I would. "What's your name?"

"Wilvor. Wilvor Parrish."

"Nice to meet you, Wilvor." I offered my hand, which he shook with impeccable grace, albeit without much enthusiasm. "You live around here?"

"Where else would I live?"

I liked the kid's style. "You live with your parents?"

"Just my father." He gazed at me with a half-opened eye. Trying to assess how much to share? "My mother's dead."

He said it casually, as if it was old news, so I just nodded. "You're out kind of late, aren't you?"

He shrugged. "I do what I want. My dad don't care."

Now, why was that? Booze? Lack of parenting skills? Or were children considered adults at 13 around here? Maybe the guy was simply an asshole. Poor kid. "You want a job?"

His eyes lit up. "A job? I'm just a kid."

"Can you wash dishes? Bus tables?"

"I guess. You the guy that took over the diner?"

"Yeah, that's me."

He nodded thoughtfully. Little flickers of hope danced in his doubtful eyes, and then, defeat. "No, I better not."

"How come?"

He studied his feet. "You're an outsider. We don't trust outsiders."

"We?"

"My dad. He says strangers don't got the Light in them."

"The light?"

"Yeah, you know. The Light." He gave me another one of those looks: head tilted; one eye closed.

The Light. Yeah, I got it. "Pity. We could use the help. If you change your mind, let me know."

"I'll think about it."

"In the meantime, if you're hungry, just come to the kitchen."

"Really?" He perked up at that. "I smelled something good coming from there today."

"Must have been the chili."

"I like chili. My dad can't cook. The only chili I get comes out of a can." Then he frowned. "But I can't pay you."

"No problem. A bowl of chili here and there won't bankrupt us."

"But I should pay."

"Consider yourself our unofficial taster. Any new dishes, you'll get to try first. You can tell me if something needs more salt."

"Or garlic?" He was grinning again.

"Definitely." This was my kind of kid. "Our way of thanking you for helping us out tonight."

That satisfied him. And me, too.

~51~

After Wilvor left, I checked on Brenda. "Nice kid," she said. "Where did you find him?"

"On the street, but I think he found me." I sat down on the bed beside her. "What happened? Did you slip on something?"

She shook her head and made a face. "No. Someone ambushed me. By the time I was aware that someone was in the house, it was too late. They cracked me over the head."

"Why would someone come in here?" I wasn't really asking a question. I was thinking out loud.

"They were probably looking for all that cash you got stashed in here. You really should put that shit in the bank."

"You know about that?" More importantly, how would someone else know?

She gave me a look, a *buddy, I love you, but Lord in Heaven, you're stupid* look. "The living room's a mess and someone's been through all the drawers." She pointed toward the dresser. Someone indeed had searched through it and hadn't been very subtle about it.

I hadn't noticed the living room, so I stepped out of the bedroom to look. Sure enough, things were turned upside down. Even the kitchen had been ransacked. They'd gotten into my room, too. My duffel bag was lying in the middle of the floor. Someone had turned it upside down. Fortunately, I had removed the cash and hidden it. I checked my hiding place. All the money was still there. The relief brought tears to my eyes.

"They sure made a mess," I said, coming back to Brenda,

"but they didn't get the cash."

Brenda tried to smile but the best she could manage was a wince. "That's a relief. See if you can find my purse."

I found it in the kitchen, beside the back door. It hadn't been touched. Brenda would have had it with her when she came home. Maybe they didn't notice it on their way out.

I made her tea and dug through her purse, with her permission, for a couple of Tylenols. "You should try and get some sleep."

"As if—" But she sighed and turned on her side and pulled the blanket across her shoulders. "Did you find Art?"

"Yes."

"Is he all right?"

"I think so."

She yawned. "Good. Leave the hall light on, will you?"

$\sim$52$\sim$

The smell of coffee woke me up in the morning. I showered first, thought about shaving—I really hated the facial hair, but as I studied Elliot's face in the mirror, I realized he had scars on the right side of his face. Burns, maybe. No wonder he had resorted to facial hair. The scars looked vicious.

By the time I got to the kitchen, Brenda had the coffee already poured and breakfast on the table. She looked like crap. "You should be in bed," I told her.

"I can't stay in bed. I'm not made that way. Just say thanks."

"Thanks." And I meant it. The eggs were perfect. "How's your head?'

"It hurts like hell," she admitted.

"You're staying here today."

She dismissed me with a sharp gesture. "Not a chance. You need me."

"I'll be fine. I doubt we'll be as busy. And didn't you say you hired a couple of people to help out?"

She nodded, and then grimaced, a hand going to brace her head. "Yeah. But they won't know what to do."

"We'll manage. You stay put. Rest. That's an order." I was firm; I might even have glowered a little. Hector was never very good at being firm, but Elliot was a master. I was liking Elliot more and more.

"Fine. But if I feel better, I'm coming in."

I nodded. No point arguing.

As I got up to go, I gave her a quick kiss on the cheek. "You're a peach, Brenda."

The morning was clear and bright so I decided I would walk to the diner. It should have been a pleasant walk and I might have enjoyed it if I hadn't been acutely aware of every curtain that parted as I passed each of those dull, dreary little houses with their cookie cutter lawns, crumbling picket fences, and beds of fading petunias.

The moment I put my hand on the doorknob of the diner, I knew something was wrong; it hit me like a sharp slap across the face.

I swung the door open and then waited a moment before I crossed the threshold.

Anticipating ... what?

A werewolf leaping out and yelling *Surprise?*

A bomb going off? That certainly was a possibility.

But there was nothing. I cautiously stepped forward.

Processing ... processing ....

It all looked the same, just as I had left it. And yet, everything about it was off-kilter, out of sync.

Where was Art? Was he still sitting in that field? Still "thinking"? How much contemplating/navel gazing/introspection can one demon do? If he was a demon. If I wasn't in some kind of fucked up trauma-induced mental hell, destined to live out the rest of my pathetic little life in a state of hallucinatory malfunction and I had fabricated the little prick out of the detritus of my screwed-up head.

On that profound note, I tiptoed into the kitchen, and then into the dining room.

Something was very, very wrong. The wrongness nestled in my gut and held onto my lungs like it was getting ready to take me on one hell of a ride.

And yet, everything looked just fine. On the surface.

But, of course, nothing was fine. Absolutely nothing. The world was going to go up in a blaze of thermonuclear glory in—how many days? Three, was it? At least, that's what that damned demon kept telling me. Not that I'd seen any concrete evidence.

I mean, really? War with Canada? Bombs? Total destruction? Who believes stuff like that, other than some crazy-assed religious nut? And what I was supposed to do about it, stuck in some backwater burg? I was dreaming, making up all this shit in my head.

It was the only thing that made sense.

      Yeah. Right. Back to the "it's all a dream" theory, are you? Silly you. Silly, silly me.

53

Enough thinking. I had work to do. I had bread to bake. Chili to make. Ribs to marinate. I got busy. Busy was much better than counting down the seconds until life as we know it ended.

I was up to my wrists in dough when the back door rattled and I jumped, scattering flour across the workstation and onto the floor. I flung open the door and found two people looking at me as if they were having second thoughts and were debating how fast they could get away.

We stared at each other until finally I said. "I'm Elliot. Are you the people Brenda hired?"

The boy, maybe 17, nodded. The girl—no, woman (sorry)—looked me over as if she were assessing my worth as a sentient being and found me sadly lacking. She looked familiar. I had seen her before, somewhere, I was sure of it.

"I'm Derrick," the kid said.

The woman peered over my shoulder, no doubt trying to determine if it was safe to come inside. "Where's Brenda?"

"Brenda had a bit of an accident. I don't expect her to come in today."

The woman weighed her options. "I don't do kitchen work."

"That's fine. I don't need you in the kitchen." That was a lie. I mentally calculated how much extra time it would take me to get everything done if I had to do it myself.

"I don't mind kitchen work," Derrick said.

"Can you peel potatoes? And carrots?"

"Yeah, sure."

"Great. I'll get you started."

"And me?" the woman said. "What do you want me to do?"

"Check the front. Make sure the tables are set properly. Menus are ready. The salt and pepper shakers are filled. That kind of stuff." The usual. "You've worked in a restaurant before?"

"Of course," she said, spraying indignity all over me. "You got a uniform?"

I shook my head. She rolled her eyes, expressing her opinion regarding my lack of proper attire. "We're informal here. What you're wearing is fine."

"Okay by me," she said, shrugging. "Do I get a clothing allowance? You want me to look good, don't you?"

"Sure. Why not?" I smiled oh-so pleasantly. Not my money, I reminded myself.

"I think I'm going to like working here."

"Good. So, you'll be waiting tables and seating people."

"I can do that. No problem."

"We were really busy yesterday. Can you handle it by yourself?"

That earned me, albeit briefly, a Death Glare. "No problem."

"Good."

"What's today's special?" she asked.

"Special?"

"You do have one, don't you? Most restaurants do."

That was true, but I hadn't thought of it. "I'll let you know." Something about this woman was bugging the hell out of me. I was sure I knew her. "Wait—" I stopped her as she turned away. "I didn't get your name."

She smiled, one of those, well-aren't-you-stupid smiles. "Felicia. Felicia Lebowski."

The wheels were spinning hard, but the hamster wasn't running. "You from around here?"

"Do I look like I'm from around here?" She didn't, I realized. Her skin was too dark.

Felicia ... and then it hit me like a freight train with no brakes going off a sheer cliff. Felicia! A parking lot, a parts store, a hotel room. A hospital room .... This was the bitch who shot me—Leroy Jackson, I mean. And possibly killed him. No, wait—wasn't he already dead? I groaned. Had she killed him twice? Was that possible? I groaned. How was I supposed to keep up? *Don't bother trying* ....

More to the point, how could I have forgotten her? Not that I'd forgotten completely. It did come back to me. Sort of. What was she doing in Jackknife, Montana?

Shaken, I retreated to the kitchen and stayed there. As I put bread into the oven, Art showed up, looking stylish in a new suit that made him look like a cross between a Mafia boss and a back-room politician on the campaign trail. "How's it going?" He seemed far too cheerful.

I instantly pounced on him. "Do you know who's out there?" I pointed to the dining room.

"Who?" He looked eager, as if we were about to play a game.

"Felicia."

"Felicia?"

"Yeah, you remember Felicia—the tall black girl who looks like she's 12. The one who shot Leroy."

"I thought she missed."

"Not completely." I glared at him. "That was her in the hospital, too, wasn't it?"

"Was it?" He smiled innocently. I wanted to bang a frying pan over his head.

"What's she doing here?"

"Working for you, is my guess. You did hire her, didn't you?" He frowned. "Are you sure that's wise?"

I sputtered but quickly recovered. "How did she find us?"

"She didn't. We found her." He patted my arm. "Relax. It's going to be fine. Stop being such a granny fuss-pot."

I opened my mouth. Then I closed it. There was no point ....

Art grinned, his teeth flashing with particular brilliance. "Got any Diet Coke?"

"You should stay away from that stuff."

"Naw. I'll be careful. I learned my lesson. No more energy drinks. That stuff is poison. Harm reduction, that's the ticket."

I pointed at the fridge. Arguing with a demon was exhausting and I had done my share for the day. I was just glad he was back to normal.

Of course, "normal" was highly subjective and probably an overstatement.

"Where's Brenda?" Art asked once he had his Diet Coke and had taken up a position at the end of my workstation.

"Recovering from a nasty knock on the head. Someone broke into our house last night."

"Oh?" He paused his gulping, can mid-air. "Now, who would do such a thing?"

"Good question. You don't know?"

"I wasn't there."

"But don't you know these things? Isn't that part of your job? To know who's doing bad stuff?"

"You're assuming it was a bad thing."

"I'm pretty sure Brenda thinks it was bad."

He shrugged. "People have a lot of different motives for doing what they do, Hector. You shouldn't assume they're always bad."

I couldn't believe what I was hearing. "What the hell is wrong with you?"

"You shouldn't swear. It will curl your hair."

This was weird. Really weird. "Are you all right?"

"I couldn't be better."

And that, friends, was the problem in a nutshell.

54

Art, once fully charged on Diet Coke, proved more than able to handle the kitchen—the hotter it got, the more enthusiastic he got. He took over making the chili, which left me time to mingle with guests.

To my ever-loving amazement, I found myself enjoying the social aspect. I'm not sure if that was really me, or if Elliot had been a super extrovert and I was channeling his energy, but I was having fun.

Mingling with guests also meant I could keep an eye on Felicia. So far, she hadn't done anything troublesome. In fact, she proved capable of charming the customers into leaving her extraordinarily large tips. Perhaps that would keep her happy and her hands out of the till.

So, I mingled, but it was exhausting. All that smiling and laughing and banal conversation and agreeable nodding. *Híjole!*

While our success made me happy, I couldn't help wondering where all the people had come from. A glance at the license plates on the cars around the restaurant revealed some of them had come from as far away as Virginia. Surprising, since we weren't exactly on a main road. How had they found us? I tried to ask, but I never got a straight answer. "You were on our way." "We heard about you from a friend." "We were just driving by and got really hungry."

Yeah, right. Just "driving by"? "On our way"? On your way to where? Hell?

There was a family from Seattle who'd taken a wrong turn

trying to take a shortcut home and stopped for lunch. They had chili and cornbread. "Best mistake we've made this entire trip," the father said. I gave the kids free ice cream.

Then there was the group of Mormon hunters from Idaho. "We don't really kill anything," one of them confided. "We're all terrible shots. Besides, all that blood is icky. We just like to get away, shoot off our guns, drink root beer, and tell tall tales." They had the ribs. "Best ribs I've had outside of Tennessee," one of them said. I packed extra for the Mighty Hunters to take home.

Nevertheless, I couldn't help but notice that there were still no locals and that perplexed me. Weren't they curious? Or did the thought of eating food not cooked in their own kitchens make them nervous? Or had all the locals abandoned the town?

At one point, I stood at the window, looking for some sign of local life. And, yes, it was there. People on the streets going about their business, shopping, walking their dogs, kids on bikes—all doing their best to avoid passing in front of our door.

Across the street, three old guys sat on the steps of the hardware store, watching; judging—oh yeah—I could feel the judgment rolling off them like sweat. They regarded the kids on bikes with disdain. They scowled at every vehicle that drove a little too fast, especially if it had an out-of-state license plate. They nodded to the women, occasionally letting their gaze linger with undisguised leers. You could practically feel the drool dripping off their grizzled tongues. Every so often, one of them would look my way, frown, and spit something foul into the street.

I moved away from the window and went back to mingling.

"How did you hear about us?" I asked one couple. The man was in his 50s, with a mass of striking white hair and the most intense brown eyes I'd ever seen. I admit, I experienced a little tug of attraction. I've always been a sucker for brown eyes. To my surprise, he didn't turn away when I stared into his eyes a fraction of a second too long.

The woman, a dark-haired woman with a bit of gray at her temples, was oblivious. "We read about you in the newspaper," she said.

"What newspaper?"

"The Helena *Daily Express*." I must have looked dumb struck because she dug into her massive purse, fished around for a moment, and then pulled out a folded section of newspaper. She opened it up, pressed it flat, and pointed.

To my amazement, there I was—Elliot, I mean—in full color, an extra-large serving spoon suspended in my hand like I was conducting an orchestra, a dopey smile on my face. Where had this picture come from? Brenda had taken the only pictures that I was aware of.

Brenda. Of course. Well, she did say she had connections.

I glanced at the article under the photo. The headline read, *New Chef Brings Jackknife Diner Roaring Back to Life*. Kind of wordy but nice.

The article was positive, though. *Small town charm - big city taste.* The chili got rave reviews. *"Best chili I've ever eaten,"* wrote the reviewer. *"It hums in your mouth, a perfect blend of sweet and spicy."* I liked that. I checked the byline—someone by the name of Barry Thomas. His picture was at the end of the article—young looking guy, kind of chubby—but I didn't remember seeing him. *"And the ribs! Holy smokehouse, but they rocked."*

"We had to check you out," the woman continued. She smiled at me like she was thinking of adopting me. She gestured at the paper. "You can keep this if you want."

"Thanks." I took it gratefully. "I had no idea we had been visited by a food critic."

"Oh, I hear they can be really sneaky," the woman said. "What do you recommend for dessert?"

"The rice pudding," I replied. "It's my grandmother's recipe. The Cuban version. It's a little sweeter than most and very creamy."

"With raisins?"

"A few, but not too many."

Her eyes lit up. "Oh, yes. Please."

I glanced at the man. He nodded, and I could feel those blazing brown eyes of his following me all the way to the kitchen.

*I am a rock star....*

55

The kitchen hummed, thanks to Art. He had a new pot of chili simmering, along with a batch of barbecue sauce. There were ribs in the smoker, neat little cups of rice pudding lined up in the fridge cooling, and a pan of golden cornbread sat on the counter, ready for cutting.

It was a relief to have Art back at full power.

He had his happy back, too. Grinning broadly, he danced from one end of the kitchen to the other. He had Derrick laughing so hard the poor boy nearly dropped a tray of glassware.

I relaxed for the first time in days.

"Enjoy it while you can," Art whispered as he passed me.

That sobered me up in a hurry. "How much Diet Coke have you had?"

"Don't worry. I'm good." He smiled brightly. "Eat something. You can't forget to eat."

I dished out some chili and sat in an out of the way spot where I could watch the action. It felt good to sit. And the chili was better than good. It was amazing, infused with a flavor I couldn't quite identify. "You've done something to it," I said.

He gave a little modest shrug. "I might have added my own touch."

"What?"

"Something special."

I eyed him suspiciously while I dished out another serving. The stuff was freaking addictive. "Nothing illegal, I hope."

"Of course not. Would I do such a thing?"

"Yes."

He didn't look at all offended. "Beer," he whispered in a conspiratorial tone. "I added a little beer."

Beer, Dr. Pepper, and chocolate. Sooner or later, we were going to kill someone...ah, well, if the world was about to end, what did it matter? At least people would go out well fed.

Was I being a bit cavalier? Well, yes, but do you blame me? I mean, did I really believe the world was going to end? I was crazy; Art was crazy. That was all. I clung to good ol' denial because, damn it, for the first time in my life I was happy.

Even crazy people deserve to be happy.

Don't they?

Just as I was about to take another tour of the dining room, Wilvor Parrish showed up at the back door. "You still need someone to wash dishes?"

"Always." I was beyond pleased to see him. I introduced him to Art and Derrick. "Eat first." I gave him some chili and cornbread. He hesitated.

"What's wrong?"

"My dad says if I eat your food, I'll—" He trailed off.

"What?"

His face turned bright red. "I'll turn ... funny."

"Funny?"

"He means gay," Derrick said. "That's a bunch of hooey, Wilvor."

"I know." He dug into the chili as if to prove he believed it truly was a bunch of hooey. There was a beat while he chewed and swallowed. Then his eyes lit up. "This is *really* good." All thoughts of conversion were apparently banished from his mind as he polished off the bowl.

"Feel any different?" Derrick asked when he was finished.

Wilvor shook his head and grinned. "Can I have some more?"

Not long after that, Brenda showed up. She was wearing a brave face, but I could see the pain behind the mask. I gave her the disapproving eye. "What are you doing here, darling? I told you to stay home."

"After I cleaned up the mess our visitor made, I couldn't

stand it anymore." Tears welled up in her eyes. "I couldn't stand being alone, wondering how things were going."

I nodded. "Come here." She complied, and I gave her a hug. "If you'd like to be useful, you could tear up some more lettuce for salads." Salads had been very popular, especially the Caesar salad with poached salmon.

She nodded gratefully and got to work.

I got it. Sometimes you need to be around people. The right people.

It was magical, watching everything fall into place. Oh, there was a mishap or two. A batch of cornbread got left in the oven a little too long. We ran out of ham and pickles for the Cuban sandwich, which was proving to be one of our most popular items. But the flow of happy customers remained steady.

Felicia continued to behave herself.

Wilvor attached himself to Brenda, and Brenda happily took him under her wing.

Art only drank two more Diet Cokes.

And I had time to read Barry Thomas' story about us in the *Daily Express.* "Was this your doing?" I showed Brenda the article.

She nodded. "I went to school with Barry's mother."

"Is this what you meant by connections?"

"Oh, he isn't my only connection."

She didn't elaborate and I didn't press her.

I slipped out the back door into the alley for a break, still clutching the *Daily Express.* A cool breeze wafted across my face. Putin came for a quick pat and pecked off a bit of cheese that had stuck to my pants. Then he casually moved off, tail flying high. "Don't get eaten by a bear," I called after him.

*Meow.*

I got up. Time to go back inside. I folded the paper, intending to clip out the review, but a headline I had missed caught my eye. *Security Increasing at Canadian Border.*

*Tension between Ottawa and Washington is at an all-time high after President Waterman threatened to expel the Canadian ambassador, among other actions, unless the Canadians agreed to start sending their oil to the US. "Consider it reparations for the damage done to the White House back in 1814," the President said. "Plus interest."*

The writer pointed out that it wasn't the Canadians who

burned the White House during the War of 1812—it was the British. A fact that Stanley Morris Waterman was choosing to ignore. *"Facts lie," he was quoted as saying.*

*"The War of 1812 has been over for more than 200 years. It's a little late to ask for reparations," said one senator.*

Apparently, Waterman didn't think so. Neither did the thousands of supporters who were marching toward the Canadian border to "make them pay."

*"It's got to be a joke," said the House minority leader.*

*"America's honor is at stake," Waterman told several advisers. "Plus, we need their oil. And their beer."*

Suddenly, I didn't feel so good. The realization hit me hard—hard like a bowling ball dropped on my head that Waterman was close to destroying not only the entire world but *my* world as well, which for the first time ever was actually a decent place. I was doing something I loved with people I cared about and who I truly believed cared about me. (Yes, I'd even grown a little fond of Art. Damn demon.) The idea that in a matter of days—no, hours—it could all end made me red-hot angry.

I still didn't like the idea of shooting him but, damn it, if that's what it took, I would do it.

Not that I expected to have the chance. I mean, I was *here* and he was *there*, in Washington. Right?

Right.

56

I went back inside to discover no one in the kitchen, except Art, sitting on a stool, legs neatly crossed, another can of Diet Coke in his hand, with the anticipatory look of impending oblivion on his face.

"Where is everyone?"

He gave me a slow, laborious glance as if he were only half in this world. He pointed vaguely. I moved toward the door that swung into the dining room. "I wouldn't go in there if I were you." He sounded drunk. I knocked the pop can out of his hands.

"What's going on, Art?"

"You didn't think your 'happy days' were going to last forever, did you?" The red in his eyes brightened until they were two blinding embers. "Gotcha."

I punched him in the nose.

It hurt like hell, but it felt really, really good.

He laughed, an icy cold laugh. "You can't hurt me, asshole. You can only hurt yourself." Smug bastard. "I got immunity."

I stood at the door to the dining room and looked through the little window that was supposed to keep those coming and those going from banging into one another.

Some guy was on his feet, punching the air with tightly clenched fists and waving around a shotgun. He was doing a lot of yelling, too. Things like "I'm going to kill that fag," and "You better tell me where he is" and "We'll all wait here until he shows up."

I didn't recognize the guy who was doing the yelling. He was in his mid-forties, stocky, hair shaved to a stubble. He wore jeans and a flak jacket.

I could see Brenda and Derrick sitting at a table with some people I didn't recognize—a man wearing a plaid shirt and a woman with bright red hair. The man was clearly enjoying the show. The woman calmly gnawed on a rib. Brenda sat on the edge of her chair, ready to pounce, but cautious. I couldn't see Derrick's face, but he sat hunched over, like he was waiting for a hole to open in the floor that he could jump into.

There were other customers, too—a group of men in the far corner, a couple of women on the other end of the room. None of them seemed particularly alarmed.

Felicia lurked near the cash register. She had this little smirk on her face, like, *yeah, man, bring it on.*

"Where's the fag?" The guy got into Brenda's face.

She looked as if she was about to bite the nose off his puffy face. "Fuck off."

He gave her a shove, sending her crashing into a table, which splintered as if it was made of delicate porcelain.

"Dad! Stop it."

Dad? That's when I saw Wilvor Parrish come out of the shadows.

This was Wilvor's father?

The man took an aggressive step toward Wilvor and the kid backed up. "I'm going to beat the crap out of you, boy. As soon as I kill that fag."

Someone twittered. Nervous laughter, I assumed. Nothing funny going on here.

I pulled back from the door, and turned to Art. "I don't suppose the fag he's looking for is me?"

"Who else? That's Jerry Parrish. Nasty dude. I wouldn't tangle with him, if you can avoid it. He thinks you've corrupted his son. Or you're going to. He thinks any guy who shows an interest in his kid is gay, but that's because he thinks his kid is gay, thanks to the kid's mother. Also, he's a latent homosexual. Complete denial. He's going to have fun in prison, mark my words, if he survives the afternoon. You won't be able to reason with him, so don't even think about it. "

"What do I do? He's going to hurt someone." Like me. Or

Wilvor. He'd already hurt Brenda, given the amount of moaning now coming from the dining room.

"You'll probably have to kill him."

"Kill him?" I considered it. I'd been hanging around a demon too long. It didn't even sound all that drastic. "With what?"

"Too bad you don't have a gun."

"I don't know anything about guns. I've never even held one, let alone fired one."

Art rolled his eyes. "You're such a pansy."

"Hey!"

"Sorry, but if the flower fits—"

"Art!"

"Okay, fine. How about a knife? You have lots of those, and I know you know how to use one of those."

"Not to kill someone."

"So, don't kill him. Just maim him. I'd aim for the kidneys." He straightened up and pointed to his torso. "Right there, I think. You'll have the element of surprise. You might get in a good thrust before he blows your head off."

I snarled at him. "You're enjoying this, aren't' you?"

"Of course. It's what I live for. So to speak." Another sip from the can. "I'd watch out for Felicia. I don't think she's on your side. She's not on anyone's side, except her own."

Tell me something I don't know.

"Also, those men in the corner—don't expect any help from them. They're some of Jerry's buddies."

"And the women?" I couldn't afford to ignore anyone.

He snorted. "A group of knitters, out for lunch and a little adventure. I doubt they'd be much help."

"The couple sitting with Brenda and Derrick?"

"He's not important. She's nothing special," he said dismissively. "You're on your own, buddy boy. Of course, you could just walk away. The keys to the truck are in your pocket, aren't they?"

Involuntarily, I patted my pocket. Yeah, they were there.

"Isn't there any law enforcement in this town?"

He laughed so sharply Diet Coke spurted from his nose. "Like they'd be any help."

Well, now, that was a surprise, wasn't it?

~57~

The urge to take off running once again seized me with full force, but I couldn't. I wouldn't. Not with Brenda out there. And Derrick. Or Wilvor. Poor kid. Or all those other people.

Art was right about two things. I did have knives and the element of surprise. But could I get to Jerry before he blew my head off?

And even if I did get to Jerry, was I strong enough to do enough damage? Jerry looked rock-solid.

Let's face it, in my heart of hearts, I was still a myopic little dipshit, despite my present rugged exterior. I didn't know how to fight. I'd always run away. I'd gotten very good at duck and cover. I couldn't count on Elliot's inner caveman to come out, if he had one.

Art continued to egg me on. "He's a freaking psychopath. He's not going to stop with you. He'll kill them all, you know, once he gets started."

Rage bunched up into a tight, explosive knot in my chest. "You could stop this."

He shrugged. "I could, I suppose, but I'm not going to. God wouldn't. Why would I? I gotta prove I'm evil enough, remember?"

"I thought you were over that."

"Well, aren't you the stupid one, my little naïve friend."

He was right. I was naïve. And stupid.

And something else.

I was mad.

Not just your ordinary mad. I was outraged. Worse than that,

I was closing in on full-throttle indignation.

I was working my way into the kind of crazy mad only the meek achieve when you've finally pushed their last button.

I grabbed the carving knife off the counter with one hand, and a boning knife with the other.

And then I charged through the door, nearly tripping over Putin in the process. Damn cat.

I went straight for Jerry. He didn't see me coming until I was nearly upon him. He grinned and raised his gun, but before he could take aim, Putin flew into his face with a Kamikaze howl.

Jerry's gun arm swung wildly, giving me time to spring on him with one vicious, well placed (and completely lucky) thrust of the carving knife.

He yelped but he was still on his feet, clawing at the cat on his face, gun swinging wildly.

The gun went off.

And then he screamed bloody, freaking murder. The asshole had shot himself in the foot. Now he was bent over, moaning, with Putin still attached to his face like a vicious little barnacle. He still hadn't dropped the rifle.

Brenda punched him in the gut.

The woman with the red hair jabbed the now stripped and neatly pointed rib bone she'd been gnawing into his throat.

The look on her husband's face was priceless—a mixture of surprise, pride, and a tinge of fear, but not to be left out, he executed a nice, sharp chop to the guy's gun hand.

Jerry finally dropped the rifle and then dropped to his knees. One of the knitting ladies picked up a chair and bashed it over his head.

He fell to the ground finally, and a cheer went up.

Out of the corner of my eye, I saw Felicia reach into the till. I sprang on her, jamming the boning knife between her fingers. She snatched her hand away, crying loudly and slumped into a corner.

Jerry's buddies were slow to react but react they did—by running out of the diner. Didn't even stop to see how poor old Jerry was doing.

Wilvor nudged Jerry with the toe of his shoe. "He's not dead." He sounded disappointed.

I patted him on the back. "Maybe not, but I don't think he's going to hurt you ever again."

Wilvor sighed. He gave me a look of wistful hope.

Eventually, someone called the county sheriff, and a big ol' bull of a guy named Harry Houser arrived about half an hour later, took one look at Jerry, and grunted. "Well, ain't this a pleasant surprise. Been wanting to get my hands on you for a long time."

Harry shook my hand. "You got balls, mister. This bastard's one nasty butt muncher. I've been chasing him all over the county for years."

"It wasn't only me." I felt magnanimous. "I had help."

He gave me a long, discerning look. Then he nodded. He wasn't the type to bother with details. He got the bad guy. That was enough for him.

"I'm worried about his kid." I pointed to Wilvor, who was presently being fussed over by the knitting ladies.

"He'll be fine," Sheriff Houser said. "His mom's folks live in Denver. Good people. I'll give them a call."

"If they need anything …" I hesitated. "Let me know. I got money."

He nodded. "I'll let you know."

When things calmed down, Brenda gave me a big hug. "Oh, my god, you were so brave."

Derrick grinned at me stupidly and whacked me on the back a few times. "Wait until I tell the guys."

Somehow, I knew the story was going to get blown way out of proportion.

Whatever.

~58~

I gave Putin his very own salmon steak that night when he finally showed up again. He even let me give him a thorough head rub. He spent the night curled up at the foot of my bed and didn't once ask to go out.

Art didn't have much to say. He smiled a lot, though. I think he was secretly proud of me. As much as I might have wanted, I couldn't stay angry with him. For one thing, it took too much energy, and I was zapped. All I wanted was sleep. And a steak. Bringing Goliath to his knees was hungry work.

We went home, and I cooked steaks for us all—Brenda, Derrick, Art, the guy in the plaid shirt, whose name was Ernie, and his wife, Shirley, who had wielded the sharpened bone. I would have fed the knitting ladies, too, but they had a bus to catch. We sat around until midnight. No one wanted to leave.

I got to talking to Ernie. Turns out his name was Ernesto Cruz. He sold used cars in Nevada, and his father had been Cuban, but his mother had been Irish.

Funny thing, he grew up in Florida. So, for the random hell of it, I asked him if he had known my grandmother and my mother. I didn't tell him they were my family, of course. I told him they had been friends of the family. Sure enough, he had. We got to talking in earnest then, me and Ernie. Seems like we had a lot in common. "Did you know Consuela had a son?"

That gave him pause. "A son?"

"Yeah, he'd about 27, I think."

An odd sort of look passed over his face. "No, I guess I didn't. Do you know him?"

I shrugged. "Sort of. Nice guy. Nothing special. He's gay." I watched his reaction. There was surprisingly little.

"So? What's wrong with that?" There was a protective tone in his voice. And it hit me like a ton of bricks—this guy was my father. My father!

I wanted to ask him a million questions. I wanted to tell him everything, but I caught Art's eye and the subtle shake of his head. "Don't push it," Art mouthed.

I didn't. I pulled myself together. Some things should be left alone. Move on and keep moving. Nothing to see here, folks. Just the usual train wreck.

By the next morning, the word was out, and the press was arriving in droves. Turns out that Jerry Parrish wasn't just a homophobic bully, he was also a key player in a group hellbent on taking down the US government. In fact, investigators found a detailed plan of attack in his house, targeting the president, Congress, the Supreme Court, and the headquarters of Amazon and Microsoft, all set to be launched in two days, just in time to take advantage of the current turmoil with the Canadians.

And the name of this little group? You guessed it: Restored Missionary Evangelical Gospel Church of the Sacred Order of Anarchy, led by none other than the Rev. Peter Knutson, who mysteriously disappeared from his Florida home, along with all the group's considerable cash assets. I was pleased that nearly a million dollars had escaped his clutches and was now in mine.

The good ol' boys who had been with Parrish at the diner had disappeared, as had everyone at their compound. All the police ever found were a lot of dead mice and rats in their houses and trucks.

As for the church, the one that dominated the town skyline, it burned to the ground overnight. Strangely enough, no one saw a thing. Not even a lick of flame. Nothing left but a pile of smoldering ashes.

Sheriff Houser stopped by the diner and shook my hand. We were very busy, thanks to the sudden influx of reporters who needed to be fed. Plus, the locals finally decided to check us out. "The President is very grateful to you," Houser said.

I doubted that, given Waterman's connection with Knutson,

but I smiled, feigning innocence, and offered Sheriff Houser a Cuban sandwich, on the house.

Brenda was in seventh heaven. She was thrilled to be chatting with reporters, yapping happily to anyone who would listen—off camera, on camera. She performed like a seasoned pro, as if this was what she'd been born to do.  It gave me shivers watching her in action.

Art said little. In fact, I didn't see much of him that day. I wanted to thank him for giving me an opportunity to meet my dad—Hector's dad. So I didn't get any of my questions answered. So I didn't get to experience the big reunion I'd always dreamed of. It was enough to lay eyes on him. It made me feel—I don't know—complete, I guess. Like a real person.

~59~

We gathered at the house that night—Art finally turned up without explanation—and Brenda made us mac and cheese from scratch, another of her grandmother's recipes. It was warm and gooey with cheese, and made me feel safe, sane and content, an existential view of middle America, circa 1964.

The only one missing from our little party was Felicia. "Anyone see her?"

No one had.

"She's a big girl," Brenda said. "She can take care of herself."

"No doubt," Art said, but he flipped me a little eye action that conveyed oh-so-much-more. Like *I hope you locked up the cash register.*

Later, I cornered him. "Where is she?"

"Who?" He looked so freaking innocent I knew something was up.

"Felicia."

He struck a "let me think about it" pose. "I haven't a clue, but I wouldn't worry about her, though. She's very resourceful."

"I'm not worried. I'm curious."

Art shrugged. "Beats me."

I didn't believe him. Not for a second. "She works for you, doesn't she?"

"No one works for me." He sounded offended.

"No one? Not even me?"

That made him laugh. "You? Don't be silly. You're my trusty

sidekick, Hector, my friend. My associate. My partner."

"Partner?" Was that an upgrade? A promotion? "Partner in what?"

"In saving the world. Remember? Speaking of which, we're not out of the woods yet. That whole church thing was just the warmup. Waterman's finger is getting very itchy. You should make a fresh batch of chili. And add a little more garlic. You can never have enough garlic." I took it under advisement.

Felicia was back at work the next day as if nothing at all was wrong. "I needed some time off. To heal." She glared at me and flexed her bandaged hand.

"You tried to rob me!" I fought the urge to apologize. Besides, I had barely touched her.

"Not true. I was merely trying to protect your assets."

Her protest was so heartfelt I almost fell for it. "Yeah, right."

"Give the girl a break, Elliot. It was a stressful situation," Benda said. Brenda was so full of forgiveness and cheer, I wondered what she'd been smoking.

"Fine." I let it go for Brenda's sake, but I vowed not to let Felicia out of my sight. We were in for a busy day. Art had muttered something that morning about a "special guest" showing up. I could only imagine what that meant. I would need all the help I could get, even if it didn't sit well.

The "special guest" turned out to be none other than Stanley Morris Waterman, President of the United States of America. Seems he was in the neighborhood, heard about the capture of Jerry Parrish *and* how fine our chili was, so he decided to stop by and say "thanks" for helping to catch a "really bad guy."

Uh-huh.

"One more day," Art whispered. "Actually, six hours. We're cutting this one really close. He's not here because of you, by the way. There's a secret bunker in the mountains not far from here. Nuclear bomb-proof. He's on his way to hide out. He's going to push the button once he gets there. Better add a little extra chili powder to the chili."

I ignored him. The chili was fine.

The cornbread, however, was a little dry.

~60~

Five minutes after Waterman arrived, Brenda came into the kitchen. "He wants to talk to you," she announced. She didn't seem happy about it.

I had no interest in talking to him. In fact, I didn't want anything to do with him, but Brenda had me in a clean apron and shoved through the door into the dining room before I could protest.

Waterman invited me to sit down and chat while he ate, so I did. I mean, I did have a few things I wanted to address with him. I got right down to business. "About the Canadians—"

"Bastards." His mouth was full of cornbread and he sprayed bits of crumbs all over me. "Can't trust them. Do you know they invaded Washington and set fire to the White House?"

"That was two hundred years ago."

"And we let them get away with it. Well, not on my watch. Besides, we really need their oil, and if they're not going to give it to us, we'll have to take it. It's the American way, you know." As if on cue, he glanced at his watch, frowned, then went back to his chili.

"Don't you think you should take the high road?"

"Screw the high road. The high road is for weaklings. America didn't become the greatest country in the world by taking the high road!" He shoved another spoonful of chili into his mouth, followed by a big bite of cornbread. "This is good stuff. Think you could give the recipe to my chef?"

"Sure." Only if I had to. And I'd leave out the secret ingredients. "About Canada—"

"You don't have to worry about the Canadians."

"It's not the Canadians I'm worried about."

He laughed so hard, he spit out more bits of yellow crumbs, this time through his nose. "You're a riot, son. Can I get some more of that cornbread?"

I got up to get him more cornbread, but Felicia beat me to it. "I got this." Waterman took it from her and gave her a good once-over.

"Now, there's one fine girl," he said to me after she'd left us. "You doing her?" He shoveled more chili into his mouth, dabbing his puffy lips with his napkin. "Could do with a little less garlic though. And it needs more salt." He reached for the saltshaker and gave it a healthy shake. I cringed. Freaking moron.

I'd had enough. "Excuse me. I need to get back to the kitchen. Enjoy the chili."

In the kitchen, I grabbed Art by his collar. "I want to kill him. I want him dead."

Art grinned merrily and patted me on the back. "Hector, my boy, I knew you'd come around."

Then he walked away and left me standing in the middle of the kitchen with a gun in my hand.

I didn't hesitate. I don't think I even gave the gun much thought. I marched right back into the dining room, raised the gun, and fired.

I mean, I think I fired.

I had never fired a gun before. It wasn't that big of a gun, but it sure made one hell of a lot of noise.

And then there was the smoke.

And fire.

And then the building fell down. Or blew up. Or disintegrated; dissolved, collapsed, or entered the vortex. One of those things, or maybe all of them.

There was one tiny, brief second when everything was perfectly clear, frozen forever in my mind's eye. A ball of fire poised at the window. A rush of wind. Felicia grinning with a gun in her hand, then frowning as a red spot on her chest blossomed. The tray Brenda was carrying flying through the air while she opened her mouth to shriek. Putin sailing through the air to land on Waterman's shoulder. Art grabbing Putin and saying, "Not this time."

There was a lot of confusion after that. A couple of guys in suits tackled me. There was some yelling and some screaming, and possibly some swearing. A whole lot of chairs and tables being overturned and dishes shattering. Maybe more gunfire. I don't really know. I was too busy trying to breathe under four hundred pounds of well-muscled Secret Service personnel who, by the way, were burping in my face. (Waterman may have been right about the garlic.)

When things finally calmed down a tad, the Secret Service boys got up, I expected them to slap handcuffs on me or possibly shoot me where I laid still sprawled on the ground. Neither happened. In fact, I'm not sure what happened after that. Time sped up again.

No, wait, that's not quite right.

It sped up all right; it went into overdrive. Zero to sixty; no, one-twenty in a heart beat.

It was like watching a movie in fast forward. People running around like little cartoon characters on speed, faster and faster until everything was a blur. A burst of orange light followed by darkness. And then quiet. And nothingness.

~61~

I woke up to the sensation of floating. Art leaned over me, a million worlds spinning in his red-rimmed eyes. "Am I dead?"

"Hector, my boy, technically, you've been dead for a while now."

"I have?" I shouldn't have been surprised, but I was. "Did I die in the explosion at Iggy's garage?"

"Nope. You survived that. Lucky you."

Lucky me, indeed. So, I could have gotten away from him.

"Not a chance, Hector. You were mine the moment I laid eyes on you."

"You're lying. You're a demon. You lie all the time and you're lying now."

"I don't lie all the time. Only when it suits my purpose. I tell the truth when it suits my purpose, too, which is what I'm doing now."

"But—" But what? Then it hit me. "I'm not getting my body back."

"Nope."

"I'm not going back to Florida."

"Not unless you want to haunt the Magic Kingdom."

"No, thanks."

"I didn't think so."

"Now what? I mean, we did stop Waterman from blowing up the world, didn't we?"

"Well, yes, we did. You can be proud of yourself, Hector.

You did well. You stopped him all right. You also saved his life."

"I did?"

"Sure did. You're a hero, Hector. Well, technically, Elliot is the hero. Close enough, though. An honest-to-god-American hero. Be proud. You stopped an assassin."

"Who?"

"Why, Felicia, of course. Little minx. If you think you hate Waterman—ha! You have nothing over dear, little Felicia. Her hatred, by the way, was strictly personal. Seems Waterman cheated her daddy, ruined his construction business, which caused him to lose millions, and the only job he could find after that was teaching in some rinky-dink high school. Had nothing to do with politics, although I'm sure she'll go down in history as a martyr to some cause or the other. The Canadians are already talking about erecting a statue in her honor."

"I killed her?" I wanted to laugh. Not because it was funny. Because it was all so absurd.

"You sure did. Lucky shot, of course, but no one's ever going to know it was accidental. It was she, by the way who broke into your house and bashed Brenda over the head. She was looking for your cash."

I thought about that for a moment. "Wait—how did she know I had money?"

Art looked at me as though I was the dumbest person in the universe. "Putin told her, of course."

Of course.

"Good thing she didn't find it, or she might have left town prematurely, and things might have turned out differently."

I considered that. I considered a lot of things. "Is this heaven?"

"Bite your tongue. We're still in Montana."

I was kind of glad to hear that. "What about Elliot? Is he dead?"

Art let loose a little sigh. "Well, yes. He died some time ago. Died trying to stop some punk from stealing gas out of his truck. But as far as the world is concerned, he died in the blast."

"What blast?"

Art grinned cheerfully. "It seems that not all the members of the Restored Church were turned to mice. Putin, bless his heart, missed a few." Putin again. Of course. Suddenly, all those "gifts" he'd left me made sense. Guess he had had my back, after all. "They heard the president was in town and couldn't pass up the chance to wreak a little havoc. You know how it goes. Anarchy is hard to give up—or control, especially when opportunity lands in your lap and you have a basement full of explosives."

"But they didn't succeed?"

"They made a big mess. I'm afraid they blew up half the town, but their explosives went off a little prematurely. The diner's toast, I'm afraid."

I was sad to hear that. "Brenda?"

"She's fine. She succeeded where Felicia failed. She found where you stashed the cash. She's on her way to Hawaii as we speak."

Good for her. "Derrick? Wilvor?"

"They made it out with only a few scratches."

"About Putin—"

"He's fine, too. He's got at least six lives left."

"So tell me, what is he?"

Art frowned. "Putin?"

"Yeah."

"He's a cat."

"Just a cat?" I tried to hold his gaze, challenging him.

"Just a cat." Not so much as a twitch.

I moved on. "And what about you? Are you still kicked out of hell?"

He shrugged and then a slow grin lit up his pale face. "You believed that?"

I stared at him dumbly. "It was a lie?" Silly me. Of course, it was a lie. And I had been sucked right in. Silly, silly me. I couldn't believe I'd ever spent a second feeling sorry for him. No wonder he picked me as his "sidekick." A true-blue sucker, that's me, all right.

"It wasn't a complete lie. I am known to be a little soft on occasion. I took you under my protection, didn't I?" He grinned, then shrugged. "I really did need your help to stop Waterman. That part was completely true. And it worked, so why fight it?"

"Is this it? Did you get what you wanted? Are you done with me?" I was more than ready for a little eternal rest.

"Ah, Hector, my naïve, young friend—I've just begun." He patted me on the shoulder. "And so have you."

~62~

I was digging myself out of the blackness, one heartbeat at a time. First, there was the smell: antiseptic and filtered. Then the sound: a buzzing, a rhythmic clicking. A whoosh. And finally voices, soft and muted at first, and then stronger—

"... he's waking up, doctor." Female; young. Shrill; excited.

"Thank god." Male; much older. Anxious; cautious.

I slowly opened my eyes, blinking hard against the sudden onslaught of light. Everything was so blurry—where were my glasses?

"Sir?" The man's voice. "Can you hear me? I'm Dr. Forbes and you're in the hospital."

I blinked in the direction of the voice. Slowly, he came into focus—narrow face, soft hazel eyes, gray hair at the temples, bulbous nose. Handsome, if you're into older men. I blinked a few more times, not trusting myself to speak. Then I realized I had tubes down my throat. I immediately began to cough.

The doctor put a reassuring hand on my shoulder. "You were hurt in an explosion, but you're going to be fine. Just take it easy. We'll take those tubes out in a moment, Mr. President."

Mister—?

I closed my eyes.

*Híjole.*

# ABOUT THE AUTHOR

Heidi Lacey is a nice old lady who used to be a journalist (of no particular renown) and a child welfare social worker. Having to live so fully in the real world was never her ambition, so now she lives on a tiny island in the middle of the Salish Sea with her cats, her books, and a few like-minded friends, real and imagined.

You can contact her at heidilacey28@gmail.com. She, or one of her cats, will reply.